A Fairy's Guide to Disaster

Away from Whipplethorn Book One

A.W. Hartoin

ISBN-10: 1475026846
ISBN-13: 978-1475026849

For Madeline
Your imagination was my inspiration.

I'm no Tinkerbell. I don't take orders from Lost Boys and Captain Hook could never catch me. I am a wood fairy though, complete with luminescent wings. Don't go thinking fairy equals weak, or timid. Because if I was any of that I could never have found my parents, my home, my future after the humans took them away from me.

I think my mom doubts aspects of my story, even though I have the scars to prove it.

I wish I could tell you what happened face to face, but being a half a centimeter tall has its disadvantages. Humans have a blind spot when it comes to fairies, no matter our size, and I'm the first Whipplethorn fairy to be seen in six generations. It was an isolated incident and I had to want it very badly to make it happen. Whether or not you see me, I want you to know that fairies exist all around you and in places you wouldn't expect. My family lives in a fireplace mantel, for instance. It's one of those big Victorian jobs, mahogany and weighing about two hundred pounds. Our home is inside the left leg of the mantel beside the firebox. Bet you never thought to look there.

Chances are we won't ever meet, and you probably wouldn't notice me even if we did, so I found a solution (I always do). I'll write you a book and I won't leave anything out, not even the stuff I didn't tell my mother.

Still, I hope you do see me someday. There's nothing like being seen, especially when your life depends on it.

Chapter I

Whipplethorn Manor was my world and I never expected to leave it. I wasn't curious about the places and creatures beyond our borders. No one told me tales of spriggans, trow, or humans. If they had, I'd have been better prepared. But no one offered answers to questions I never thought to ask. Instead, I was wrapped up in my little life in a crumbling mansion and content to be so, if only my mother would let me have my way.

"Matilda." Mom stuck her head through my door, her long black hair swooping down and brushing the floor. "Come down to the kitchen. We need to talk."

I flopped back on my bed and studied my ceiling's wood grain. Talking was never good. Talking meant Mom was about to change her mind. She'd make it sound like it was for my own good and she was doing me a favor. I was great at getting out of stuff but lousy at getting my own way. I managed to avoid unwanted activities with a series of excuses and fake injuries like overwhelming homework, or blinding headaches. I had a fake limp that was pretty useful. It came on suddenly and lasted for two weeks. Getting what I wanted was much more difficult. Limps didn't help with that. Mom caught on to the limp thing and used it against me. That's how she blocked my last babysitting job. She said if a person with a limp couldn't possibly clean bathrooms, they couldn't babysit either. The limp wasn't the real reason I didn't get to babysit though. That was just the excuse. It was my ears' fault. I had snail pox when I was two and the fever cost me a good deal of my hearing. It wasn't a big deal to me. I could hear what I needed to hear.

Since the snail pox, Mom and Dad worried about me like crazy while at the same time saying I was just the same as all the other girls my age. Except the other girls were all babysitting and I wasn't.

The thought made me feel rebellious, but it wasn't a good idea to make Mom wait too long, so I heaved myself off my bed and went down the hall toward the kitchen, my long purple and green wings limp on my back and sweeping the floor with my every step. Mom was in the kitchen, but she could hear a gnat's wing beat and that was on a bad day. The sound of my wings on the floor drove her crazy. She hated dusty wings and said it was a sign of dusty mind. Whatever that meant. If she wouldn't let me babysit again, I could at least annoy her.

The glowing mushrooms on the hallway walls lit the way as I slowly passed by. They grew in pots and cast a warm green light. Each cap was bigger than my fist and watering our fungus was my favorite chore. I stopped to say hello to my favorite, a frilly clump of Foxfire I named Barbara.

Mom walked out of the kitchen, her long silver and blue wings draped over her shoulders like a cape. "Are you coming?"

I dropped my hand and continued to the kitchen. I slipped past Mom and plopped down on my dad's stool at the big acorn top table. Mom bustled around, eyeing me as she rearranged her hand-painted eggshell plates. I crossed my arms and waited. She could rearrange those plates all day. I wasn't going to make it easy for her. Finally, she stopped and put her hands on her hips, assuming her battle expression. It only showed up when she wanted to make me or my little sister, Iris, go to the dentist or eat a lima bean.

"There's been a change of plans," she said.

I slumped over. My long black hair fell in my face and pooled in my lap.

"Really," I said. "I'm shocked."

"You're going to do Eunice a favor."

I peeked at her through strands of hair, afraid she was pulling a fast one. "Babysitting?"

"Yes."

I jumped up. "Really? You'll really let me this time?"

"Yes, that is if you don't have a headache or limp."

I ignored her implications. "Who's Eunice?"

"You know Eunice. Gerald's mother. He's in your sister's class."

I dropped back onto Dad's stool with my mouth open. Gerald Whipplethorn? I wanted to babysit, but Gerald wasn't worth it. The kid annoyed me like an itchy scab you couldn't pick off. He was the worst. The absolute worst.

I suddenly remembered an essay I had to write, my eyesight started to go in my left eye and I gripped the stool in an effort to ward off what was sure to become a crippling case of vertigo.

"No way, Mom." I wavered back and forth on the stool. "I don't feel so good after all."

"Stop that nonsense. You've been pestering me about babysitting for a year. Now's your chance."

"I can't babysit for Gerald. He's a nightmare."

"Matilda Grace Whipplethorn, you are babysitting for your sister and Gerald. He's already upstairs. His mother needs a break."

"Everybody needs a break from Gerald. I need a break and I haven't seen him in a week."

"You're just nervous."

"I'm not nervous," I said.

"Well, there's no reason to be. Babysitting is a pretty boring job. Nothing will happen." She picked up a roll of parchment off the counter. "Why don't you look over the list and see if you have any questions."

The emergency procedures list. My mom's collection of paranoid fantasies, including every awful thing that might happen if she left me in charge. I took Mom's list off the counter and skimmed it. The thing was ridiculous. It insisted I be capable of handling such calamities as a rogue fly attack, snail pox, and spurting arterial blood. There hadn't been a rogue fly attack in twenty years and I didn't even want to know what arterial blood was, much less what to do about it. I wasn't old enough anyway. Adult wood fairies could manipulate liquids, like making it rain in one spot instead of another, or staunch blood flow. My Grandma Vi could stop a cut from bleeding with just a look. As far as I could tell, my magic hadn't come in yet. At least no magic I wanted anyone to know about.

"Well, any questions?"

"I never have any questions."

I never would either. I was afraid Mom might actually answer and tell me how to pop snail pox pustules. That was information I didn't want in my thirteen-year-old brain. But on the other hand, the list implied that a horrendous calamity might happen if Mom left me in charge. For once, it was in my interest to encourage the idea.

"Mom, I don't think I'm ready for this. The stuff on the list is pretty serious. I'd freak out or something."

"I told you nothing's going to happen. You're fine. Perfectly fine."

She said I was fine, but she looked like she needed to breathe into a paper bag to keep from hyperventilating.

"If spurting arterial blood isn't going to happen, why is it on the list?" I asked.

"The list is just a precaution."

"I don't care. I'm not doing it."

Mom bent over and kissed me on the forehead, enveloping me in her wings. She smelled like violets and the scent soothed me as it always did since the time I had snail pox pustules.

Then she placed her forehead against mine. "It will be fine. You can handle him. You can handle anything."

I looked into her dark brown eyes and found the usual worries. "You don't really think so, do you, Mom?"

"I do too," she said. "Plus you have the list."

Then Mom darted out of the kitchen with just one glance over her shoulder. I caught a glimpse of a puckered brow, but I didn't care. I'd always known I could do it, and soon Mom would know she didn't have to worry about me. If I could watch after Gerald, I could do anything.

I rolled up the list and went to the kitchen window, a carved rose the size of a nickel. I pushed it out so that it was completely open and I could see all of Whipplethorn Manor's formal dining room where our mantel was placed by humans a hundred fifty years before. My ancestors carved out their home in the left leg of the mantel, so they would have a good view of the humans' whereabouts back when there were humans still living in Whipplethorn. Now I had a good view of nothing. The room was empty and had been for fifty years. An earthquake had cracked the foundation and the humans fled, leaving an extraordinary house to rot. This decision had always caused me to question the wisdom of humans. We wood fairies hadn't abandoned Whipplethorn. We simply adapted to our new more isolated circumstances.

Mom flitted in front of my window, her lovely wings creating a canvas behind her and bathing me in a warm glow with their luminescence. She flew back towards me one last time, cupped my cheek and spoke in my ear, so I'd be sure to hear. "Don't let that Gerald fly all over you. Have fun, darling."

I didn't have a chance to respond. Mom zipped away, across the dining room toward the enormous bank of windows. She stopped at a broken window pane and waved. A wide, joyful smile lit her face. I would keep that image of her safe within my heart in the days to come. Then she flew through the jagged hole. I watched as her silver streak crossed the overgrown lawn. She dodged a collapsed rose arbor, passed over the disintegrating iron fence that surrounded the mansion, and disappeared into the dense forest surrounding Whipplethorn. Mom was traveling at her top speed to catch up with the rest of the Whipplethorn fairies. Within minutes, she'd be miles away at the blueberry harvest.

I fanned myself with the list, trying to ignore its dire predictions. Especially the part about bandaging a head wound in three easy steps. That would be a lot less messy if I could staunch blood flow. But Grandma Vi had told me a million times that there was nothing to be done about it. Magic came when it came and one couldn't choose the gift. I wished I could do something about it. I really did.

I turned around, still holding the list, and found Gerald staring at me from the kitchen doorway. He had his arms crossed and a fierce scowl marred his broad forehead under his light brown hair. He was wearing a grey suit with a navy blue bow tie. Leave it to Gerald to be overdressed for every occasion.

"Where's my breakfast?" he bellowed. "Mother said you'd give me something good."

I glanced down at the list, but there wasn't anything on there about dealing with Gerald and there should've been. He wasn't a vague possibility like explosive diarrhea. He was definite. My mother should've replaced rogue fly attack with obnoxious kid attack.

"Your mother probably already fed you."

I turned my attention to a dozen red maple leaves dancing across the dining room's wide-planked floors.

Gerald met my remark with silence, which wasn't like Gerald. Of course it's possible that I just didn't hear him. When I looked up to see if I could catch a word or read his lips, all I caught was a glimpse of Gerald's wings rounding the corner toward our storeroom. I tucked my hair behind my ears and stuffed the list of things that weren't going to happen in the pocket of my blue jumper. Mom dyed it especially to match my eyes, but I think my eyes are more purple than blue.

I followed Gerald down the hall, sweeping my fingers over the book shelves adorning the wall. Three sad little books sat on the middle shelf and I couldn't help frowning at them as I passed. It seemed so pathetic to build shelves for books we didn't own. All the books in Whipplethorn wouldn't be enough to fill the shelves my father built. He seemed to think that if he built shelves, books would find their way to them. I plucked the thickest tome off the end, an instruction on advanced woodworking. Maybe it could occupy Gerald for a bit. I pressed the book to my chest and arrived in the storeroom just in time to see him bite into our last bit of blueberry.

"Gerald, what are you doing? That's our last one. You're not even hungry. I know you're not," I said, slamming the book on a flour barrel.

Gerald stuck his tongue out at me and then licked the blueberry with a big slurp. I decided right then that his classmates were right. Gerald wasn't a wood fairy. He was a stink fairy, just like everyone said.

"What are you going to do about it? Refer to your stupid list?" he asked. A wicked smile spread across his pale face and his wings fanned out. He always did that when he was being obnoxious. I assumed he was trying to make himself bigger, not that it did him any good. Gerald was small, even for an eight-year-old wood fairy.

I wanted to drag him through the storeroom by his vicious tongue and throw him out of the window, but since it was my first babysitting job I thought I'd better not. Instead, I took a breath and counted to three.

Gerald's smile widened and he yelled, "Can you hear me?"

I took a step toward him and lowered my voice. "I heard you just fine. Get away from that blueberry and go play."

Gerald's wings spread a little wider. They operated like my wings, folding down like a moth's against his body and spreading open to resemble a butterfly's, but they were much too small for his age and lacked a defined pattern. His blues and greys were dull and muddled even with the bit of sun coming in through the storeroom windows. No matter how much Gerald pretended, his wings just weren't very impressive.

Gerald plunked down on a stool and crossed his arms. "You can't make me."

"I'm the babysitter. I can make you do anything." Babysitting was starting to sound like more fun than Mom let on.

"You're not really," said Gerald. "Everyone knows I'm smarter. I should be babysitting for you."

"Nobody would let you babysit, Stink Fairy."

I marched across the dusty wood floor, grabbed Gerald's arm and hauled him to his feet. Gerald jerked away from me and toppled backwards into my mom's neatly stacked grains of wheat and barley. The grains fell down around him and one particularly large barley grain clunked him on the head.

"Ouch." Gerald reached up to touch his ear. He smirked at me and held out his hand. A smear of crimson coated his palm.

"You shouldn't have pulled away from me," I said, thinking I was lucky he was still conscious. So much for the list being just a precaution. I'd only been watching Gerald for a few minutes and I already had my first head wound. I knew babysitting Gerald wouldn't be as boring as Mom claimed. Gerald was a lot of things, but I'd never known him to be boring.

"You shouldn't have grabbed me," said Gerald. "I'm telling my mother."

"Go ahead and tell her, Stink Fairy." I waved for him to come over. "Come on. I've got to bandage that big head of yours."

"You're an idiot," he said.

"I'm an idiot?"

I stomped towards him, spreading my wings out to their full span. My tips touched the ceiling and the bottoms trailed on the ground. The whole room became awash in my purple and green luminescence. I was about to reach for Gerald's arm again to drag him to the kitchen for a bandage when he said, "Somebody's running this way."

It had to be Iris and it had to be bad, because Iris never ever ran. I turned in time to see my little sister bounce off the doorframe of the storeroom. She got to her feet and squeezed through the narrow storeroom door, panting and brushing the wrinkles out of her sparkly blue dress that matched her wings.

"Matilda, you'll never believe what I saw," Iris said.

Gerald brushed past me and stood in front of Iris with his arms crossed. "What did you see, big and stupid?"

Iris sucked in her lips. "I'm not stupid."

"And you're not that big either," I said, even though Iris was way bigger than I had been at her age. She might turn out to be larger than our father, who was nearly as tall as the dime Mom propped up on the parlor wall for decoration. "You shouldn't talk, Gerald. You're not even a real Whipplethorn."

"I am, too," said Gerald.

"No, you're not," I said. "You can tell by your wings. They don't shine at all."

"Yes, they do, idiot."

"No, they don't. Look how muddy and dull they are." I pulled out one of his wings. "Real Whipplethorns have luminescent wings."

"That doesn't make you better," said Gerald, pulling his wing away from me.

"It makes me a Whipplethorn."

"Humans," yelled Iris.

We turned to stare at her. She clapped her dimpled hands and grinned.

"I saw humans," she said, her grin growing larger.

"Where?" Gerald and I said together.

"Right out in the great hall. You could hear them if you stopped fighting."

I held my breath and listened. Maybe I heard something, deep tones from outside the mantel. I never would've noticed if Iris hadn't pointed it out.

"Are they loud?" I asked.

Iris hesitated. "They're not that loud."

Gerald sneered at her. "Are you kidding? They're humans. It's like they're bellowing out there." Then Gerald's face went another shade of pale. "They're talking about tools."

I pulled out the list and scanned the thing from top to bottom. Nothing. Humans weren't on the list. And why would they be? It was like humans had forgotten Whipplethorn Manor existed at all. Of course, I'd seen humans before, but never in the house. Sometimes Dad would find some hiking on trails in the national park nearby, and we would go to look at them. If I was very good, Dad would let me fly right up to them and look up their nostrils. No Whipplethorn fairy had been seen in six generations and I wanted to be the one to break our cold streak. So I tried everything I could think of to get their attention, including pulling ear hairs and biting noses, but they never noticed tiny wood fairies. Dad said I had to want it very badly to make it happen. He'd never been able to do it. I couldn't imagine wanting a human to see me any more than I already did.

Iris and I ran to the storeroom windows and leaned out. Three human men in faded overalls were walking around and pointing at things. Once I was in the window, I could just barely make out what they were saying.

"What do you think, Sal?" asked the tallest.

"Gold mine. It's a flipping gold mine," said Sal.

The third one pulled a notebook out of his pocket and began writing things down. "You got that right."

My sister and I glanced at each other. "Do you think they're moving in?" asked Iris.

"No." I'd spent a lot of time imagining humans living in Whipplethorn. Three men with rough hands and pit stains didn't match my fantasies at all.

"What are they doing here then?" Iris leaned over the window sill to get a closer look. "Do you think they could see me? Can I go out?"

I pulled Iris back. "Better not. Mom wouldn't like it."

She turned around with a petulant frown on her face. I was about to chastise her when I spotted Gerald backing out of the room.

"Don't you want to see?" Iris asked him.

Gerald didn't answer, but he stopped moving. His eyes darted from one of us to the other.

"Maybe he's too smart to be interested in humans," I said.

Gerald remained silent. A feat I'd never before experienced. Gerald always talked, whether anyone wanted to listen or not.

"What's wrong with you?" I stepped closer to Gerald, eyeing him with interest.

Iris tapped my shoulder. "Look."

We crowded into the window again. The three humans were standing in front of our mantel, rubbing their giant hands together and filling the mantel with their odd stink, a combination of sweat and pungent soap.

"May as well start here as anywhere," said the tall one. "You got it, Sal."

"You bet," said Sal as he slapped a long, thin piece of metal in his palm.

Iris leaned forward again. "What's that?"

"I don't know," I said as I felt my blood run cold. I'd read about that happening in books, but the description always seemed silly and melodramatic until it happened to me. It was like taking a bath in ice cold fear. Something was about to go terribly wrong.

The humans went to the sides of the mantel, out of our sight. There was a dull thump and the mantel shook. Iris's eyes went wide and she reached for me. A cracking noise rang out and the mantel jerked forward, throwing us into the window frame. Iris slid onto the sill, her torso hanging over the edge. I dropped the list and grabbed Iris's right wing, jerking her back in. There was another crack and the mantel twisted. Grains of wheat and barley flew everywhere, knocking us off our feet. Dad's woodworking tools clattered onto the floor. Their sharp edges menaced us as we screamed and clung together. Another jerk. Iris and I were thrown against the outside wall again. Another body width and we would've fallen out the window.

I grabbed a wall bracket, securely bolted to the wall supporting Dad's shelves. I held onto it with my right hand and looped my left arm around Iris's waist. We lay there for a second on the wall that was now a floor and screamed while the dust floated down. Before it had a chance to settle, the mantel flipped upright and we were back on the real floor with me still clinging to the shelf. Then the mantel jerked again and we began to slide toward the door to the hall. Another's screaming reached me through Iris's hysteria.

I looked past Iris's head and saw Gerald, bloody and bruised, sliding across the floor to the open doorway to the hall. The list fluttered past him, useless. Then my woodworking book glanced off his forehead, and his shriek went to a higher pitch. His fingernails gouged into the floor and his mouth was stretched open wider than I'd ever seen it.

"Matilda!" he screamed.

"Gerald!" I wanted to reach out to him, I really did, but I couldn't let go of Iris and letting go of the shelf wasn't an option either. We'd all fall. A sudden jerk of the mantel and I found myself dangling from the shelf with Iris's arms tight around my neck. I looked down in time to see Gerald disappear through the doorway, still screaming my name.

Chapter 2

I lost my grip on the bracket and Iris and I landed next to the doorway Gerald had fallen through. The wall kept jumping and bumping. That's when I realized our mantel was being carried off. Sometimes it jumped so much we'd float in the air for a second before slamming against the wall again. I looked for something to hang on to, but found nothing. Worse, the shelves I'd clung to before were now over our heads, and didn't look secure at all. They were dangerously close to falling on top of us. Every time the mantel jerked or bounced, the shelves shook and bolts pulled a little further out of their holes.

The mantel creaked and we bounced into the air again. The shelves groaned. The bolts were holding by a thread. Iris stopped screaming. Her mouth formed an O that kept getting larger. I didn't know if Gerald was still screaming. I hadn't heard him since he went through the door to the hall.

The mantel did another terrific bounce, slamming my teeth together.

"We've got to move," I said. "The shelves are coming down."

Iris clung to me and cried, "No."

"We have to. We'll get squashed." I dragged Iris toward the door and Iris started screaming again.

The mantel bounced and we flew into air again, landing on the door frame. I leaned over and looked down, through the two doors, across the hall into our parents' bedroom. It took me a second, but I spotted Gerald wedged between the bed and the bureau. I couldn't see his face, and he wasn't moving.

"Come on, Iris," I said as the shelves wavered above us.

"No," yelled Iris. "I want Mom."

"Mom isn't here. I'm in charge. Now I'll hang onto the door frame and you climb down me," I said.

"I'll fly," said Iris.

"There's no room to spread your wings. Just do what I say. The shelves are going to drop."

I swung myself over the edge of the door frame and held on, digging my fingernails into the wood as Iris shimmied down my back. At last she let go and landed on the hallway wall, then scooted out of the way. I dropped down just as the shelves broke free and crashed into the wall above. Bits of wood and debris fell through the doorway into our parents' bedroom, but Gerald didn't respond.

"I'm glad we moved," said Iris between gulping sobs.

"Me, too," I said.

The mantel stopped moving and I put my hand over Iris's mouth to stifle her cries and tried to hear if the humans were talking. If they were, I couldn't make out a word. The mantel lurched upward, driving us against the wall and then dropped.

I held on to Iris as we flew into the air for a moment and then back down.

"You have to stop crying, Iris. I can't hear anything. Are they talking? What are they doing with us?" I squeezed her and took my hand off her mouth.

"Something about crown molding and flooring," said Iris, voice still quaking. "I think they're walking away."

Iris buried her face in my neck and hugged me. I rubbed my sister's back and looked around the dim hall that used to be tastefully decorated. A few windows in the bedrooms must've remained open. Slits of light came through the doors, highlighting the debris. Particles of dust hung in the air and shone multi-colored, taunting me with their beauty amid the destruction. Broken furniture, clothing, plates, and cups littered the hall. All the mushrooms we used for illumination were damaged and fading. I didn't see my favorite, Barbara, anywhere. Then I remembered we weren't alone.

"Gerald," I called out.

"He's awake," said Iris. "He wants to know where we are."

"We're in the hall above you." I let go of Iris and patted her shoulders. "It's okay. I'm going to get Gerald."

Iris nodded, stuck two fingers in her mouth and began sucking them like she did when she was two. I struggled to my feet on legs that felt loose and wobbly like the bones had been removed. My head swam a little when I stood up.

"I'm coming, Gerald," I said, not at all sure if I could get to him and afraid of what I might discover when I did.

I walked with mincing, painful steps to the door of my parents' bedroom and looked down. Gerald lay below me to the right, pushing at the bureau and muttering. I squatted, held onto the door frame, and swung myself down into the bedroom. I dropped, hitting the side rail of my parents' bed and bonking my head on one of the bedposts. I was glad nobody was there to see me falling all over the place except Gerald and I didn't care what he thought of me.

When I straightened up, rubbing my head and cursing under my breath, the sight of Mom's special place stopped me cold. Everything was ruined. From the delicately carved furniture my father made, to the Venetian glass mirror Mom prized. There were spots of wet where her perfume bottles had struck the wall and left their contents. The smell of Mom's scents brought tears to my eyes. What would Mom and Dad say? I knew it couldn't possibly be my fault. Mom didn't even put humans on the list, but still I suspected my hearing didn't help the situation any.

"Matilda?" Gerald's voice broke into my thoughts. For once, his face didn't hold a resentful expression, only frightened and pained. Blood coated his left cheek and an angry bruise bloomed below that. His wings were crumpled and a bit frayed, but since wings healed quickly, I wasn't too worried about them. Gerald's arm, which hung from his shoulder at an odd angle, was a much bigger concern. I was the worst babysitter ever. It couldn't have been any worse if I'd set him on fire.

"Is the bureau on you?" I asked.

"No. I think I'm just stuck between it and the bed."

I pushed the bed away from Gerald and it collapsed. I slipped and fell to the floor, banging my knees and ripping holes in my black tights. Gerald shifted his weight and cried out when his arm touched the bureau.

"Don't get up yet." I rubbed my knees. "I have to think."

The woodworking book flew past my head and landed at my feet. I looked up to see Iris waving in the doorway to get my attention. "Matilda, I hear something."

"What? Is it Mom and Dad?" I asked.

"No. It's crying," said Iris.

Crying? Who would be crying? Everyone else had gone to the berry harvest.

"Matilda, pull me up," said Gerald.

"Wait," I said. "Can you hear it?"

Gerald's face screwed back into its usual expression of resentful self-righteousness.

"You're supposed to be helping me," he said.

"Gerald, do you hear it or not?" I stomped my foot, crushing a bit of glass into a powder.

"It's that baby," he said. "Now help me up."

I took his left arm, the uninjured one, and hauled him to his feet. He winced at the pain in his right shoulder. "I think it might be disconnected," he said.

"I'll have to pop it back in," I said. How to fix a dislocated arm was on the list. I'd read the instructions a dozen times, but the thought of wrenching Gerald's arm back into its socket made me nauseous.

Gerald raised his eyebrows. "Has your magic come in yet?"

"No, it hasn't. But the instructions were on the list. It is good for something."

"No way. You won't be able to stop the swelling. My dad will do it."

"Suit yourself, but it could be hours before your dad comes back. Listen again. Are you sure it's a baby?"

"Yes," Gerald said in a long, bored tone.

I strained my ears, but I still couldn't hear a thing. "Iris, do you think it's the baby, Ezekiel?"

Iris's face appeared over the edge of the door frame above us. "I think so. Why's he crying like that? Where's his mama?"

I shrugged. I thought our neighbors in the other leg of the mantel had gone to the berry harvest like everyone else. The Zamoras were new neighbors and I didn't know them well. They'd moved into the mantel after my grandmother died and I didn't visit because I didn't want to see Grandma Vi's home changed. Plus, they had the new baby, Ezekiel, and didn't get out much.

"He's still crying," said Iris.

"Mrs. Zamora will take care of him," I said.

"If she's there," said Gerald, sitting down on the floor and rubbing his arm. "Maybe she flew off and left him when all this happened."

"Shut up, Gerald. She'd never do that," I said.

"Then why's he still crying?"

"I don't know. Will you let me think?"

"Sure. It'll be fun to watch you try," said Gerald with a smirk.

"He's still crying," called down Iris. "And he's getting louder."

I threaded my way through the mess to my parents' windows and peeked out. All I could see was cream-colored metal.

Gerald came up beside me. "Where are we?"

"I don't know, but we have to get out of here now."

"No kidding. Your parents' furniture just about killed me."

I pushed at the window, but it wouldn't open any farther. I might be able to fit through, but Iris never would.

"Iris, see if you can open the front door," I said.

I waited as Iris scurried off and returned. Her round face peered over the edge of the door. "It won't open. It's too heavy. I'll try the other door." She left and returned a few seconds later. "It's worse than the front."

"We'll have to wait until the mantel's upright again to get out," I said.

"What about the baby?" asked Iris.

"What about my arm?" asked Gerald.

I looked around my parents' room as if I might find some answers in the mess. My hand went automatically to my jumper pocket, but the list was gone. My first thought was to wait for some adult to come along and fix it. But even if someone did come, how would they get in? I felt Iris and Gerald watching me, waiting for me to decide what to do. And even though I couldn't hear him, I knew Ezekiel was out there crying, also waiting. But I wasn't completely on my own. I had Iris for ears and Gerald might prove useful if I needed to annoy someone. The decisions were all mine and I found I didn't mind so much. It was better than asking permission.

"All right," I said. "Iris, I want you to come down here and help me. Just come down the way I did, and I'll catch you."

Gerald snorted and would've said something nasty about Iris's weight no doubt when I stepped on his foot. He yelped in pain and I held up my arms to my not-so-little sister. Iris dropped and just about flattened me. There wasn't an ounce of breath left in my lungs and a pain cramped my neck that probably wouldn't go away for days.

"I'm sorry. I'm sorry," Iris said as she rolled off and helped me up. "I won't eat any more maple syrup, I promise."

"Good idea," said Gerald.

"Don't be ridiculous." I glared at Gerald as he stuck his tongue out at Iris. "Eat whatever you want. Now let's take care of Gerald."

"What do you mean by that?" he asked, trying to scoot away from us.

"We're going to fix your arm, dufus. What do you think?" I smiled at him. Fixing his arm might not be that bad after all. I might even enjoy it after all the nasty things he said to Iris.

"No, you're not. I'm waiting for my dad."

"When it's time to get out of here, you have to be ready. Sit on him, Iris."

Iris grinned and plunked down on Gerald so hard a big whoosh of breath rushed out of him.

"At least use that stupid list," Gerald said with what little breath he had.

"I don't have it. I'll have to do it by memory," I said.

Gerald pointed frantically at the spot where he'd been trapped. The list lay, unscathed, next to a bed post. I went over and snatched it up. The three step instructions for popping an arm back into its socket were fifteenth of the list. Mom was big on three steps to anything and, for once, I was grateful. I could handle three steps.

I stuffed the list in my pocket. I stepped into position, grabbed Gerald's arm the way the list said and yanked. There was a grinding pop and Gerald screamed.

"You did it!" yelled Iris.

"Get off, fatty!" yelled Gerald.

I helped Iris up, and we watched Gerald fuss and flex his fingers. His arm was back in its socket, but he didn't appear to be grateful about it.

"I could've done that," he said. "It's not that big a deal."

"Only if your grandmother was a healer," replied Iris. "Matilda has talent. Grandma Vi said so."

"Your grandmother wasn't a great healer. My dad could …"

"Shut up, Gerald," I said. "Is the baby still crying?"

"He's kind of screaming," Iris said with big tears in her pale blue eyes.

I went to the window and shoved it open as far as it would go. "I'm going to go get him."

"I'm going, too," said Gerald.

"No, you're not. Stay here with Iris."

"It's not my fault she's too big to fit through. I'm leaving. I'm going to find my dad."

"No, you're not." If I knew one thing for certain, it was that they had to stick together. Iris couldn't leave, so we were all staying. What kind of babysitter would I be if I let Gerald run off? What if something happened to him? I wasn't totally against something happening to Gerald, but I had to keep him with me, and I couldn't leave Iris.

"I'm going," said Gerald. "You can't stop me."

I grabbed his good arm and wheeled him around toward my parents' ruined wardrobe, lying on its side. My dad had decorated it with dozens of pieces of delicate inlaid wood, but they'd all popped off and lay scattered around the floor. I felt a little sick when I thought of the hours he'd spent making the piece perfect for Mom's Christmas present the year before.

I pulled open the door. "In you go."

"No way!" Gerald yelled. His face turned bright red and a vein popped out on his forehead as I shoved him in the wardrobe. He may have been smarter, but he definitely wasn't stronger.

I slammed the wardrobe door in his face, turned the key in the lock, and handed the key to Iris.

"Wow," said Iris.

"Yeah. I'm going to pay for that, but I couldn't trust him not to leave."

"Wow." Iris looked at the key in her hand and then back at me.

"Don't let him out unless … unless I, you know, don't come back or something." I went to the window and tried to ignore Gerald hollering and banging in the wardrobe. It was hard to concentrate with all the fuss. I pushed at the window, but the wood didn't give. It would be a tight squeeze.

"What do I do while you're gone?" asked Iris. A worry line appeared between her eyes, just like the one our mom had.

"Nothing. Just wait with Gerald."

I pushed all the air I could out of my lungs and pulled myself through the window. I scraped my nose and tore my jumper on a nail, but I managed to squeeze out onto a huge hump of cream-colored metal next to the mantel. My eyes smarted from the bright sunshine after the dimness inside the mantel.

After my eyes adjusted, I saw that we were in the back of a pickup truck. I'd seen a few in the national park, but never so close. The mantel fit neatly into the truck's bed between the two humps where the truck's wheels were. There was a big rope over it and thick blankets underneath.

I stretched my wings and flew up onto the side of the truck. Whipplethorn Manor was yards away and teemed with humans. I'd never seen so many in one place before. I hoped to see Mom's silver streak weaving through their numbers or Dad's glowing purple wings fluttering in the garden. My ears might've been bad, but there was nothing wrong with my eyesight. I searched among the humans measuring the front porch and shouting at each other. Others pointed at the mansard roof and the grey slate tiles that decorated it. But my parents weren't there. None of the Whipplethorn fairies were. If I could've heard what the humans were saying, I could've at least figured out what was happening.

Iris stuck her head around the edge of the window and waved at me. "Matilda, did you get him?"

"I'm going right now."

I flew up over the mantel and hovered for a moment above the shelf. From my position, the mantel looked like a U. The legs, that usually framed the fire box, extended away from me and I saw them in a different light. Upside down the curves and carvings looked more beautiful and refined. I'd never truly appreciated the mantel's beauty before. Whipplethorn Manor was always bathed in dusty darkness and I was used to it that way. The sunshine revealed the magnificent detail of the carvings and the shine of the mahogany to me for the first time. I thought I knew my home, but now I was seeing it for the first time as a stranger might and it was glorious.

I fluttered over to the right leg of the mantel. The sight of the Zamoras' front door jerked me back to my task. I flew down and landed on part of the pillar on the right leg. The pillar had a curvy section in the middle that resembled a bunch of long columns meshed together. The door was hidden among the pillar's many lines and bumps. I'd rarely used that particular door when I visited Grandma Vi. She was usually in her sitting room at the top of the mantel near the shelf, so she could get the most sunlight.

I felt around the door until I found the carved button that unlocked it. I pushed and heard a faint click, and then wedged my fingers under the edge. I pulled, but I couldn't budge it. I imagined Ezekiel's cries and my heart rate rose with every imagined shriek.

"I'm coming!" I yelled through the door, knowing he probably couldn't hear me. And even if he could, it wouldn't make him stop crying.

I flew back up into the air and looked for a window on the side that might be open. I found it near the bottom. One of the windows for a storage room lay cracked open. I wedged myself through the opening. But as soon as I did, I found myself in completely unfamiliar surroundings. In Grandma Vi's time the storeroom was filled with plants and medicines. Now it contained musical instruments of every conceivable type and most of them were smashed to bits. The door to the hall was still recognizable and I picked my way across the room over broken cellos and punctured drums to the door in the floor. I stomped on the door and it flew open. Ezekiel's screams rushed into the storeroom, although to me they were more like frantic whispers.

I dropped to my knees and peered over the edge of the door into the hall. "Ezekiel! Ezekiel!"

The screaming paused and started again slightly louder than before. Ezekiel wasn't very old, just over a year. Like all wood fairies, he could comprehend language at birth, but wouldn't be able to speak until he was two or three years old.

"I'm coming!" I yelled into the darkness. The Zamoras' side of the mantel was darker than ours. Barely a sliver of light found its way in. I kept looking into the dark, hoping I'd be able to make out more than just dim shapes, but nothing became clearer. It stayed dark. I would have to drop into the darkness and hope for the best. Unless I did the one thing wood fairies weren't supposed to be able to do. It didn't seem fair that the one magical gift I had was the one that would make my mother cry.

I could make fire. Not a good thing if you live in wood, plus kindling was notoriously hard to control. My dad always said kindlers couldn't be trusted, so I'd hidden my so-called gift since I was eight. I'd been on the verge of telling

Grandma Vi when she died. She was the one person I knew wouldn't mind.

I leaned down into the darkness and tried once more see Ezekiel, but it was no use. I had to do it or I might break my legs and that wouldn't help anyone. Besides, the baby wouldn't be able to tell on me for at least a year and by then I'd have figured out a way to break it to Mom and Dad.

I put my hand into the darkness, ignoring Ezekiel's screams, and concentrated on my palm. I'd practiced some, but since the idea of burning down the mantel terrified me, I didn't have much experience. I took a deep breath and blew onto my palm. For a second, nothing happened and then a tiny blue flame ignited right in the center. I blew again and it grew, flickering and flirty, tickling my hand and making me grin. The flame grew to the size of a large ball, sending its light around the corners of the hallway.

"I did it!" I cried.

Ezekiel's screaming got even louder than before and I imagined his little throat was raw and burning by now. I lay down on my stomach with my chest balanced on the door frame and my lighted hand extended down into the hall. Shattered remnants of pictures and a hall table littered the wall that now served as a floor. I saw no sign of Ezekiel, though his screams were slightly more clear.

"Mrs. Zamora! Mrs. Zamora!" I yelled.

There was no answer, not even a tiny whispery one. Seeing the way was clear for me to jump, I closed my fist and extinguished the blue flame in my palm. As the hall went black, Ezekiel's screaming began to have a keening quality, like he was beginning to despair. I felt the weight of his fear and loneliness in my chest. Then he stopped crying and that was worse.

"I'm coming, baby," I called, but he didn't start crying again. Maybe he didn't believe me. Maybe he thought I would go and leave him like his parents, but I wouldn't. I would never do that.

I grabbed onto the door frame, swung over the edge, and dropped into the darkness, landing painfully on my knees. The hall seemed darker now that I was down in it. Without Ezekiel's voice to guide me, it was heavy and oppressive, like being covered in a thick blanket and not being able to get out from under it. I held out my hand and blew on my palm. The flame appeared quicker and brighter than before. It sent wavy shadows around the hall and I almost wished I hadn't made it. The shadows were rather creepy. I reminded myself that light was necessary to find Ezekiel and I got to my feet. I wished I could hear Iris and Gerald next door. If my ears had been normal, I would've had their voices to comfort me. But my ears were practically useless. I couldn't even hear Ezekiel breathing, which would've been a comfort, too.

"Ezekiel. Ezekiel," I called. "Where are you?"

I picked my way through the darkness, avoiding furniture and broken glass until I came to an open door. I stuck my hand down through the doorway and saw him. Ezekiel was against the opposite wall, pinned underneath the remains of his crib. His black hair curled down low over his forehead, nearly covering his brown eyes which usually matched his skin. But now he looked pale to me and a bit greyish. When he saw me, he took his fat fist out of his mouth and held it out to me.

"I found you," I said. The baby blinked and started squalling again. "All right. All right. I'm coming."

I put out the flame, which made Ezekiel squall louder, and dropped into the room next to him. I relit the flame and touched his face with my other hand.

"Quiet down. You're hurting my ears and they don't work so well in the first place."

Ezekiel stuck his fist back in his mouth and began making sucking noises. His big eyes kept going back and forth between the flame and my face. He knew what I was. There was no mistaking it. I ran my free hand over him. He appeared to be all right, despite having a crib on top of him. I lifted the railing and braced it with my hip, and then held the fire far out away from the baby and slid him out from under the crib by his foot. Then I got down on my painful knees, pulled him onto my hip, and struggled to my feet.

"You're not going to tell anyone about me, are you?" I asked.

He looked me in the eyes and gave me a slow blink. I'm pretty sure that meant he agreed not to rat me out.

"Okay. We have to get out of here," I said to the baby. He looked back at me with wide brown eyes and sucked harder on his fist.

I picked my way across the ruined nursery to a window. It was shut tight and there was a smear of blood on the frame. It must've been from Mrs. Zamora, since Easy wasn't bleeding. I rammed the window with my shoulder, but it didn't budge.

"Great," I said. "It can't ever be easy."

What should I do? Put down the baby or put out the light? Neither seemed a good option. The wall began to shake beneath us. A little bit of dust fell onto my face from a shelf still attached to the wall above my head and made me sneeze. Ezekiel sneezed, too, as the wall shook harder.

"Oh, no. What now?" I put Ezekiel down and extinguished my light. I rammed my palms against the window as the wall jumped and I fell on my knees. Ezekiel began shrieking again, but I couldn't stop to tend him. My hands felt their way up the wall and fumbled for the lock. I found it and felt a click. "Come on. Come on." I pushed against the window and it gave a bit. The light made me blink. Then the mantel shifted again and threw me against the wall. I picked up the baby and looked out the window. A human's hand was resting on the side of the truck and he was probably talking. Oh, to have normal ears. I clutched Ezekiel tight to my chest and stuck my leg out the window. My toe touched another cream-colored wheel well and I pulled us both out of the window.

Across the bed of the truck were a couple of red-faced humans coming towards the truck with a load of crown molding in their hands. I gasped when I saw it and I'm not a big gasper. My friends Sadie and Ursula lived in the crown molding. It looked like all of Whipplethorn was being torn apart. My only consolation was that Sadie and Ursula weren't home. They were out berry-picking with their parents. I pushed the thought of them out of my mind and spread my wings. I tried to take off, but Ezekiel's weight was too much for my aching wings. The humans went around to the back of the truck and placed the molding in behind the mantel with a lot of other moldings that hadn't been there before.

"Let's go," one said. "This is enough for one trip."

"Yeah, I'll drive," replied the other.

Drive, I thought. Then I slapped my forehead. Trucks were for going places. The humans were taking the mantel away from Whipplethorn. I jumped for the mantel and managed to pull myself and Ezekiel up onto the top. I ran across the face of the mantel toward the storeroom as the humans slammed the truck doors and the machine rumbled to life.

"Iris," I screamed. "Get out! Get out!"

I didn't know if Iris heard me or how she would get out if she did. I only knew she had to escape, or we'd be taken away, away from Whipplethorn and everything we knew.

Chapter 3

I leapt off the side of the mantel onto the wheel well. The truck lurched forward and I fell, clutching Ezekiel to my chest. I threw my arm out and my fingers caught a brace on the side of the truck bed. As I held on, I saw the storeroom window cover shaking. Iris must've been ramming herself against the wood. I couldn't imagine Gerald doing any such thing. I crawled across the wheel well to the window to see my sister's terrified face peeking around the edge.

"Get out!" I shouted.

"I can't!" Iris shouted back.

"Get one of Daddy's axes!"

"I couldn't find one!" Iris rammed herself against the cover again.

The truck picked up speed and the wind blew Ezekiel and me a couple of inches away from the storeroom window.

The truck went over a bump and we hung in the air for a moment. A gust came and blew us farther away.

Iris stuck her hand through the opening in the window. "Come back in," she yelled.

I fought the rising wind as I scampered across the wheel well. Another gust and we'd be gone. Iris couldn't get out, so I had no choice but to go back in. I made it to the window and grabbed Iris's hand. I pulled myself close to the opening and used my body to thrust Ezekiel through.

"Take him!" I yelled.

Iris let go of my hand and took the baby. I tried to get a grip on the window frame, but a gust came and swept me away. I tumbled through the air, bits of dust and debris buffeting me, getting in my eyes and scratching my skin. I shut my eyes tight until I hit something with my hip. The sharp pain made me open my eyes and I saw the truck gate speeding toward me. I spread my wings and managed to miss it. Then I was out of the truck, behind it, in a swirl of choking dust.

"Iris!" I yelled, gagging on the dirt that coated my mouth.

I beat my wings to fight the air currents and steady myself. Then I flew straight up, out of the truck's wake and into the calm air above. I flew, extending and beating my wings hard to keep up. The truck surged ahead, but I managed to match it. I may not have had good hearing, but there was nothing wrong with my wings. It almost felt good up there in the bright sunlight, stretching my wings to their full potential. I rarely got to fly fast. There was usually no call for it, and Mom disapproved. She feared I'd sprain my wings, even though Grandma Vi pointed out numerous times that sprains were rare and didn't amount to much when they did happen. I did feel a pain across my shoulders, but it was a good kind of pain. It made me feel strong, like I could do anything.

The truck slowed down to make a turn and I dove. I flattened my wings against my body and zipped through the air like a dart. I flipped my feet down at the last second to land by the window just before the truck picked up speed again.

"Matilda," yelled Iris.

I touched the window edge and Iris grabbed my wrists and hauled me inside, scraping my shoulder and tearing the puffed sleeve of the shirt under my jumper. We tumbled to the floor and lay for a moment, gasping.

"Wow," I said.

Iris buried her face in my shoulder. "I thought you were gone."

"No way. Not a chance," I said. "I'd never leave you."

Iris started weeping, little sobs of relief. Behind that gentle sound came a not-so-gentle sound. An angry rant rattled the wardrobe. Gerald. Dear Lord, I'd forgotten all about him. Ezekiel sat near the wardrobe, staring at it with his fist in his mouth. He had a look of utter distaste on his little face. Apparently, even babies didn't like Gerald.

I rubbed Iris's shoulders and took the key from her. I went to the wardrobe, took a deep breath, and turned the large wooden key in the lock. The door sprang open and Gerald burst out of the wardrobe. His face was a strange kind of purplish-red and he sputtered with rage, practically incoherent. I scooped up Ezekiel, who was wagging his finger at Gerald and looking quite disapproving.

"Now Gerald, I had to do it," I said as I backed up. "I'm your babysitter. I couldn't let you run off."

"I'll kill you. I'll pull off your wings and beat you with them." Gerald stalked toward me with his hands curved into two claws, sharp and furious.

I put out my hand and caught him by the forehead before he could strike me. I held him at arm's length while he sputtered and swung at me.

Iris came around from behind me, tisking and wagging her finger at Gerald, like Ezekiel. "Gerald, you look so silly. Is that any way for a genius to behave?" Iris sounded just like her teacher Miss Molly when she was lecturing Gerald on one of his many misdeeds. Miss Molly had a way of handling Gerald, which was probably why Mr. Thomas let him skip two grades so she could deal with him.

Gerald dropped his hands and backed away. "I am not silly," he said. Even as he spoke, he gave the impression of puffing up like one of those weird tropical fish I'd seen in a book.

"That's right. Geniuses are never silly," I said, thinking that they weren't very much fun either.

"I am a genius, you know," said Gerald. "Everyone says so."

"Well," I said. "You're something all right."

"Just so you know," said Gerald.

"I know exactly what you are, Gerald."

Gerald's eyebrows knotted together and he threw me a suspicious look. Then the truck turned and we all stumbled to the right. Gerald and Iris ran to the window, crowding together in their excitement. Their wings spread wide, the colors complimenting each other. They looked quite beautiful together.

"What is it?" I asked.

"We're in town," said Iris.

"Downtown," corrected Gerald.

Iris lurched into him and jolted him away from the window. "How would you know, smarty-pants?"

"I know lots of things you don't know, stupid."

"Name one," said Iris.

Gerald stepped back from her and glanced back and forth between us. He clamped his lips together so tight they turned white and trembled.

Iris crossed her arms and narrowed her eyes at him. "Go ahead, Genius. Name one. One thing. Come on, name it."

Gerald fairly vibrated from the force of holding back whatever he knew. He was famous for blurting out facts that nobody cared about. But I thought this fact might be one we would care about. We might care about it very much.

"What is it, Gerald?" I asked softly.

He turned away. "Nothing," he said.

I shifted Ezekiel to my other hip and he nuzzled into my shoulder. The warmth of his small body soothed me, and was a reminder that Gerald, despite all his obnoxiousness, wasn't so very old either. He was just a little fairy, really, and I was supposed to be taking care of him, like Ezekiel, no matter what.

I walked over to him, balancing carefully in the shifting mantel, and touched his shoulder. "I'm sorry about all this, Gerald."

He raised his eyes to me, angry and defiant. "I just want to go home," he said.

"I know. Maybe I should've let you go when you had the chance. I was trying to do what babysitters are supposed to do. You're the genius. You understand that, right?"

Gerald shrugged. "Whatever. I'm hungry."

I looked up at the door in the ceiling. Getting food wasn't going to be easy, but I'd have to figure it out. The truck turned again and skidded to a halt. I fell onto the remains of the bed, narrowly avoiding squashing little Ezekiel. Iris and Gerald made their way back to the window and listened.

"Well?" I asked.

"We stopped," said Gerald.

"I know that, Gerald," I said, rolling my eyes at him.

"Maybe if you want to know, you should listen." Gerald sneered at me.

"Stop it, Gerald," said Iris. "I can't hear everything either."

"I can hear just as well as you and I even understand what they're saying."

"Shut up, Gerald," Iris and I said together.

Gerald stomped across the room, muttering about his superiority and being unappreciated as Iris leaned out the window to hear better. Then she turned back to us, her eyes large and full of wonder.

"We're being sold," she said.

"They can't sell us," said Gerald. "We're … we're Whipplethorns."

Iris stomped her foot at him. "You mean we're Whipplethorns. You're just an Ogle."

Gerald bowed up. "We're Whipplethorns, too."

"Not really," said Iris. "You changed your surname, but you're really still Ogles."

I stepped in between them. "Stop it, you two. That's not important. And they're not selling us. They don't even know we're here. They're selling the mantel. Who are they selling it to?" I asked as Ezekiel nuzzled my cheek.

"An antique dealer," Iris replied.

"A what?"

Iris shrugged and turned back to the window. After a moment, she said, "They're coming to get us. Hold on."

There was nothing for us to hang on to but each other. Gerald looked around, his wings opening and closing. I pulled Gerald to me and then Iris. I wrapped my arms around the three of them and held on as tight as I could.

"What should we do?" Iris asked as something snapped above us.

"I don't know yet," I said.

Gerald grinned up at me. Little spots of pink appeared on his cheeks and he glowed with malicious joy.

"Shut up, Gerald," said Iris.

He pulled back from us. "I didn't say anything."

"You were going to."

"I was not. I …"

The mantel lurched and threw us into a corner. I braced my feet against the floor and clung to Iris and Gerald. Iris screeched as the bed slid past and knick knacks started flying. Then the mantel settled into a walking rhythm and we relaxed. Things shifted back and forth, but, at least, nothing was flying around and whacking us in the head.

Just when I let go of the deep breath I was holding and started to feel this comforting rhythm might go on awhile, it stopped. The mantel shot violently upright to its normal position. It happened so fast, we didn't have time to scream. We bounced off the wall and landed in a heap on the floor. The mantel was tilted slightly so everything, including us, slid a little towards the back wall and then settled quietly.

"I think it's over," I said.

Iris propped herself up into a seated position. "Maybe."

"What do you mean, maybe?" I asked as I tried to pry Gerald off me. He was clinging to my waist and so glassy-eyed, I wasn't sure he knew he was doing it.

"We're not alone," said Iris.

My mind started racing. Mom and Dad didn't like to tell us stories about species they thought we'd never encounter in isolated Whipplethorn. Mom didn't want to scare us, but I'd picked up a few stories at school and I figured I could handle about anything, except mindbenders because there was no way to fight them. They could read your mind and manipulate you. Trolls weren't good either. I'd have been pretty worried about kindlers, if I wasn't one. The gory tales about us were rampant at recess along with stories of humans, which were the most likely scenario.

"You mean there are humans here," I said.

Iris wrapped her arms around her legs and rested her chin on her knees. "Not just humans."

Chapter 4

Iris leaned out the window, balancing on her stomach and exposing her dimpled thighs. She teetered as though she might tumble out at any second and glanced back over her shoulder at me with a grin.

"Give me a second," I said as I adjusted Ezekiel's diaper pin.

"You have to come see," she said.

"It is pretty cool," said Gerald. "Let's go out."

I jerked my head up. "Nobody's going out."

"Oh, yeah?" Gerald shouted. "Try and stop me."

Gerald pushed Iris aside and started worming his way through the narrow window opening.

"Grab him, Iris," I said as I laid Ezekiel on a quilt.

Iris tugged on Gerald's ankles. He was halfway out the window and cussing up a storm.

"Stop it, Gerald," Iris said. "They're out there."

"Who's out there? You don't even know. Let go," said Gerald.

"They're there," said Iris. "I don't know what species exactly. It could be Kindlers or those weird Bogles."

"Bogles just hurt murderers," yelled Gerald over his shoulder.

I grabbed his leg and tugged. "You're going to have to tell us more than that, Iris. What's out there?"

"I don't know. Bad things."

Then my stomach got a swirly, queasy feeling. It reminded me very much of the stomach flu I'd had last winter. Then a loud voice came from behind me.

"I believe she may be referring to me. Although I don't appreciate being called a thing."

I started and turned around to see an odd little creature standing in the doorway. He was the same height as Gerald with a bald head, greenish-brown knobby skin and oversized hands and feet. He wore a brown suit that looked like it was made out of a greasy paper bag and he smelled like a dead frog.

Iris and I stood frozen, our hands still on Gerald's legs. My mind was blank. If someone had asked me my name, I wouldn't have known the answer.

"Hello?" the creature said while wiggling its fingers at us. It started walking with an odd hopping stride around the room, eyeing things and occasionally stopping to sniff them. He came close enough to make me gag. My eyes watered and my nose began to run.

"How did you get in here?" I managed to choke out.

"Through the door, naturally," the creature replied.

"You shouldn't be in here," said Iris. She let go of Gerald's leg to cover her nose.

The creature moved over to Iris. She backed up against the wall, her face puckered up like she'd just sucked a lemon. It stuck its head close to her face and its tongue came slithering out like a snake's would. "Too old," it said. "What a shame. What a pity."

Gerald twisted around in the window. "What is it? What's going on?"

The creature lowered its tongue to Gerald's bare calf, almost touching it. It jerked its head back. "Sour."

I let go of Gerald's other leg and pushed the creature away. He was much softer than he looked, a sort of wet sponge texture.

"Get away," I said.

"Is that any way to speak to your new neighbor? Your new friend?" it asked.

"You're no friend of ours. Get out. Go away."

The creature clicked its tongue at me in a very disapproving way as Gerald wiggled back through the window. He straightened his shirt and looked to me. "What's going on?" asked Gerald. "I heard somebody."

I pointed at the creature and Gerald turned around. As soon as he laid eyes on the creature he fell into a dead faint and hit the floor with a soft thump.

Iris shook her head. "Not a Whipplethorn."

"What is this Whipplethorn?" the creature asked.

I grabbed the creature's sleeve. "We're Whipplethorns and this is our house." I pushed it to the window. "Get out."

"Is that the kind of fairy you are? Whipplethorn? I thought you were wood fairies. You look it." The creature stood its ground and wouldn't let me shove him out the window.

"We are wood fairies. Whipplethorn is our last name. Now get out."

It hopped away from me and placed a large finger on its chin. "And he's not a Whipplethorn. Does that mean you don't want him? I could take him off your hands. For a price, of course."

Gerald stirred on the floor, saw the creature, and fainted again.

"Not very sturdy, is he? I'm afraid that will cost you. What have you got to trade?"

"Nothing." I advanced on the creature and tried to push him out the door. For being so small, he was surprisingly strong. "We're not selling Gerald."

"Oh no, my dear sweet girl. Not sell." Its voice lowered. "Get rid of."

"Well, we're not doing that either. What are you, anyway?"

"I am a spriggan. A proud race of, um how shall we say, fixers."

Iris came at him, her face screwed up with distaste, and starting pushing with me. "We don't need any fixing. Go away."

The creature backed out the door into the hall. "You'll be sorry. This trade could've spared you much trouble."

We backed it down the hall to the side door, which hung open. We pushed the creature to the threshold.

"Is this how you treat your neighbors?"

"We're not staying," I said.

The creature winked at me. "That's what they all say. Good day."

"Same to you." I booted it off the threshold and it landed with a wet splat on well-worn linoleum.

We stood in the doorway watching as it disappeared between two ancient trunks piled on the floor next to the mantel. In fact, things were piled everywhere around the mantel. I'd never seen so much stuff. There were rocking chairs, picture frames, disintegrating clothing, crockery, beds, and anything else I could've imagined.

"I heard the humans call it an antique mall." Iris grinned. "Kind of cool, isn't it?"

"I guess."

All I could think about was our parents. How was I going to get us home when we were in such a huge mess?

"What's a spriggan?" asked Iris.

"We can look it up in Dad's book." I glanced around the messy hall. "When we find it."

"Check it out, Matilda," said Iris, pointing out the door at shelves piled high with dozens of books.

"Wow." I began counting the books, but swiftly lost count after forty. "That's a lot of books."

"They're all dusty and just piled up. Don't the humans care about them?" asked Iris.

"I guess books aren't rare in the human world."

"It would be so cool to read some." Iris looked like she was ready to take off.

"It would be, but we've got bigger things to worry about." I hooked my arm through Iris's and we walked down the hall back to the bedroom. Ezekiel sat on the floor. His fine brows were drawn together and his mouth formed a worried pout.

"What's wrong, baby boy?" asked Iris.

Ezekiel raised his chubby arm and pointed at the window. It was empty and Gerald was nowhere to be seen.

"Oh, no," I said. "That's just what we need."

"What?" asked Iris. "Where's Gerald?"

Ezekiel shook his finger at the window and chirped. I went to the window, feeling beat up and tired. The antique mall appeared more cluttered than ever as I tried to spot Gerald amongst the mess. I looked for some tiny movement, for a flutter of wings or a glimpse of his resentful face, but there was nothing.

Iris grabbed my arm and tugged it hard. "He's gone. What do we do?"

My head jerked back and forth as Iris yanked on my arm. Gerald was gone. I'd lost Gerald. And worse, I'd have to go find him. I'd have to go out. There were bound to be more spriggans and probably worse.

"What do we do? What do we do?" Iris kept chanting.

I finally pulled away from Iris's hand, went to the window and leaned out. My eyes roamed past glass cases filled with knickknacks, past kitchen chairs, and wardrobes, all with price tags dangling. A well of sadness rose up around my heart. All those things crammed into the space were things that someone had once cared about, probably cared about very much, and now they were to be sold to whoever was willing to pay. And Gerald was out there, by himself with very little common sense to guide him. How could I find a boy who didn't want to be found in a place so immense and confusing it would take days just to figure it out? What if I couldn't find Gerald before the spriggan did?

Chapter 5

I hefted Ezekiel onto my hip and yelled after Iris as she disappeared into the hall. "Make sure you lock all the windows."

Iris's answer was lost to me, an unpleasant reminder that I would be leaving the safety of the mantel to search for Gerald with rotten hearing. An army could sneak up on me with no problem. Ezekiel put his arms around my neck and nuzzled my cheek like he could hear what I was thinking. Then he chirped loudly and patted his mouth.

"Right. You're hungry. I almost forgot."

I slammed all the windows in the bedroom, but had to look for the locks. I couldn't ever remember locking our windows or doors before. In Whipplethorn Manor it simply wasn't necessary. I ran my fingers around the window sills until I found each tiny wooden hook. Then I fastened them onto their equally tiny eyes. There must've been some time in my family's history when locks were necessary or my ancestors wouldn't have made them. Lucky for us someone had been afraid of something. I wondered if it could've been a spriggan. I was certainly afraid of them. Enough that I considered using some of Dad's special glue to seal the window against its return.

"Maybe Gerald'll get some sense and come back on his own," I said to the baby.

Ezekiel screwed up his mouth and blew air out of his nose.

"You're right," I said. "He's too smart for sense. At least, he thinks he is."

I carried Ezekiel into the hall and started going from room to room, slamming and locking windows. Ezekiel's stomach growled so loudly that even I could hear it. I walked him to the kitchen sat him on a clear bit of floor. I put my hands on my hips and surveyed the damage. The kitchen was worse than the rest of the house. Food, utensils, and containers covered the floor. The chandelier my great-grandfather had carved lay in pieces in the corner.

"I guess I don't have to wash the dishes anymore," I said.

Ezekiel snorted.

"Well, we probably won't be staying."

Ezekiel picked up one of Mom's long cooking spoons and banged it on the floor. He gave me a disappointed look and tossed it on a pile of cups.

"Fine. I'll clean up. Probably. Eventually," I said to the baby. "Now what do you eat? Do you have teeth?"

I rummaged through a cabinet that was lying on its back on the floor and pulled out a jar containing peach fruit leather Mom made in the summer.

"Peach?" I asked Ezekiel.

He stuck out his tongue and made a raspberry at me.

"Okay. No peach. Grape?"

Ezekiel considered the strip of grape fruit leather in my palm and held out his hand. I gave him the piece and watched as he bit it with tiny white teeth that I'd never noticed before. Iris came into the kitchen and watched for a moment.

"What does he drink?" she asked.

"I don't know." I looked at the water jugs which were on their sides in pools of their former contents. "The water's gone. I don't suppose we can give him wine."

Ezekiel blew another raspberry and we both laughed until we found ourselves hugging with tears dripping down our faces. The laughter felt so good like a spring had uncoiled inside me.

"I'd better go find Gerald now," I said, picking up a water jug as I wiped the tears off my cheeks.

"I locked all the other windows and doors." Iris handed me a cork and a carrying strap. I put the strap over my shoulders and bit my lip, looking at Ezekiel. Leaving him felt wrong. Iris was only ten. What if she didn't know what to do? I felt ridiculous questioning Iris's capabilities, when I wasn't certain of what to do myself. Iris could at least hear.

Iris hugged me. "We'll be okay. Find Gerald so I can kick him."

"Get in line," I said. "Now come on. You have to lock the door behind me."

Iris picked up Ezekiel, stumbling to the right before she got used to his weight.

"Okay."

I walked out of the kitchen, stepping over various broken articles of our life and went to the front door. Iris walked close beside me, murmuring comforting words to the baby, such as "She'll be right back, don't worry." I felt down the door frame, found the tiny lock, and unhooked it. I lifted the clasp that kept the door closed and pushed. The door swung open and revealed the antique mall in all its disarray. I stood on the threshold and looked into the cluttered world that I had no wish to enter. From that angle the mall seemed even bigger. It was an enormous warehouse divided by shorter partitions. I could see above the partitions that the long tubed lighting went on and on. They'd need millions of mushrooms to light the place. Even our smaller section was as big as one of the Whipplethorn bedrooms.

"It's really big," said Iris.

"It's not so bad. I have a great sense of direction. I won't get lost." Even as I said it, I wasn't so sure. I'd never been lost, whether in Whipplethorn Manor or out in the forest. But I'd never been in a place like the antique mall.

"Maybe I should come." Iris hugged me. "I could help."

I knew what she was saying. She could hear for me. Tell me when things were coming, but it was no good. I couldn't take Iris and the baby out of the safety of the mantel just because of my stupid ears.

"No. It'll be fine. You stay and take care of Ezekiel," I said.

"We can come. He's easy."

I pulled back and patted the baby's cheek. "You are easy, aren't you? I expect you to live up to that name while I'm gone, little guy."

"I don't know, Matilda. I hear lots of stuff." Iris's lower lip trembled and a flush spread over her pale cheeks.

"Is anything saying it eats wood fairies?"

Iris giggled and wiped away a tear. "No."

"Then I'll be fine. Just listen for me knocking, okay?"

"Okay. Bye." Iris looked steady and capable, but her voice quavered.

I turned and leapt off the threshold the way Dad taught me and let air catch my wings. The air was very warm in the building and held me more readily than the cool air of Whipplethorn Manor. I hovered a foot down from the door and tested this new buoyancy. Any little flutter moved me much faster than I expected. I did several flips and zipped back up to the door.

"How are you flying like that?" she asked me in awe.

"The air's different."

"What's different?" Iris stuck her hand out and waved it around.

"It's warmer than at home. Feels good." I did a flip and a dive in front of them just for the fun of it. "Guess I'd better go find the stink fairy."

Iris and Ezekiel waved.

"Bye, Iris. See if you can find Barbara for me." I waved to the baby. "Bye, Easy. That's what I'll call you, if you're good."

I fluttered to the top of the partition, so overwhelmed by the size of the antique mall that I sat down on it with a thump. The metal felt cool through my jumper and I shivered at both the cold and at the immense place before me. The section where the mantel rested was large, but it seemed tiny in comparison to the rest of the building. Rows of lighting tubes stretched on forever across a vast ceiling. Partitions fitted together and formed a crazy kind of maze where humans chatted and wandered around, picking up objects and looking as overwhelmed at the sheer volume of stuff as I was.

I'd never seen that many humans and I had no idea they came in so many shapes and sizes. A tall man lugged a large crock past two smaller, rotund men arguing over something. I couldn't hear what they were saying, but their faces were red and sweaty. An enormous woman tried to squash herself through an opening between two partitions and succeeded, only to knock over a basket, three picture frames and a delicate-looking chair. The woman picked them up quickly and looked around to see if anyone had seen her. No one, but me.

A couple of elderly women walked past my partition. They smelled of lavender and cookies. Their grey hair was swept up off their necks into knotted, swirling designs. They were close enough that I could hear their words, just barely.

"Are you sure that's what she wants, Sarah?" asked the taller of the two.

"I know my granddaughter," said Sarah.

"I thought I knew mine and look where she is today. Pregnant by a carhop. Ridiculous," said the one on the right.

"Bellhop, Marie. He's a bellhop," said Sarah.

"It amounts to the same. Another nowhere man introduced into the family," said Marie.

"Well, no offense, but my Rebecca is nothing like that. I'm certain she wants a roll top desk for completing her master's degree. She's been hinting about it for years," said Sarah.

"Strange thing for a young woman to want."

Sarah peeked in the area where the mantel was. "Not really. My dear Thomas used to tell her tales about the roll top his father had. Oh, how she loved those stories. And besides, she's not that young. She has children of her own now."

"I keep forgetting that. You know you're old when your grandchildren have children."

"That hasn't happened to you, Marie. You still don't act your age." Sarah brushed past her and walked up to the mantel.

"There's a big difference between acting your age and knowing it." Marie leaned on my partition. "Thomas never acted his age as I recall. And what tales did he tell his granddaughter anyway? What could a person possibly say about a roll top desk to make it interesting to a child?"

"Oh Marie, you knew Thomas. He had such a way about him." Sarah stood still and brushed her cheeks. I thought I saw the sparkle of tears on her fingertips.

"Well?" asked Marie. "What did he say?"

"He said there were fairies living in his father's desk. Bunches of them, whole families living inside the wood."

I jumped to my feet and flew off the partition to get closer to the chuckling ladies.

"Dear man," said Marie.

"He was the sweetest, no doubt."

"Fairies! Imagine that," said Marie. "Do you have it? The fairy desk. You should give her that one."

Sarah brushed her cheeks again. "Afraid it was sold after the big crash in '29. Thomas said the family lost almost everything in the stock market. Apparently, his father felt just terrible about all those fairies being displaced."

Then the two ladies stopped at our mantel.

"My, what a beautiful piece. Mahogany, I think."

The ladies began discussing the mantel and looking it over. Sarah ran her fingers over the carved designs and murmured. "Beautiful, just beautiful. It has a nice feel about it, too."

"We better get going or we'll never find a desk in this place," said Marie.

The ladies walked out of the mantel's area and I followed them. I fluttered around in their lavender wake, soaking up the scent. They reminded me of Grandma Vi. Plus Sarah and Marie seemed to know where they were going and that was comfort. I had no idea where to go or where to look for the wayward Gerald.

I swooped around the ladies, looking on bookshelves and behind furniture. There was no sign of Gerald, and there were thousands of places a tiny wood fairy could hide. It might be impossible to find him even if he wanted to be found, which he probably didn't.

"Gerald!" I yelled.

I don't know why I bothered. If he yelled back, I wouldn't be able to hear him unless he was right in front of me. It was all beginning to seem pointless. I dove down and landed on cool linoleum to look under a beautiful hope chest. No Gerald, but the paintings on the side were lovely and I stepped back so I could see the entire design. Painted in ancient gold lettering was 1855 and the initials M.M. and J.M. with birds and flowers swirling around the letters. The chest was the kind of thing I imagined would have belonged in Whipplethorn Manor when there was still furniture in it. It was so elegant and clearly made with love by a master woodworker. Maybe Dad could make me one.

Dad. Not until that moment had I thought of him and the future together. For the first time, I considered that I might not see him, or Mom or any of the other Whipplethorn fairies again. I don't know when I started doubting it. The feelings seemed like they'd been there all the time. I wanted Mom and Dad to find us, but what if they didn't? What if I couldn't find a way to get us back to Whipplethorn?

I touched the hope chest and then rested my cheek against the wood. The smell of the green paint was old and faded, but still there. The woodworker must've mixed and painted with great care; Dad did. Tears burned my eyes and I squeezed them shut until I smelled something else and it wasn't paint. I sniffed deeply and opened my eyes, the tears forgotten. The smell was odd, but not wholly unpleasant. It was like cattails from the pond mixed with lemongrass. I looked around for the source and that's when I saw them.

A group of beings were piled under a low table across the aisle from me. I assumed they were some species of fairy. They were too small to be anything else. The pile was brown, lumpy, and unremarkable. I might've thought it was a pile of dog poop, if it hadn't been for the smell and the occasional leg sticking out. And I wouldn't have thought the pile alive, but the legs twitched and kicked. A hand covered with thick brown fur stuck straight up and waved around, only to disappear again.

I crept alongside the hope chest, eyeing the mass of bodies. I stopped and looked for the Sarah and Marie. They were down at the end of the aisle, looking at a roll top desk the size of a small car. The sight of them made me braver and I dashed across the aisle to crouch by the table leg. I listened to the faint snores and grunts. They didn't make it any easier to tell what type of fairies they were, even close up. They had legs and arms covered with brown fur, but little else to distinguish individuals. I couldn't remember any fairy description like what I was seeing.

I started to move towards the pile, but stopped short. They could be dangerous. I took a deep breath like Mom taught me and examined my feelings, my senses. Mom said that all wood fairies had a sense that told them when there were dangerous creatures about. The trick was to listen to the sense and not ignore it. I'd never had cause to use it at Whipplethorn, unless I counted sensing Gerald's innate skunkiness. I tried to find something inside myself that said these creatures were dangerous, but nothing was there. If they weren't dangerous, they might've seen Gerald. It was too good a chance to pass up. Still, it seemed prudent to get a weapon, just in case.

I flew into the air and fluttered down to the ladies still at the desk. On it was a stack of paperwork, a stapler, and several bins of costume jewelry. Two sharp metal points stuck out of the stapler. I landed next to it and eyed the points. A nice sharp staple was just the thing. Dad used them in his woodworking. They were his most precious tools, quite hard to come by. Staples were good for gouging and weren't very heavy. I jumped on the base of the stapler, grasped the point and pulled. Nothing. It was stuck on something. I should've been able to wrestle it out. My strength, while unremarkable for a wood fairy, was more than a match for a staple. I whacked it with both hands. Still nothing. I glanced back toward the table that the pile of creatures was under. Hopefully, they wouldn't wake up and get away before I got the staple. I flew to the top of the stapler and landed as heavy as I could. The stapler didn't even tremble. My strength was good, my weight a joke. I jumped and jumped, but nothing would make that stapler spit out a staple.

I sat down on the end, panting. If I couldn't think of something, I'd have to go wake up those fairies without a weapon. I crossed my legs and rested my head in my hands. Think. There must be something I could use. Sarah and Marie chatted above me about the merits of the desk. They kept waving their hands and the air currents they created nearly brushed me off the stapler. Maybe I could get them to see me and push the stapler. Even if they only thought I was a bug, they might try to squash me and release the staple.

I jumped up and down. "Hey! Down here. Hit this stapler. You know you want to."

Sarah and Marie ignored me. I yelled myself hoarse, but they never looked in my direction.

"I don't know, Sarah. It's quite expensive. Are you sure you should?" asked Marie.

"It's perfect. Rebecca will love it." Sarah turned and craned her neck to look over a low bookshelf. "There's never someone around to help when you need them."

Then she spun completely around and her purse swung straight at me. I saw it coming, but only had time to shield my face before the great big black leather box swept me into the bin of costume jewelry. Sharp points poked me all over. Dozens of earrings stuck me in the wings, back and legs. I struggled to get on top of the mound, but kept sinking deeper amidst the golden quicksand of clinking metal against metal. Strands of beads wrapped around my legs and pulled me deep into the abyss.

Chapter 6

As I sank deeper into the jewelry bin, Marie said, "Look here, Sarah. I swear my mother used to wear a necklace just like this one."

A hand, wrinkled and smelling like baby powder, came toward me and grasped one of the necklaces. It rose, flashing its multi-colored Bakelite beads and teasing me with the hope of escape. I lunged at it, but the slippery beads brushed past my hands, eluding me. I lunged again, ignoring the jabs into my feet and legs. The tag ($1.99) rose in front of me and I grabbed the tail end of the string. Then I was dangling above the bin and its many flashing points as the ladies discussed the likeliness that it was the same type of necklace that the mother had worn. How could they not see me? A tiny wood fairy with glowing purple and green wings, dangling right in front of their faces.

"It's very like it," said Sarah. "Your mother wore that necklace nearly every day. Whatever happened to it, Marie?"

"I don't know. After she died, most of her things disappeared. I think my father couldn't take the sight of them. I wish he would've set aside something for me."

"You should have it then, even if it's not exactly the same," said Sarah. "It'll be my treat."

"Don't be silly," said Marie. "I'll buy it."

Sarah took the strand from Marie and I let go, flying up over the ladies heads.

I hovered and examined my arms and legs. Aside from a few new scratches, I'd come off pretty easily.

"It's my day to buy gifts," said Sarah. "Two memories to purchase, and it'll be my pleasure."

"Two?" asked Marie.

"Yes. The desk for Rebecca to remember my dearest Thomas and the necklace for you, Marie, to remember your dearest mother. Now no arguments; let's go find someone to ring this up."

The ladies discussed the purchases and how many men it would take to move the desk. Then they walked away. I couldn't imagine how many it would take. The thing was huge. Bigger than anything I'd ever seen. As I fluttered above it, eyeing the points that had so recently poked me, I had an idea. I landed on the worn green felt on the desk's writing surface, went to the nearest bin, and clambered up the side. Resting my arms on the edge, I peered inside. Weapons. They could all be weapons. I spotted one with just a tiny golden ball, the size of my head, on one end and a wicked sharp point on the other. The earring would be heavy, but wood fairies weren't weak. I could handle it.

I let go of the bin, flew up, and hovered over the jewelry. Grabbing the earring would be difficult. I hadn't mastered the delicate art of flying upside down and the thought of landing in the bin again was very unattractive. The brown pile under the table was still snoozing, but who knew how long they'd stay that way. If they woke up and attacked, I had to have a weapon, so I decided to go for it.

I took a deep breath, closed my eyes, and flexed my wing joints the way Dad instructed me. When I opened my eyes, the world was inverted. I'd done it. Not very well, Dad would've said. My wings refused to hold me steady. I rocked back and forth, bouncing up and down with every air current, but I was right over the bowl and the desired earring. With a shift of my wings, I lowered myself within arm's reach. My hand was just big enough to get a good grip on the shaft. I flexed my wings again, but before I could rise out of the bin, an air current caught my wings and drove me down. My forehead hit a necklace bead and the blow unbalanced me. I flipped upright, scraping my knees on several other earrings, but I managed to hang on to my prize. I flew straight up and hovered above the bin, shaking from the effort.

"Not so bad, Dad," I said, a little embarrassed to be talking to someone who wasn't there. But the words felt good. I liked to think that he'd be proud of me. I was doing things he would've encouraged if Mom wasn't always so worried about me getting hurt.

I flew back down the aisle and landed on the floor in front of the table where the brown fairy pile lay quivering. I found myself quivering, too. Maybe this wasn't my best idea after all. But it was the best I had and besides, I was curious. I'd never met another species before.

I walked under the table, holding my earring with the point toward the lump. I couldn't hold it still. The point kept jumping around until I rested the shaft on my hip. I felt like a knight ready for a joust with my trusty lance. All I needed was a horse and perhaps a bit more courage.

"Hello, there," I said to the pile, my voice barely more than a whisper.

The pile did not move.

"Um, hello. Wake up." I stepped closer and held the earring farther forward.

A couple of hands shot out, but they didn't wake. I took more steps until I was close enough to distinguish the silky texture of the brown fur and tried again.

"Hello. I need some help. Wake up," I said.

I tucked my hair behind my ears, bit my lip, and poked what looked like a hip with the tip of my earring. Nothing.

"Oh, for goodness sake. What's wrong with these things?" I asked as I poked another one. The pointy end of the earring was quite painful. I knew that from experience. What was wrong with them?

I jabbed another one without any care for the damage I might cause, but the creature didn't do anything but snore.

"They won't wake," said a voice from behind me.

I jumped and spun around, holding my earring tightly. In front of me stood a curious creature that looked as though it'd been carved from the table leg it stood beside. It was a golden brown complete with wood-grained skin, long spindly arms and legs, and no discernible clothing. Long, thin sticks stuck out of its head and it hurt my neck to look up at it. The creature was twice my height and had black eyes beneath wood-grained lids. Although I couldn't tell whether the creature was a boy or a girl, in my heart I instantly categorized it as a male about ten years older than me.

"They won't wake," he said again.

"Why not?" I asked, my voice shaking despite my efforts to hold it steady.

"They're trow. They wake at dusk, never before," he said.

"Oh." I couldn't think of anything else to say.

The wood-like creature lifted its knee, then extended a leg and took a carefully balanced step toward me. The step was so slow it disarmed me completely and I nearly giggled.

"What happened to you?" he asked.

I clutched my earring. I no longer felt like giggling.

"Nothing," I said.

"You're covered with bruises and scratches."

I looked down and realized he spoke the truth. Some of them were fairly fresh from the jewelry bin. The rest were dried and flaking from when the mantel had been torn off the wall.

"There was an accident," I said.

"A bad one, looks like. Do you need help?"

"I'm looking for someone. A little boy."

"A wood fairy like us?" it asked.

I stared at the creature. Did it mean us as in the two of us? How could we both be wood fairies? He didn't even have wings. The creature took another slow step forward and I took a step back.

"I am a wood fairy, although a different type, as you can see," he said. "I'm Soren Maple. And you are?"

"Matilda Whipplethorn. What type are you?"

"I'm a dryad."

"I'm just a plain old wood fairy, I guess," I said.

Soren's face looked as hard as oak, but it curved into a gentle smile. Warmth, sweetness radiated off of him. I could find nothing inside myself that said to fear him.

"There's nothing plain about you," he said.

I smiled back at him.

"Come with me, Matilda Whipplethorn, and we shall see," said Soren.

"See what?" I asked.

"If we can find your little boy." Soren turned and walked away with his high-stepping, slow gate. I glanced around. The antique mall lay quiet and deserted except for the occasional human. I wasn't sure I should take his help, but neither did I want to wander around aimlessly. It really wasn't much of a choice. I hefted the earring and followed him through a warren of wooden chair legs and hoped for the best.

Chapter 7

The furniture stood like a gleaming maple forest in a quiet corner of the antique mall, each piece elegantly carved and smelling of lemon oil. I stared with wonder at the canopy bed in particular. Its four posts twisted toward the ceiling and the silk lining in the top formed a beautiful sun-burst pattern. The huge headboard below was a riot of scrollwork and various fruits carved with such artistic talent as I had never seen.

"Oh," I whispered.

Soren ducked his head. A tinge of pink bloomed on his golden cheeks. "Welcome to my home."

"It's so beautiful. Do you live on the inside?" I asked, although I doubted it. Soren was so big, how could he fit?

"No, we nest on the outside." Soren waved at the furniture.

I eyed the area Soren was waving at, but couldn't see anything.

"You should wave as they're waving to you," he said.

"Where?" I asked.

"Everywhere. You only have to really look in order to see. Just like humans. Although humans never bother to look."

So I really looked. I ran my eyes carefully over the beautiful bed, the matching highboy, the bookcases, and dressers. And then they were there, dozens of spindly arms just like Soren's, waving at me in a most cheerful fashion.

"I see them. I see them," I said, waving wildly.

"My family," said Soren as the dryads climbed slowly down the furniture, stopping to wave every few steps. When they got closer, I felt a blush come over my own cheeks. They didn't seem naked, but I couldn't make out any clothes either. I was able to ignore this with Soren because there was only one of him. A whole family of possibly naked dryads made me want to run the other way, no matter how friendly they seemed. I backed up a few steps, uncertain about what to do.

"What's wrong, Matilda Whipplethorn?" asked Soren.

"They're …" I hesitated. Should I say it? I didn't want to insult anyone.

"Yes?"

"Are they wearing clothes?" I asked at last.

Soren grinned at me. His wood-grained lips stretched farther than I'd thought possible.

"Oh, thank you. So kind of you to say."

I bit my lip. "Um."

"Mother," said Soren, waving to the closest dryad who was walking toward us with painfully slow steps, even slower than Soren's. She had the same intricate wood-graining, but she was slightly shorter with large eyes and a small bow of a mouth.

"Mother, this is Matilda Whipplethorn and …" Soren grinned even wider, "she thinks we're naked."

Soren's mother clasped her hands together. "Music to a mother's ears."

I looked back and forth between them. Soren's mother laid a warm hand on my shoulder. Again, I felt nothing but sweetness coming from the dryad.

"We're not naked, dear. We're painters," Soren's mother said.

"Painters?" I asked. "What do you paint?"

"The greatest canvas. Ourselves." She held her hand up in front of me and rubbed away a strip of wood-graining, revealing pale brown skin.

"Oh." I didn't want to state the obvious. Paint wasn't clothes. No one with sense would think so. Maybe Soren and his family weren't dangerous, but they might be crazy. "I think I'd better go."

"Does this help?" Soren's mother stepped back and appeared to lift her skin right off her hip.

"What is it?" I asked.

"Our clothing, dear. We're painters. We paint everything to match our beloved trees. It is a huge compliment that you thought the illusion perfect."

I dropped my hands. "It is perfect." I turned to Soren. "I was worried you were naked the whole time."

"I should've known. You looked at me so oddly." Soren laughed and was joined by his family. They all crowded in, patting me and giving thanks for my compliments.

Soren's mother put her long arm around my shoulders and led me away. "Don't crush the child, people. I suspect Soren brought her to us for a purpose, not just to feed our vanity. Vanity is our great weakness, that and walnuts. You don't have any walnuts, do you?"

"Sorry, no," I said.

"Too bad," she said. "What would you have us do, my son?"

"I would have us help." Soren put a hand on my shoulder. "Tell them, Matilda Whipplethorn."

"I'm looking for someone. A little boy. He's a wood fairy. A wood fairy like me, I mean."

"He's your brother?" asked Soren's mother. "Another Whipplethorn?"

I grimaced. "Not a bit. He's not my brother and he says he's a Whipplethorn, but he's not."

Soren examined my earring and tested the sharp tip with his finger. "What is he then?"

"He's an Ogle. His family moved into Whipplethorn Manor late and changed their name. My family is original to the house. We came with the first stick of wood. We're real Whipplethorns."

All the dryads nodded as one. "So sad," some said.

"I thought it might be something like that. Such a sad thing," said Soren's mother.

"Sad? It's not sad. He's just pretending to be a Whipplethorn and going around acting better than us when he isn't even one of us." I planted the ball of my earring on the floor and held it like a flagpole.

"Perhaps you're too young to understand. Take us for example. We dryads are tied to our trees." She gestured to the furniture. "First we lived in our trees in the forest, and then our trees were cut and fashioned into furniture. We've traveled from house to house and finally to this antique mall, but we'll never willingly be separated from our trees. Something terrible must've happened to separate the Ogles from their home. You're wood fairies like us. You must feel the same about your trees as we do."

I considered what she was saying. I'd never thought about it before, but my parents said we came with the first stick of wood to Whipplethorn Manor. They said that our family had always been with the mantel. Did that mean we were with the mantel before it was a mantel? I did know Gerald's family didn't belong to any particular bit of wood in the house. They just found an empty spot and burrowed in. Nobody minded. Other families moved in when they needed a place. It was the changing of the name that bothered people. I once heard Grandma Vi describe it as disloyal. Disloyal to what? Was Gerald's family disloyal to their original tree?

"I don't know," I said. "I guess they must've left the Ogle house for a reason. I never thought about it."

Soren's mother squeezed my shoulder. "About this little boy, who are you looking for?"

"Gerald. He's about this tall." I gestured the appropriate height. "His wings are not as ..." I stopped. I was going to say that his wings weren't luminescent like mine because he wasn't a Whipplethorn, but it didn't seem like the kind of thing Soren's mother would want to hear. "His wings are blue and grey."

"Why did he leave you?" asked Soren.

"He wanted to find his parents. I tried to tell him to wait, that they would find us. But he climbed out the window and ran away."

"So your parents are gone, too," said one of the other dryads.

"Yes, but they didn't leave us. It was an accident." I flushed and looked around, daring anyone to say otherwise.

"I'm the babysitter and I decided we had to stay together when the humans came. Maybe I should've let him go when we were still at Whipplethorn."

"Tell us what happened," said Soren.

He gestured for his family to sit in a semi-circle around me. They carefully folded their long legs and arms in and waited for me to tell my tale. I bit my lip, searching for the words to explain what had happened.

"Humans came," I said.

"They always do," said one of the dryads.

I told them everything about the humans, the mantel, Gerald, baby Easy, and my sister, Iris. The dryads asked few questions. They seemed to know everything before it happened in my story. When I finished, Soren rose to his feet and told his family to do the same. It was a slow process.

"You must find Gerald immediately," he said. "Your sister is right. It's not safe out here for little ones on their own."

I looked around at the dryads standing around me with expressions of worry on their painted faces. "What could happen?" I asked.

"Well, there's the spriggans for one," said Soren.

"We met one," I said. "He came into the mantel."

The dryads murmured to each other. An intense worry radiated off them and settled in my chest. All I could think about was Iris. She was alone with Easy. Alone.

"Was the spriggan very interested in Gerald?" asked Soren's mother.

"He offered to take him off our hands," I said.

Soren's mother turned to him and he began giving orders. He told certain dryads to organize a search and another one to get supplies. He ordered his mother to take care of me and she led me around the back of the bed to one of the legs. It looked normal from a distance, but up close it was out of proportion. The Maples' home was built right on the leg and painted to match. Soren's mother opened a long, narrow door at the back and ushered me inside. Tiny pinholes in the walls let in light. My eyes took a moment to adjust in the dim glow after the glaring light of the antique mall. When I could see, I was astonished by what I found. The house was bigger than it looked, with several rooms and comfortable furniture. Everything was wood or painted to look like it. Soren's mother sat me on a cushy couch and left the room. The fabric on the couch was silky and painted to look like Birdseye maple, my favorite wood. I ran my hands over the fabric again and again. It was so perfect I wished my parents could see it.

Soren's mother came back into the room with a warm cloth and a set of clothing, wood-grained, just like hers. "Here, dear. Tend your scratches and change your clothes. They're ruined, anyway. There are some here in the mall who would help you, but they'd be shy of you in your present condition." She turned and left, closing the door behind her.

I brought the clothes to my nose and sniffed them. They smelled like Dad's wood shop just after he'd cut a fresh piece of maple. I breathed the scent in until my lungs could take no more, and then slowly let the air out, pressing the fabric to my face. I heard the door open and looked up.

Soren's mother peeked around the edge of the door. "Hurry, dear. There's no time to lose." Then she disappeared again.

I nodded and wiped my face and scratches. There must've been an antiseptic on the cloth because all my scratches tingled and left a pink tinge on the cloth. I realized how awful I must look. It was a wonder Soren didn't run the other way when he saw me. I probably looked like I'd been in a war, and in a way, I had. A war where I seemed to lose every battle.

I slipped off my tattered jumper, blouse, and tights. The blouse survived all right, but my jumper and tights were trashed. The new clothes were way too long for me, but fit in every other respect, except that there was no place for my wings to emerge. The clothes felt wonderfully clean and new against my skin. They were soft, probably woven from cotton and painted with intricate detail.

The door opened again and Soren's mother asked, "Are you finished?"

"Yes, but the clothes are too long and I can't get my wings out."

She came in with a piece of glass. "No matter. We'll fix that." She cut the hem of the pants and the cuffs of the sleeves. Behind me, she cut long slits down the back of the top and pulled my wings through.

"Done," she said, patting my shoulder.

"If the spriggans got my sister, what would they do to her?" I asked.

"How old is she?"

"Ten."

"She's too old for them. We're lucky you're long past the valuable age. You'd have brought a pretty price," she said. "We must go. Soren will already be leading the search."

We went out the door to find most of the other dryads were gone or still walking away. They didn't move very fast, but they looked determined with their straight backs and strong steady strides.

"What would they do to Gerald then? He's eight," I said.

"They'd sell him. They're traders. Children are their favorite merchandise."

"Sell him. Like a slave?"

"Exactly like that. Children are easier to work with. They adapt better than adults," said Soren's mother.

I walked beside the dryad in silence. It was unbelievable. Slavery. I had heard of it, but didn't know it was still practiced. My parents definitely should've told us about spriggans. Sometimes scared is better than ignorant. But who would buy Gerald? All he could do was annoy people. As worried as I was about Gerald, I still had a queasy pit in my stomach about Iris. I couldn't remember a time when my little sister wasn't dogging my heels. We were always together, whether I wanted to be or not. Now Iris was all alone with Easy. I didn't think she'd open the door to the spriggan, but maybe he could trick her. Iris was as curious as she was sweet.

Soren's mother took my hand. "It's not too late. We'll find him."

I nodded. All I wanted to do was get back to the mantel and check on Iris but I couldn't, because of Gerald. If anything happened to Iris because of that stink fairy, he'd regret it.

A.W. HARTOIN

Chapter 8

I spent the whole afternoon searching the antique mall with Soren and the other Dryads, but sometimes I went off alone, flying up high and fast.

No luck, not even a glimpse of Gerald. That stink fairy. Was he hiding from me? Or worse, had something happened to him?

Soren Maple waved at me from beside a large woven basket. I took one last look from my high vantage point near the ceiling, tucked my wings, and dove straight down to the dryad. I smiled at the nervous look on Soren's face as I pulled up at the last second to land beside him. When my feet touched the linoleum, my knees nearly went out on me. Soren caught me and held on while I caught my breath and forced my legs to support me.

"You're tired," he said. "We must return home now."

"What? Home? No," I said.

"It will be dark soon. The humans will close the mall and turn off the lights." Soren spoke slowly as if I were a very young child. If I hadn't been so tired, it would've irritated me.

"So?" I crossed my arms and frowned.

"It'll be dark."

"I don't care. We haven't found Gerald yet. I have to find Gerald."

"You have a water jug," Soren said. "Do you need to bring water to your sister?"

I fingered the jug. I'd gotten so used to it bouncing against my hip, I'd forgotten all about it. "Yes," I said. "But I can't stop now."

He clasped my hand. "It's all right. We'll get the water and take you back to your sister. My night forces will take over from here. If they find Gerald, they will bring him to me."

I looked up into his kind eyes, no longer surprised at the wood-graining surrounding them. All I saw was my friend, someone I could count on. Soren squeezed my hand and I squeezed it back.

"How far is the water?" I asked.

Soren pointed at a large grey box mounted on the wall ahead of us. "It's right there."

"What is it?"

"The humans call it a water fountain." Soren gestured to several other dryads walking our way. "It will take several of us to operate it."

Soon I was walking in a forest of long thin stalks of wood. I let my mind turn off and walked without thinking. It was so pleasant to not be worried, to feel completely safe in that forest of friends. I closed my eyes and Soren swooped me up in his arms.

"You don't have to carry me," I said.

Soren's warm breath was a gentle nuzzle on my cheek. "Rest awhile. Your weight is nothing to me."

I faded into sleep, and then jerked awake some time later. Soren held me with one arm and scaled the water fountain with the other.

"You can really climb," I said.

"You can really sleep." Soren smiled down at me. "We're at the top."

He set me down and the metal's cold seeped right through my shoes. The top had a lip around the edges, a flat portion, and then it dipped down into a basin with a big metal dome in the middle with holes. Off to one side was an odd, curvy metal stand with an enormous button behind it.

"Where's the water?" I asked.

Soren pointed to the metal stand "It's in there. We almost went mad with thirst before we figured out how to use it."

The other dryads gathered on the top, talking to each other in their quiet, gentle voices.

"We're ready," said Soren. "Matilda, go down there to the bottom of the faucet and get ready to catch the water in your jug. Be careful. It can sweep you away."

Soren and the rest of the dryads climbed up on the button one by one. I watched as more and more stood together on the button. I was about to ask what was supposed to happen when a small pool of water appeared at the base of the tall metal thing. I thrust the jug under the stream and looked up. The dryads were cheering. Water out of metal. It was like magic. Magic that took twenty dryads standing on a button to make happen.

The dryads climbed down off the button and gathered around me, smiling. "Wonderful, isn't it?" asked one.

"Thank you," I said.

I looked at Soren and found him with an odd fixed expression on his face. He grasped my shoulders and turned me around. There on a shelf next to the water fountain was Gerald, tucked up between long, thin pieces of what looked like hard paper. He was curled up in a ball and one of his wings was draped over him. He was still, very still.

I ran to the edge of the water fountain to see Gerald better. He was in one piece. I thought. The Dryads gathered behind and Soren put his hands on my shoulders. His warmth melted into me as the cold penetrated my feet from below. Caught in the middle was a burning knot in my stomach. It didn't seem possible. We'd found Gerald. I feared that if I blinked he'd disappear.

"Is that him?" asked Soren.

I nodded ever so slightly.

"Matilda, you should go to him."

"He's not moving," I said, searching for any sign of life.

Soren lowered his head beside mine. "He's breathing. We can hear him."

A whoosh of breath came out of my lungs and I wobbled a little with relief.

Soren tilted his head closer to mine. "You can't hear very well, can you?"

I nodded and, for once, I wasn't embarrassed. My hearing didn't matter. I'd found Gerald and he wasn't dead. I wasn't the worst babysitter ever in the history of the world, only moderately terrible, and I could live with that.

Then a flash of anger passed through me. "I'm going to kill that little stink fairy."

Soren laughed. "That didn't take long."

"He made me worry so much. I'll just … I don't know what I'll do." I was so relieved, so mad, and so altogether exhausted I felt loose and limp.

"You're happy." Soren wrapped his arms around me and squeezed.

"Happy? I'm not happy. He's a jerk. Look at all the trouble he's caused." I stomped my feet on the metal, making little clinking noises.

When I said "jerk," Gerald stirred. He raised his head as I was stomping my feet. His eyes grew large and wandered around, looking at the dryads. I stopped stomping and put my hands on my hips. What did he mean by running away and causing so much trouble? Stink fairy. Worthless know-it-all. I spread my wings to fly over, but as soon as I did, Gerald shuffled out of sight back between the paper boards.

"Oh, no! Gerald!" I yelled.

I zipped over and landed between the boards myself. I looked down the narrow passageway he'd run into and could make out some movement, but, of course, couldn't hear anything. The last thing I wanted to do was walk down that long corridor in the dark without knowing what might be at the other end. On the other hand, it was my chance to snag Gerald. That stink fairy wasn't going to get away if I had to walk through a tunnel filled with cats.

"Gerald. It's me."

He didn't materialize, so I crept into the tunnel. I ran my hand over the paper wall to my right. After my eyes adjusted, I could make out a picture on the wall of humans holding instruments and grinning like lunatics. At the end of the passage, Gerald appeared, or a form about his size. He was standing with his wings up. It was just like little Gerald to try to be intimidating, despite his shaking wings. When I got closer I could see that his whole body was shaking, too.

"Gerald, it's me. Matilda."

Gerald didn't answer, but backed up a step. He looked as if he wasn't sure whether to run to me or run away.

"Gerald. Come here this instant."

I sounded like my mother on a bad day. I don't know why I used that voice or why it worked, but Gerald stopped shaking and stomped his foot.

"Don't order me around," he said.

"Don't be an idiot," I replied.

"I'm not an idiot. You're the stupid one. Stupid fairy."

"Stink fairy."

With that, Gerald ran to me. He flung himself into my arms so hard we fell to the ground.

"I wasn't sure it was really you," he said.

"What convinced you?" I asked, sitting up.

"Nobody else calls me Stink Fairy, except your fat sister."

I rested my head on Gerald's. "Stop calling Iris fat."

"Stop calling me Stink Fairy."

That was a tough one, since he was a stink fairy, and I sort of enjoyed calling him that.

"If I must," I said, standing up and pulling him to his feet.

"She is fat, you know," Gerald said.

"Why does it matter?" I took his hand and led him back down the corridor toward the dryads.

Gerald shrugged. "It doesn't. I'm just saying."

"Well, don't."

Gerald shrugged again as we came out into the light to face the dryads on the water fountain. They cheered, cupping their hands around their mouths and jumping. I waved and felt a sharp tug on my other hand. Gerald had fainted again and lay toes up on the shelf. I knelt beside him.

"Gerald," I said. "Wake up."

Gerald cracked an eyelid. "Are they still there?"

"The dryads? Of course, but they're nothing to worry about."

Gerald shut his eye. "Make them go away."

"I will not. They've been nothing but helpful to me. I've been searching for you for hours. Come on. Get up."

"Hours?" Gerald opened his eyes to slits. He looked exceedingly suspicious, even for him. "Really?"

"Yes, Gerald. Hours. Now we have to get back home to Iris and the baby." I propped him up into a seated position.

Gerald stared at the dryads. "What are they made of?"

"Flesh, like you and me. They just paint themselves to look like wood."

"Why?" he asked.

"I guess they like wood a lot."

"I like wood," said Gerald.

"It would be strange if you didn't. We are wood fairies, after all." I pulled him to his feet. "We have to go. Iris is waiting."

We dove off the edge of the shelf and flew to the water fountain. I kept a sharp eye on Gerald, but I needn't have bothered. He kept as close as possible without us colliding. I landed near Soren and Gerald landed behind me, grabbing my hand. I began to think he wasn't so bad after all.

"So you've found your little boy," said Soren, towering over us.

Gerald stepped out from behind me and dropped my hand. "Little? Who said I'm little?" He eyed me. His face was back in its usual resentful expression.

I sighed. Truces with Gerald never lasted long. Dealing with him made me tired again.

"Gerald, it's just a description. I had to tell them what you look like," I said.

"I'm not little," Gerald bellowed.

A chuckle ran through the crowd of dryads. Some of them clamped shut their painted lips together in order not to laugh out loud. Soren and I exchanged a look of understanding. I would've laughed myself if I hadn't been sure it would've chased Gerald off and I didn't have the strength to go after him. Instead, I patted his shoulder.

"I didn't mean you're little. You're just the right size for you," I said.

"All right then," said Gerald, still glaring up at Soren, who was at least three times as tall.

"We need to get home," I said.

"You know where we are, if you need us." Soren glanced at Gerald. "Come to us for anything at all."

Gerald crossed his arms and stuck out his chin. "We don't need any help. I can handle anything."

"Of course," said Soren. "Matilda, come and visit us if you can."

I crossed my arms. Not in an attitude of resentment, but one of restraint. I wanted to hug Soren and have him hug me. It'd been so easy being with him. I didn't want to leave, but my need to get back to the mantel was greater. Soren touched my cheek and I turned, swallowing down the sadness of leaving him.

"Come on, Gerald," I said as I flew off the water fountain.

I glanced back to make sure Gerald was right behind me. He was, keeping close as before. Then I pivoted in the air and hovered. All the dryads were climbing down the side of the water fountain, except Soren. He stood in the same spot, waving at me.

"Thank your mother for me," I yelled.

Soren yelled something back. I couldn't make it out. Gerald flew past me and stuck out his tongue. I sped up and passed him easily. We soared over rows of furniture and past glass cases. I led the way back to our mantel and I didn't need good ears to do it.

The antique mall began to feel cozy and quiet with fewer humans milling around. I forgot that I couldn't hear them and just enjoyed the wind rushing past me. Everything was going to be fine. Soren had said so and he'd been right about everything else. We'd found Gerald and he wasn't dead. If I could find my way through the antique mall, I could get us back with our parents and somehow life would go back to normal.

Chapter 9

We rounded the last corner and saw the mantel leaning against a wall. The wood gleamed warm and wonderful under the bright lighting tubes and I couldn't wait to get inside to smell familiar smells and hug Iris. Coming home when home was no longer a sure thing was a wonderful feeling. Gerald's wing brushed mine and I'm sure I saw a warmth in his eye, although his expression was as resentful as ever.

I reached for his small hand, but before I grasped it, there was a clunk and the lights went out. A red glow bathed the area and distorted everything. I stopped short and heard Gerald cry out beside me. I pivoted toward Gerald, but he was too close and I ran into him. We tumbled downward, entangled.

"Tuck!" I yelled.

Gerald obeyed instantly, tucking his wings and wrapping himself in a ball. I grabbed him and righted us just before we hit a table.

"What was that?" Gerald asked, still in his tuck.

"Soren said it would be dark soon. I guess that was it. I just didn't expect it to happen so quickly." I tossed Gerald away from me like a ball. He spread his wings and hovered.

"Everything's red."

"Yeah, it's weird. Let's go home," I said.

Gerald glanced at the mantel. "Home."

We flew to our front door, hovered and knocked. I hoped that Iris would hear and come quickly. Before I could knock a second time the door flew open. Iris stood in the opening, grinning so wide it looked painful.

"You're back," Iris said, shooting out of the doorway into my arms.

I hugged Iris and flew her back through the doorway. Gerald landed on the threshold behind us and made discontented sounds at our reunion. He scowled at us and said, "Something smells weird."

Iris put her hands on her hips. "Our house doesn't smell weird."

"If you think this smells normal, there's something wrong with your nose."

I turned to look around the dark hall. Something did smell a little off, but all the feelings fit in the right places in my heart. Suddenly, I never wanted to leave the mantel again. It was my tree, like Soren's mother said. I never wanted to be separated from it.

"I found Barbara and picked up the rest of the mushrooms, but they're still not putting off any light. Should we use the torches?" asked Iris, gesturing to a bracket on the wall that held a bundled bunch of sticks dipped in sap.

"I guess we'll have to. Since the mushrooms are damaged," I said.

"Do you think Mom and Dad will be mad? Torches are only for extreme emergencies and you know how they feel about fire."

"I think today counts as an extreme emergency, but I don't know where Dad keeps his flint."

"I found it," said Iris, holding up pieces of flint and metal.

The metal had some fresh scratches on it and I raised my eyebrow at Iris. She ducked her head and handed them to me.

"It's dark in here without the mushrooms," she said.

Gerald squeezed past me and pushed up his sleeves.

"I'll do it," he said. "I'm the best at making fire."

"Go ahead, Gerald. Give it a try," I said.

"Try? I don't need to try," said Gerald. "I'll do it."

Gerald went to get one of the brackets, but tripped on a wad of blankets on the floor.

"What's this?" he asked.

"I was taking a nap, if you must know," said Iris. "I wanted to be right here when you came back. I sleep so soundly, I knew I'd never hear you knock unless I was right by the door."

"Where's Easy?" I asked.

"Ezekiel? Are we calling him Easy now?"

"We are. It's loads better than Ezekiel. Where is he?"

"Sleeping. He was really tired. I didn't know babies slept so much." Iris turned to Gerald and stuck her chin out at him. Her plump face wry and disbelieving. "Go ahead, Gerald. Make fire. We're waiting."

Gerald grabbed a torch and handed it to me. He kicked the blankets out of his way, shook his shoulders like an athlete, glanced at us, and then with the showy affectation of a magician, he struck the flint on the metal. Nothing happened. Not a spark or a hint of one. Iris stifled a giggle as Gerald tried again. His face turned red. He struck and struck until little beads of sweat formed on his brow and still nothing happened.

"Good try, Gerald. I'll just do it," I said. The dark was getting to me and the reddish glow from outside wasn't helping.

"I don't need any help," he said.

I made a sideways chopping motion at Iris before she could utter a reply "Fire's really hard to make. Most wood fairies are terrible at it, which is good considering where we live."

Gerald's face got redder than ever and his lower lip trembled. "Of course Iris wouldn't be any good. She's so f ..."

I clamped my hand over Gerald's mouth before he could finish the word, but Iris crossed her arms and lowered her eyes anyway. I dropped my hand and gave Gerald a hard look. I put everything I had into that look. We had a deal and he was going to stick to it. Gerald surprised me by lowering his eyes and looking away.

"Go ahead," he said.

I positioned myself so that Gerald and Iris couldn't see what I was doing. I struck the flint while concentrating on the torch. A pretty little flame ignited on the tip and lit my face with a warm glow. Iris clapped her hands and Gerald looked with admiration at the flame.

"I guess one's enough. Mom will be upset that we had any fire at all," I said. "Where'd you put Easy?"

"In my room. It's not so bad and there's no broken glass in there," Iris said as she stared at the flames. Its light gave her face lovely shadows and defined her cheekbones so that she appeared more adult and prettier than she normally did.

"I hear him. I think he's awake," said Gerald. He was looking at Iris, too, and his voice was soft.

Iris turned away from the light. "Better go get him."

"I'll go," I said. But they followed me as if they were afraid to be alone. Perhaps they were. I held the torch high as we trooped down to Iris's room. We passed our parents' room, still in distressing disarray, and then approached my room.

I popped my head in to see how it had fared and held the torch up to light the area. My heart sunk to see it in such a state. I'd always been particular about my room. I had the prettiest lace curtains and Dad made all the furniture in a style he called French provincial. I'd collected colorful bits of glass and mounted them in frames. Mom called it my art. Now all that loveliness lay in ruins. Gerald and Iris crowded in around me. I looped my arm around Iris's shoulders and laid my cheek on the top of my sister's fair hair.

"Well," I said. "It's not so bad."

Gerald snorted in reply, but I decided to just go ahead and let him snort. If it made me feel better to dissemble a bit, what was the harm? If it wasn't so bad, then I could fix it, quick as anything. If I said it was a disaster, it would never be the same, and I very much wanted things to be the same.

Iris patted my arm. "You're right. We'll fix it in no time."

"The bed is shattered and there's stinky gunk on the walls," said Gerald. He might have gone on, but Iris and I gave him such fierce looks that he stopped numbering the defects of my room and gave it a derisive look instead.

Iris grabbed my arm "Easy sounds funny. He might be sick."

I turned, squeezed past Iris and Gerald, and ran the twenty steps to Iris's room. I flung open the door and saw on the floor a sight I'd never forget. A baby sat on Iris's mattress in the middle of the floor, but it wasn't Easy or like any baby I'd ever seen. It looked like a small brown boulder with patchy greenish mold on it. Tiny black eyes with a beetle-like quality blinked at me and it opened its mouth to show off jagged pointy teeth. My mouth opened, but I wasn't aware that I was screaming until Iris came up beside me.

"Why are you screaming?" yelled Iris.

Iris looked past me and starting screaming herself. I pulled Iris back, and tried to slam the door only to find Gerald passed out in front of it. I pulled him by the foot out of the way and slammed the door. Iris had backed up against the opposite hall wall. She'd stopped screaming, but her pale face had lost every ounce of color it ever had.

"What was that?" Iris asked, her voice wavering.

I swallowed. I wasn't sure I could choke a word out if I tried. Instead, I put the torch in the nearest bracket and leaned on the wall next to Iris. Gerald sat up. He lurched back and forth like he'd been into the elderberry wine.

He looked up at us. "That thing ate Easy!" Then he looked quite sick and fell over in another faint. His head hit the floor with a dull thump as we stared at him with disbelief.

"It didn't really eat Easy, did it?" asked Iris.

"Of course not," I said, although I was by no means sure.

"Do you think Easy's in there with it?" asked Iris.

I jumped over Gerald's inert body and flung open the door. The boulder baby stood in the middle of the mattress on lumpy legs that looked way too small to support it. The baby waved at me and proceeded to poop on Iris's mattress. A stench that would've made a latrine smell good in comparison wafted over me. I pinched my nose and stepped in, looking around the room for Easy. He wasn't there. The window lay on the floor. Its hinge pins scattered among the debris.

"Is Easy in there?" said Iris.

"No," I said.

Gerald came up beside me with his shirt pulled over his nose and mouth. "What is it? It smells like dead frogs."

The boulder baby did smell like dead frogs, lots of them. Even with the window open the smell seemed to get worse and worse until I started to gag. I backed out of the room and shut the door again. It stopped the worst of the stench, but it was still strong enough to make nose pinching necessary.

"Where's Easy?" said Iris.

"I'm telling you it ate him," said Gerald.

"Shut up, Gerald. It didn't eat Easy. It's a baby," I said.

"That's not a baby," said Gerald. "Smells like gross dead stuff."

"That's because it's a baby spriggan," I said.

Gerald crossed his arms. "Oh yeah? How can you tell?"

"You said it yourself. It smells like dead frogs, just like the grown-up spriggan and it kind of looks like the big one did. I mean, it looks worse, but similar."

"But what's it doing here? And where's Easy?" Iris asked.

"How should I know?" Just when I thought I'd fixed one problem another replaced it. I wanted to bang my head on the wall.

"Hey!" a voice yelled from behind Iris's door.

All three of us jumped and my skin tingled in a most unpleasant way.

"Hey!" The voice got louder and sounded quite annoyed.

"Oh, no," whispered Iris. "What'd we do?"

"Something else got in," said Gerald. "Maybe it'll eat the spriggan."

"We need to lock the door," I said. "Where's the key?"

"It's in the room," wailed Iris.

"We can't lock it in?" asked Gerald. "Great, Iris. Why'd you leave the key in your room?"

"Well, I didn't know I was going to need it to lock a monster in, did I?" Iris tucked her head into my shoulder and sniffed.

"Hey! Come back! I'm hungry!"

"Who are you?" I yelled, wishing I still had my earring to protect us.

"Are you coming back or what?" yelled the voice with something that sounded like a juicy belch.

"Did you eat the baby?" asked Gerald.

"It's gone," yelled the voice.

"What's gone?" I asked.

"I'm hungry."

I gestured at the door. "One of you see if you can hear exactly what's in there."

Iris pressed her ear against the smooth wooden plank, while Gerald glanced around the hall as if I couldn't possibly have been talking to him. I gave him a wry look and stepped back from the door.

"Well?" asked Gerald, when looking nonchalant became a chore.

Iris straightened up and smoothed her dress. "I think it's alone in there."

"What's alone? The baby?" I asked.

Iris nodded and I made a decision. "All right. Here we go. Iris, you and Gerald go to my room and lock yourselves in. I'm going in there."

"No way," said Iris.

"Forget that," said Gerald. "We're staying with you."

We? When had Gerald and Iris become a we?

"Fine, but don't blame me if that thing tries to gnaw your legs off," I said.

From behind the door, the voice yelled, "I'm not a thing and I don't bite … much."

Gerald and Iris nodded at me as I grasped the door handle and pulled. The door swung open easily and revealed the baby now sitting on Iris's mattress next to its pile of poop.

"It's about time," the baby said. "I'm hungry. Where's the food?"

I ignored it and began looking around the room. I peeked in Iris's closet, under her broken bed and even under a pile of clothing.

"What are you looking for?" asked the baby. "I'm right here."

The baby appeared to be speaking, but I couldn't reconcile its age with the voice coming out of its mouth. It couldn't be real. Something or someone else had to be speaking for it. We searched the room, keeping well away from the baby. It tilted its head and watched us. Intelligence glimmered in its eyes. It was an odd thing to witness. The baby was easily the most repulsive thing I'd ever seen and its smell was unspeakable.

Gerald took a couple of tentative steps toward the mattress. "It's not a baby," he said.

"I certainly am a baby," said the spriggan.

Gerald jumped back. "It heard me."

"Of course I heard you. I'm sitting right here, numbskull."

"It can't be," said Iris. "It just can't."

"It's not a baby," Gerald said again.

"I am a baby. Am. Am. Am." The spriggan got to its feet and hopped up and down on the mattress. The poop began to jiggle back and forth with each hop and the sight made me feel ill. It was hard to say what was worse, the hopping baby or the jiggly poop.

"Oh, please stop that. It's too gross," I said.

It sat down and said with an air of expectation, "I'm hungry."

"How come you can talk?" I asked.

"Why wouldn't I?"

"Babies don't talk."

"Obviously we do."

"Wood fairy babies don't talk."

"True. Your babies are slow, but valuable," it said.

"Valuable?" Iris's brow wrinkled as she puzzled over the idea of a baby being valuable.

"Yes. Very valuable or I wouldn't be here."

I went over to the window and breathed in the fresh clean air until my lungs were ready to burst. "Why are you here?"

The baby's expression turned glum. "I'm payment in full."

A queasy knot formed in my stomach. "Payment for what?"

"That other baby, naturally."

"You mean your family stole Easy and just left you here like we wouldn't know the difference?"

"They thought you might notice. But, really, why would you care?" The baby spriggan shrugged. "I'm Horc by the way, and about the food."

"No food. Where's Easy? Where's our baby?" I resisted the urge to yell or to stamp my feet. The only thing I didn't want to do was to shake the truth out of it. That would require touching it.

"They took it."

"We know that. Where did they take it, I mean where did they take Easy?" I asked.

The baby got to its feet again and slowly said, "I'm hungry."

"You, you better tell us where they've taken him or I'll, I'll spank you," I said, raising my hand.

"What's spank? Is it tasty?"

"It's not tasty. It's a spank." I was going to have to touch it. The idea was absolutely repulsive, but I would do it, if I had to.

The baby gave me a blank look. "I'm hungry."

"Look, you," I said as I kicked the edge of the mattress. "I'm not feeding you until you tell me where our baby is."

The baby raised its eyebrow lumps at me. "Feed me and I'll tell you."

I couldn't believe it. I was being blackmailed by a baby.

"Maybe we should just feed it." Iris had left the room and was peeking around the door with her fingers pinching her nose.

"I agree," said Gerald.

I didn't want to feed it. If I fed it, we might never get rid of it. But what choice did I have. I couldn't starve the thing. I glared at the baby with my hands on my hips. If I'd been the baby, I would've been frightened, but it just sat there looking at me, blinking.

"What do you eat?" I asked.

"Everything, but I'm partial to stink bugs."

"Gross. You eat stink bugs?"

"You don't?" The baby's eyebrow lumps knotted together.

"Maybe that's why you smell so bad," said Gerald. "Eating stink bugs can't help."

The baby got to its feet and wagged a finger in Gerald's direction. "I'll have you know, my scent is perfect. My mother worked for hours to get it just right."

"You mean, you don't smell like that naturally?" asked Iris.

"My natural smell is quite odious, but my mother thought I could use a little help," the baby said.

I turned to Iris. "Go see if you can find some hoecakes in the second storeroom."

Iris returned with a basket heaped with round corn-colored cakes. She handed it to me, and then rushed out of the room. I handed a cake to the baby. He sniffed the cake, and nibbled the edge. Then he shoved the whole thing in his mouth and swallowed without chewing.

"I'm hungry," he said.

"No kidding," said Gerald. "You should chew your food. It's bad for the digestion."

"Quiet, wood fairy. What you know wouldn't fill my stomach." The baby belched and held out his hand for another cake.

Instead of giving him one, I gave one to Iris and Gerald. I put another to my own lips and took a large bite. The baby made a sound that was a cross between a growl and a whimper.

"Don't worry," I said. "You'll get more if you cooperate. Now where's our baby?"

"Home, I expect."

"Where's that?"

"Underneath the second cash register. The smell of money is delightful."

"Where's that?" I asked.

"You really are as slow as my uncle said. It's in the center of the mall." He held out his hand.

I handed him another cake and watched him gulp it down.

"So wood fairy babies are valuable," I said. "Why? Easy can't do anything. He can't work."

"They're valuable because they don't come on the market very often, but that baby was something more. When my uncle came back and told everyone what he'd found, they all got very excited." He held out his hand again.

"Why? What's special about Easy?" Iris asked.

"No idea," said the spriggan.

I handed it a cake. "If you tell me, I'll give you another one."

The baby snorted, took the cake from me and scarfed it down. When he finished, his eyes closed halfway and he rolled over on his side, belching and farting. I didn't think anything could make Iris's room smell worse, but I was wrong.

"Don't go to sleep," I said. "How do we get him back?"

"You don't. He's theirs now, fair and square."

"Fair and square? Are you crazy? They stole him," said Iris, coming back into the room.

"They traded. Him for me. Fair and square." The baby closed his eyes until I kicked the mattress again. "What?" he asked.

"If you help us, we'll take you home. Don't you want to go home?" I used my most comforting tone. It was a baby after all. He must want to go home and I wanted him there, too.

The baby snuggled and grunted himself into a more comfortable position. "I'll stay here."

"Really?" I asked. "What about your mother?"

His eyes popped open and narrowed at me. "She traded me. Will you?"

I didn't know what to say. Of course, I'd never trade away a baby, but I didn't want to keep the baby spriggan either.

"No," I said. "I guess not."

"Good, then here is better. Good food. It's not stink bugs, but maybe you'll get one for me."

The baby started snoring and we went down the hall to the kitchen. I found a carrying bag in the rubble and filled it with some fruit leather.

"What are you doing?" asked Iris.

"Going after Easy." I didn't look at Iris when I said it. I didn't want her to see how worried I was.

"But it's dark," said Iris. "And …"

I handed my water jug to Iris and slipped the carrying bag over my shoulder. "And what?"

"Remember the things I heard earlier?" Iris rubbed her hands together like they were ice cold.

"I went out before and it was okay."

"They weren't all awake then." Iris turned to Gerald. "Tell her, Gerald."

Gerald's resentful expression returned to his face. "I don't see why you have to go after that baby anyway."

"Gerald! How can you say that?" Iris's face turned pink and her hands trembled.

"He's not ours. Why should you go out there in the dark and leave us here? Those spriggan could come back and take us, too." Gerald advanced on me with his wings spread.

I smoothed down Gerald's wings and put my hands on his shoulders. "You're not ours either and I went after you."

Gerald ducked his head and pulled away from me. "At least wait until morning. There's too many of them."

"I can't wait. It might be too late. What if I'd waited to go get you? Something terrible could've happened."

"That's different," Gerald said.

"Why? Because Easy isn't a Whipplethorn?"

Gerald's head jerked up. He looked like he was waiting for me to say he wasn't a real Whipplethorn either. But I didn't. I patted his shoulder again. "I'm going."

Iris took my hand and led me to a window. She unlatched the lock and swung it open. "Look there," she said with a gesture into the darkness.

The mall was dark, but not as dark as I would've expected. Besides the strange red glow, there were other lights. Pinpricks and patterns of lights shimmered all over the mall. I couldn't hear anything, but I sensed a great deal of activity.

"I can hear them all," said Iris. "If you're going after Easy, then I'm going, too."

I watched as Iris disappeared into the darkness. Her giggles faded and then returned with wondrous joy as she entered the ring of light produced by my torch. Iris stopped short of landing on the front door threshold and hovered in the air. Her round face flushed and smiling.

"I've never felt so light," Iris said, doing a flip and spin all in one.

"It's amazing, isn't it?" I smiled back at my sister.

"Stop smiling," Gerald said to me. "So the fat fairy can flip out there, so what? Anybody could do it in that air."

I watched Iris spin away into the darkness again. "Quiet. You said you wouldn't call her fat anymore."

"You said you wouldn't leave me."

"I'm not leaving you for good."

Gerald tried to push past me and I snatched his wing before he could take off.

"Let go," he said.

"You're staying. Just lock the doors and everything will be fine."

"I bet you said that the last time, and Easy got stolen."

I pulled him down the hall and placed him against the wall next to Iris's room. We both coughed from the smell and Gerald's nose started to run.

"I had to leave Easy to help you. You owe him. We can't take that baby with us. He must weigh a ton. So somebody has to stay, and that's you. It's your turn. Understand?" " No." Gerald crossed his arms. "Iris can do it. She let Easy get stolen."

I turned my back on Gerald and walked down the hall to the door. Iris landed, hopping up and down with excitement. She hooked her traveling bag strap around her neck and attempted to find a way to carry it comfortably. The bag bulged with snacks and a juice flask she'd filled with water. I told her we wouldn't be gone that long, but Iris's excitement blocked out any sense.

"I'm ready," Iris said.

We flew off the threshold into the lighter-than-air air and grinned at each other. I turned back to the doorway and found Gerald standing there, his face a mixture of rage and fear.

I fluttered back to him. "Lock the door. We'll be back as soon as possible."

"What if the spriggans come?"

"They won't. They already got what they wanted. Lock the door and put a diaper on that baby."

Gerald nodded and closed the door. I pulled on it to make sure it was locked and turned back to Iris. We flew straight away from the mantel until we'd passed the partition opening. I stopped and hovered. Hundreds of lights flickered beyond the partition. Iris joined me, no longer joyful. Two lines formed between her eyes and her little pink bow of a mouth puckered into a frown.

"We'll go to the dryads. They'll help us," I said.

"We're in the soup now," Iris said, imitating Dad's gruff voice.

"We'll be fine."

"You only say that because you can't hear them." Iris gestured to something scurrying across the floor beneath us. It paused as if it'd heard and looked up from beneath a smooth, shiny black shell. In the darkness, all I could make out was gleaming white eyes and a set of teeth, curved into a grin.

"Better go," I said.

Iris nodded and I flew between glass cases and furniture. I spotted the bridal chest and swooped down to see if the brown pile of furry fairies was gone. It was, with no trace. We flew up high and I felt safe in the air. So far we'd seen nothing else flying. I felt something touch my foot and saw Iris red-faced, struggling to keep up. I slowed slightly and went around a corner. The closer we got the dryads, the more determined I felt. I pictured Soren, smiling and nodding. He'd help. He'd know how to get Easy back.

We turned the last corner and the dryads' home appeared before us. The furniture stood bathed in the glow of a red sign over the mall door that read, "Exit." I landed, looking around for some sign of the dryads. They were hard enough to see in the light, but I had a creepy crawly feeling dozens of eyes were on me.

Iris caught up and landed next to me.

"That was horrible," she said.

"I know I flew fast, but we had to get here. You'll be all right."

"It's not that. We better find those dryads right now." Iris squeezed my arm and gave me a frightened look that made me feel wobbly.

I turned and pointed. "That's Soren's mother's house."

Iris let go of me and ran. She'd gone at least ten steps before I reacted. Iris never ran. The last time she ran our mantel got torn off the wall. I stared for a second and then slowly turned to look in the other direction. Advancing out of the murk was an army of dark creatures. They scuttled out from under furniture and from around glass cases. The red glow of the exit sign didn't touch them. I didn't wait until it did. I ran.

Chapter 10

"Where is it?" Iris ran around in a circle, flailing her arms over her head. I ran past the door and banged on it. "They're coming!" Iris screamed beside media banged with both fists. "Help! Help!"

No one answered. I heard some faint scuttling sounds behind me. Iris backed up against the wall next to the door.

I grabbed her. "Get behind me." I spun around with my hands spread out to shield Iris. It was ridiculous, like a mosquito shielding a fly.

Out of the dark, dozens upon dozens of shiny black shells advanced on us. The shells together formed a diamond, each shell fitted to the next like scales on a fish. I couldn't see any heads, arms, or legs. Once the scuttling stopped, the diamond was completely silent. Iris breathed hard on my cheek and she trembled so much, my teeth chattered from the vibration. Still the shells didn't move. I put my left hand down on Iris's hip and pressed. We stepped sideways, but as we did, the shells countered with a shuffling movement. I held my breath and waited. When the shells didn't do anything else, we tried moving to the left. The shells matched our movement again.

"This is ridiculous," I whispered. As the word ridiculous escaped my lips, the shells rocked back.

"Hello," called a voice from the shells. It was impossible to tell which one.

"Hello," I said.

Then the shells rocked back and lifted, exposing the dark creatures beneath. One creature stood up and revealed itself completely. It was half my height and pitch black with skinny arms and legs with large knobby knees and elbows. Where its nose should've been was a flat section over a wide slit of a mouth, filled with bright white teeth. Its gaze made me feel cold all over. The whites were the whitest I'd ever seen and the pupils the blackest.

"You're Soren's girl, aren't you?" asked the creature.

I just stared at him, my mouth agape.

"All right, boys. It's okay. They're just the new wood fairies," said the creature.

The rest of the shells rose up and showed their inhabitants. Every single one seemed a copy of the first.

"What are your orders, Commander?" asked one in the first row.

"To the east. Fan out in the snake pattern. Report back when you hit a wall," said the commander.

The shells dropped back down, hiding the creatures beneath and scuttled away in a wavy pattern, leaving only a few behind. The commander eyed Iris and me, popped off his shell, and sat on it.

"What's a couple of wood fairies like you doing in a place like this?" he asked.

I said nothing. I couldn't seem to find my voice.

He pulled out a thin stick from some concealed spot on his abdomen. "You got a light?"

I could only blink at him. A light?

"You know, fire. You can make fire, can't you?"

I went cold. How could he possibly know I was a kindler?

"Let's have it." He stood and held out the stick.

I swallowed. "I don't have any fire."

"Really? Are you sure about that?"

The creature stared at me hard. He knew about me. Somehow he knew.

Iris continued to shake, but said, "Of course she's sure. We're normal wood fairies. Kindlers are dangerous."

"Interesting." He snapped his fingers and another shell lifted. The creature came forward and sparked a tiny flint. The commander stuck his stick in the flame while puffing on the other end. The stick sizzled and he pulled back, blowing out a ring of smoke. "So you met Soren this afternoon? You're one lucky girl. You never know who you'll run into out here."

I wasn't sure whether I should confirm or deny meeting the dryads. Would knowing us put Soren in jeopardy in any way or us for that matter? I examined my feelings about the creature before me. I wasn't afraid exactly, but I wasn't comfortable either. He was small, half my size, but something about him made him seem much bigger. He wasn't going to out me as a kindler at least for the moment and I appreciated that.

"Gnat got your tongue?" the commander asked.

"No, sir," I said, without knowing why I used sir, except that the other creatures made it clear he was their leader.

"Very polite. I like that. So are you Soren's wood fairy or not?"

"We're friends," I said.

The creature nodded again. "Good. Good."

I felt Iris relax beside me and then tighten up again. "They're coming back."

Nothing had changed in our vicinity, but Iris's lips were a thin line, and her breathing grew rapid.

"Good hearing," said the creature. He looked at me. "You, not so much."

"What do they want?" asked Iris, her voice shaking.

"My boys are reporting back. No need to worry," he said. The shells scuttled out from under a dresser a few feet away.

Iris's breathing became a pant. She starting shaking again and I looped my arm around her shoulders. I couldn't take my eyes off the shells. They moved as one, formed into a diamond shape again. In the middle of the diamond was a dead fly. No one held it. It jostled around on the shells with nothing to restrain it, almost as if it were still alive, except that it was on its back with its legs crossed in the air.

"The sound," said Iris with her hands over her ears. "It's terrible."

"What sound?" I asked.

"Their sound."

The scuttling sound came to me only when they got very close, and it did make me shiver. Just when I wanted to put my hands over my ears, they stopped. One popped up and came forward to the commander. His sound alone wasn't so bad.

The commander sat back on his shell, sucking on his stick. He made the other one wait as he looked at Iris.

"Our sound isn't very loud," he said to Iris. "Your hearing is exceptional. We could use someone like you. Bet you can hear them before they die."

"Before what dies?" asked Iris.

"Anything." He turned to his subordinate. "Report."

"First prize of the night, sir."

"Bring it here," he said.

The shells scuttled forward. The ones in the back rose up and the fly rolled off to land in front of the commander. The fly rocked back and forth for a second until it settled on its back. I leaned forward to get a better look. Flies weren't very common around Whipplethorn Manor. The ones I'd seen hung around the humans hiking in the national forest. Mom worried about rogue fly attacks, which were extremely rare. Dad said flies were harmless, but unpredictable. There'd been flying accidents and he said it was best to be careful lest you ran into one.

Iris shifted her hands from her ears to her nose. The fly was newly dead and gave off a scent that wasn't unpleasant unless you knew it came from something dead. The commander chuckled at Iris's reaction.

"Smells bad, tastes great," he said.

The commander snapped off a leg and held it out to Iris. Both of us leaned back, sounds of disgust escaping our lips. He chuckled again and bit off the foot. He snapped his fingers while chewing and several of the shells popped up. Their inhabitants gathered up the fly and tossed it on top of the other shells. Then they went back into formation.

"I'm sorry," I said. "But what are you?"

"Phalanx fairies. You don't recognize us? We're rather distinctive, wouldn't you say?"

"We're new here."

"I can see that, since you're trying to wake the dryads after dark. Good people, but hard core sleepers. You won't get anything out of them until morning."

"What'll we do?" Iris tugged my arm with both hands.

"I don't know. We'll figure something out."

The commander jumped to his feet. He stalked up to us, almost jittery with excitement. "Do about what? Is there an invasion?"

Iris and I looked at each other. "Who would invade the antique mall?" I asked.

"You look like you've been in a battle." He puffed on his stick while assessing our conditions. "Multiple injuries. Some blood spatter. What happened?"

"Humans tore our mantel off the wall. We were still inside," I said.

"It was pretty scary, but there wasn't any fighting," said Iris.

The commander shrunk down like all the excitement leaked out of him. "Pity."

I nudged Iris with my hip. "Well, we better get going. Don't want to keep you from your … hunting."

"Sure you don't want a taste?" He brandished the remains of the fly leg at us.

"No, thank you," I said, nudging Iris again. "We don't eat … meat."

The commander's mouth turned down into a grimace. "Vegetarians. I should've known." He waved us away, picked up his shell, and popped it back on.

Iris nudged me and I bit my lip. I didn't relish asking for help from those things. The commander knew about me and they were too weird for words. Who ever heard of fairies eating flies? It was so disgusting. I'd almost rather go it alone than ask for help from some pint-sized weirdoes.

"Excuse me, sir," I said. "Isn't there any way to wake the dryads?"

"There are procedures for emergencies. Do you have an emergency? I thought you found your boy."

"I did, but we have a new situation and Soren said I could come to him for help."

"What's your situation? I won't disturb Soren unless it's serious."

I took a deep breath. "The spriggans came and ..."

The commander cut me off. "The spriggans. Are all your people accounted for?"

"They stole our baby."

"This happened here within the confines of the mall?"

"Yes, sir."

The commander reached into his abdomen and produced a red thread with a minuscule key on it. He snapped his fingers and a shell came forward. "Farue, awaken Soren and locate the council members." He handed Farue the key and he scuttled away into the darkness.

"What are you going to do?" I asked.

"Fairy trafficking is a serious offense. It goes on outside, but the mall is under Soren's rule. Soren and the council will decide how to proceed. When did they take the baby?"

"We're not sure. It was during my search for Gerald."

Soren emerged from under the bed, carrying my earring. A group of dryads fanned out behind him. Their faces were tight and drawn. They didn't wave this time. Soren's eyes rested on me for a second, but then he went to the commander with his slow, patient steps.

"Soren," said the commander with a slight bow of his head.

"Kukri. What is the situation? Farue said there's been a kidnapping."

"Baby from the Whipplethorn mantel."

"They don't usually take babies. Anything special about him?" asked Soren.

"No. I don't think so," I said.

"We better move fast," said the commander. "Spriggans will traffic the child sure as sin."

"I agree," said Soren. "They've become bold since my father's death."

"They deserve what's coming to them. Want me to summon the council?"

"No." Soren steepled his long fingers. "There isn't time."

The commander took a long drag on his stick. "We're in good shape. I hear the sluagh are already hibernating, so they won't be coming to the spriggans' defense."

I stepped forward. "Are you going to attack them?"

"We're going to ..." the commander smiled, "discipline them."

"That sounds like attack to me. Can't we just tell them to give Easy back?"

Soren gave me my earring. "We could, but they'll use the time in negotiation to spirit Easy out of the mall and my jurisdiction. Once he's gone, he's gone for good."

The commander's voice rose. "I say we attack. Two teams per dwelling. We'll have that baby back and teach those bags of frog filth something in no time."

"Are you going to kill them?" asked Iris. Iris'd been so quiet I'd forgotten she was there.

"If necessary," said the commander.

"You can't kill them. Wood fairies don't kill," Iris said, her face flushed with indignation.

"I'm not a wood fairy. Do you want your baby back or not?" asked the commander.

"But I am a wood fairy," said Soren. "My father believed the spriggans could see reason if given the right motivation and I think we have the right motivation."

"You mean her." The commander gestured to me.

"You want me to do it," I said. "That's crazy. They won't listen to me."

Soren looked down into my eyes. "They will if you make them. Your journey home begins here. You have abilities. It's time you honed them. You'll need all your gifts to accomplish your goals."

"I still say we attack," said the commander. "Skills or no skills, let's get straight to the point."

Soren placed his large hand on the tiny phalanx fairy's shoulder. "She shall be allowed to try. If Matilda can't get them to see reason, we attack. I leave the details to you, Kukri."

Chapter II

I soared just over the heads of the commander's troops with Iris at my side. She carried Soren's banner, a flag with a maple pattern on it. The banner would show the spriggans that Iris and I were under Soren's protection, but I insisted on carrying my earring anyway. I held it tight to my chest and it proved to be much less unwieldy than I expected. Soren and his group were somewhere behind us, heading toward the center of the mall with their slow steps.

Soren had mapped out the spriggans' nest for me. It was in the humans' cashier area, a rectangle made of high counters. There were three nests in old cash boxes on the shelves below the registers. We didn't know where Easy was. It would be Iris's job to listen and figure it out. Then she and I would confront the spriggans under Soren's banner and ask for Easy back. Soren seemed to think I would be able to persuade them, but all I had was the threat of the phalanx attacking. Maybe that would be enough.

The white counters of the spriggans' area were easy to spot. We flew around the rectangle until we found the entrance on the other side and landed. The phalanx caught up with us in a couple minutes and the commander popped off his shell to give us last minute instructions.

"You hear anything?" he asked Iris.

"There's a lot of them," she said.

"Sixty-eight at last count. Lucky for us they don't breed well. You hear your baby?"

"Not yet."

I planted the tip of my earring on the linoleum. "Are you sure?"

"Sure, I'm sure. What's the plan?"

The commander tapped his white teeth. "They might've taken Easy somewhere else for pickup from a buyer. That could be anywhere. We won't find him before the transaction takes place unless we get some cooperation."

"You don't think I can do it," I said.

"On the contrary," said the commander. "I think you can, but it won't be words that do the trick."

"Words are all we have," said Iris.

"I won't be the one to disagree with you." The commander gave me a curious look. I suppose he meant my fire, but what was I going to do with it, light the spriggans' torches for them, help them cook their dinner? I wasn't going to out myself to Iris for apple strudel.

Iris pointed to the third register on the far right. "That one. They're talking about an impending sale. It must be Easy."

"Nice," said the commander. "I'll give you ten minutes, no longer. Iris, you listen for the countdown."

"Yes, sir."

I hesitated and then picked up my earring. "Let's go."

The air in the mall was still and warm. I only had to beat my wings a couple of times to stay on track as we flew over yellow slips of paper littering the floor and past rolls of newspaper and bubble wrap. I landed on the lowest shelf under the third register with Iris close behind me. Iris pointed at a rusty old cash box shoved deep into the gloom. I saw a rusted out hole in the side of the cash box and hefted my earring. Soren's banner trembled in Iris's hands, but her face remained determined.

When we reached the hole, we found a dime slid across the opening. The smell of spriggans was thick in the air and I started breathing through my mouth. I thought nothing could be grosser than the baby spriggan, but I was wrong. A bunch of adult spriggans smelled much worse. Iris gagged beside me and the banner wobbled above her head. Before I thought about it, I tapped the end of the earring on the dime. The sound was blunt and dull, less impressive than I'd hoped for.

"They heard," said Iris.

I stepped back from the dime and planted the ball end of my earring firmly on the shelf and put my hand on my hip. Iris stood the banner in front of her so the spriggans wouldn't miss it.

"Open up!" I yelled.

The dime slid back, revealing a dark, stinking hole.

Iris gripped my shoulder. I stared into the darkness, my stomach feeling as twisted and hard as a piece of driftwood. My anger rose and my face flushed, hot and red. What were they waiting for? If they thought I'd just go away, they'd find out how wrong they were.

"One of them just said come in," said Iris. "It sounds like the spriggan who came to the mantel."

Iris made a move as if to obey. I hissed over my shoulder a sharp dissent and she froze.

"You come out here," I said.

When the spriggan didn't answer, my palms began to prickle and itch. I couldn't remember Soren's plan. The spriggans were ignoring us. I couldn't talk them into giving back Easy if they ignored me. The thought of being ignored made my palms prickle more.

"What should we do?" asked Iris.

My palms were unbearably itchy. I stared into the hole and remembered Soren's words.

"Soren said I had to make them listen," I said.

"How?"

I glanced down at my palm and saw a flame erupt in the center. It was nothing like the pretty little yellow flames I'd produced before. This one was snapping in anger and blue in its intensity. It grew larger every second and, without thinking, I drew back my hand and launched it at the hole. The blue flame streaked into the darkness. Iris gasped. Panicked shrieks came from the hole. The spriggans' panic wove its way around us, so thick I could feel it in the air. I smiled and continued to stare into the hole that now had a faint blue glow in it. Spriggans ran around, emitting more stink in their panic. Another blue flame appeared in my palm and I itched to throw it.

"Don't do it," said Iris.

"Why?" My flame grew larger.

Iris backed away from me. "You can't. You can't."

The blue glow in the hole disappeared and the spriggan from our mantel stepped into the opening still wearing his oily paper bag suit. He crossed his arms and leaned on the edge. His tongue slithered out, slow and slimy. I had the impression that he was tasting us, looking for something in particular. The thought made the flame in my hand grow larger still.

"Very impressive," he said. "You don't seem the type."

"Where's our baby?" I banged the earring on the floor and held up my flame. The blue burned so bright that it was beginning to turn white.

He produced a hairy black stick from his pocket and started picking his teeth with it. "Not that impressive."

I pointed at Soren's banner. "How about that?"

The spriggan yawned. "That is even less so. Soren is a weaker version of his father."

"Soren isn't weak."

"He must be or you wouldn't be here. Two little girls to beg our indulgence."

"I don't beg," I said. "Soren wanted to give you a chance."

"So he's stupid as well. Perhaps now is the time to end his reign, starting with you."

I drew back my arm, but before I could throw the flame, a cold stream of water washed down from above. My flame went out and darkness overwhelmed us. I blew on my hand. Nothing, not a sputter, not a spark.

"That will teach you, little girl," said the spriggan. "Never attack your betters in their own home."

"Our betters? You thieving, disgusting piece of rotten frog filth! Where's our baby? Give him back." I pointed my earring at the spriggan.

"I imagine your baby is back at your mantel. His name is Horc, by the way. Do take good care of him."

"That's not our baby. We want **our** baby!" I yelled.

My eyes adjusted to the darkness just as the spriggan wrenched the earring out of my slippery hands and pointed it at me. "I don't know who you are, but it's time you take your leave."

"I'm not leaving. The phalanx will attack if don't give our baby back."

"Let them. We're prepared."

The spriggan jabbed the earring into my stomach, piercing my clothing. I felt the pain, but it didn't bother me. I eyed the spriggan, feeling cold and so self-assured it was almost as if I'd become another person entirely.

"Interesting," said the spriggan. "Let's try the sister. Perhaps she's easier to persuade."

The earring's tip swung toward Iris, who gasped and stumbled backward, falling with Soren's banner. The spriggan marched forward, jabbing the earring at Iris.

"I knew there couldn't be two so fearless," he said.

I grabbed at the earring. The spriggan shoved me with it and I stumbled back, landing next to Iris. Dozens of spriggans gathered behind him. They laughed and chewed on bits of fly as we scooted backwards toward the edge of the shelf. I scrambled to my feet and picked up Iris.

"You better give him back," I said.

"I'm exceedingly worried." The spriggan jabbed the earring at us again. Iris lost her balance and fell backwards off the shelf, dragging me with her.

We landed hard on the linoleum. My whole body went red hot with pain and anger. My chest constricted and air refused to enter my lungs for a moment. Finally, I drew a long raspy breath. The spriggan came to the edge of the shelf and looked down at us, smiling.

"Go home, girls," said the spriggan. "Know when to quit."

I jumped to my feet and prepared to launch myself at him, to scratch the hateful grin off his face. The spriggan looked down, daring me to try. His cohorts pointed and laughed. Iris grabbed my arm and held me back.

I turned to scream at her, but found myself staring at a stream of black rushing by instead. The phalanx fairies formed a barrier between us and the spriggans. One phalanx fairy climbed on the back of another.

"Up to your old tricks, ain't you?" said the commander.

The smiles faded from the spriggans' faces and the sharp scent of fear wafted off of them. The majority stepped back and let the leader face the commander alone.

"I don't know what you mean, Kukri." The spriggan crossed its arms and looked at the commander with an air of indifference.

"Sure you do," said the commander.

"You wouldn't take the word of these girls over mine, would you?" asked the spriggan.

"I'd take the word of practically anyone over yours," said the commander.

"Can't we discuss this like gentlemen?" asked the spriggan.

"We could. Do you know any?" The commander jumped off the back of the other phalanx fairy and winked at me. I turned to Iris, who was bright red and avoiding my eyes.

Around us, the phalanx fairies took off their shells. They flipped them in front of themselves and held them like shields. The spriggan backed up a step.

"You know the rules," said the commander.

"You wouldn't attack us over slanderous lies, surely?"

"It ain't possible to slander you. Now do you yield and surrender all ill-gotten gains?"

"I do not. You have no authority here."

"Soren does and he commands it."

The spriggan stood up straighter. "I do not recognize Soren."

"I was hoping you'd say that," said the commander.

The phalanx fairies swarmed forward, climbing onto the shelf without benefit of flying or ladders. They moved so quickly that the spriggans appeared too stunned to move. Only when their leader was grabbed did they retreat into the darkness. Iris clamped her hands over her ears. I moved forward, straining to hear anything.

"What's happening?" I asked.

"They're fighting."

"I know that. Who's winning?"

Iris looked at me like I was as smart as a box of rocks. Before I could ask again, a spriggan flew off the shelf and landed at our feet. He lay gasping with a nasty slash across his chest. Yellow ooze dripped down his side and his eyes rolled up in his head. The ooze was the worst smell yet and we backed up as the phalanx fairies launched more spriggans off the shelf.

"Look out!" yelled Iris.

More spriggans carrying short wicked swords came from under the other cash registers. Their mouths formed caverns and I knew they must be screaming. The spriggans made straight for us, their beady eyes fixed. I flew straight up with Iris clinging to my waist. Two armies of spriggans merged beneath our feet. The spriggans shook their fists at us. I beat my wings as hard as I could, but we began to sink.

"Iris, Iris! Let go!" I yelled.

Iris didn't let go. Her grip tightened. Her eyes darted around, not focusing.

"Iris!" I smacked her, but she didn't respond. We were sinking fast. Below, the spriggans waited, their moist brown hands stretched upward. Still, Iris wouldn't let go and down we went.

Hands grabbed at me, pinching and pulling. All I could see was brownish-green skin and moldy teeth. Iris clung to me. Her nails tore my clothes as the spriggans wrenched her away. She screamed at me for help, but I couldn't break free. I had to watch as the spriggans dragged my sister off, slapping her and pulling her hair.

The spriggans passed me from hand to hand. I twisted and arched my back, surprising the spriggans by managing to get on my feet. One spriggan grabbed me by the shoulders. "Going somewhere? I think not."

His breath would've dropped a rhinoceros beetle, but I clutched his dry coat in my damp hands drawing him close. He jerked back and gave me a stinging slap. The room spun. I caught glimpses of the phalanx near me as I fell. They used their shells as weapons as well as shields. They slashed at the spriggans with the edges.

I got to my feet and my palms began to prickle. Blue flames formed in each one. A spriggan grabbed me and I pressed my palms against his chest, burning holes through his coat. He shrieked and let go. In the distance, I spotted Iris being carried toward the exit. I threw two fireballs in a great arch and hit the spriggans carrying her. I held out my hand and my fire spread into a round shield, protecting me. I ran through the battle to Iris. Two more spriggans were dragging her by the legs. I hit them with fireballs and pulled Iris to her feet. Then I spun in a circle and formed a ring of fire around us. The spriggans backed away, the fire glittering in their eyes.

"Stay here," I told Iris.

I jumped through the ring and ran toward the third cash register. The spriggans and phalanx fairies battled on, but it was clear who was winning. The phalanx overwhelmed the spriggans even though the spriggans outnumbered them two to one. Working among the wounded were little fairies with silver wings half the size of mine. Their long, fine hair, the color of wheat, flowed around their heads like they were underwater. They bent over the wounded, soothing them with drinks from a long-handled water dipper. I saw one bandage the head of a phalanx fairy. When she rose to go to another of the wounded, a spriggan rammed into her. Instead of being thrown to the floor, she melted into a pool of water and then reformed. I ran past her and flew up onto the shelf. The battle was less intense there and I spotted the spriggan leader in his paper suit. I blasted my way through his guard and grabbed him by the throat.

"Where's my baby?" I screamed in his face.

His eyes were wide with fright. "I don't know."

"You know." My palms prickled and his eyes went wild. "Stop!"

"Tell me and I'll end the battle. Don't and I'll end you."

"He's in the apothecary cabinet by the front door," he gasped.

I shoved him back and formed a fire ring around him. I ran back to the shelf edge and looked out over the battle. For a second, I considered letting it go on, but Iris's words echoed in my head. Wood fairies don't kill. If I let it go on, I'd be confirming what people thought of kindlers. I could control myself. I could do the right thing.

I shot flames out of my palms. They exploded over the melee in a beautiful burst. Both sides froze and looked up.

"Stop," I screamed. "It's over."

After a pause, the phalanx retreated and formed ranks near the exit. One phalanx climbed up the shelf before me.

"Why'd you stop us?" asked the commander.

"We got what we came for. I have Easy's location," I said.

"Well, I can't say that I'm not disappointed, but Soren will be pleased. He's not the fan of bloodshed that I am."

"I have a gift," I said with a smile.

The commander cocked his head at me and I pointed at the spriggan leader running around like a nut within my fire ring.

"Ain't this just like Christmas." The commander rubbed his hands together and grinned, showing every one of his numerous teeth.

Chapter 12

I landed beside the charred circle of Iris's fire ring. She stood next to Soren, staring at the ring.

"Are you okay?" I asked her.

She peeked at me from under long lashes and nodded. Soren's eyes roved over the battlefield and its combatants. Spriggans were melting away into the darkness under the registers. They left their wounded behind to be cared for by the silver-winged fairies. The phalanx wounded formed up in ranks and disappeared under their shells.

Soren put his arm around my shoulders. "You did well to end it when you did."

"You wanted me to use my fire," I said.

"I did. Gifts should be used, not hidden away."

"My family might not agree," I said, reaching for Iris.

She shrunk away, avoiding my eyes. "You should've told me."

"That's what you're mad about. My fire saved you. I got Easy's location."

"You should've told me. I'm your sister. You know everything about me."

Soren pushed us toward each other. "It seems you have underestimated your sister, Matilda."

I hugged Iris hard. "You're really not afraid of me?"

"People say kindlers are bad because they can't control themselves. They have accidents that burn down houses and set people on fire." She looked at the charred ring. "You won't have any accidents. If you burn anything up, it'll be on purpose."

"I'm sorry I didn't trust you. I should've."

Iris hugged me and I wobbled from relief.

Soren laughed. "You have Easy's location?"

"The apothecary cabinet by the front door."

"Let's retrieve him before the buyers show up." Soren left orders for the commander to join us when the spriggan leader was secured.

We left the cashier area and walked around the side past more of the commander's troops, resting under their shells. A loud clunk startled us and light flooded the antique mall. I clapped my hands over my eyes and stumbled. Soren caught me before I fell and held me for a second. I peeked out between my fingers, squinting and blinking. Glaring white light bathed the antique furniture to the right of us and made it look stark and cold. Every detail of the grungy linoleum floor showed in the harsh light and my lip curled up at the sight. I'd gotten comfortable with the dark. The dimness was closer to the light of Whipplethorn Manor than the glaring whiteness.

"Open for business," said Soren. "I should've warned you. That light can be shocking until you get used to it."

We walked alongside the counter until Iris grabbed my arm. "Humans are coming."

Soren nodded and told us to get close to the counter. Then a human came around the corner. Her enormous shoes stomped past us. The wind she created blew our hair back.

"Christ, Larry. Did you see the mess in here?" The woman's voice boomed. She was so loud, even I heard her clearly.

"What mess?" said a man.

"There's a burn on the floor and paper's strewn all over. Yuck. It smells like something died in here."

"What about the cash registers?" asked the man.

"They seem okay and the alarm wasn't tripped," said the woman. "I guess it was that worthless Joe. I swear, he can't do anything right."

"True enough."

The humans kept talking about Joe and his worthlessness while Soren, Iris, and I walked to the front of the mall. We passed the edge of the counter and saw huge glass doors with morning sunlight streaming in. Flecks of multi-colored dust hung in the air, and heat from the sun on my face made my skin prickle like my palms when I made fire.

Next to the doors was a small area stuffed with antiques of questionable age. Festoons of plastic flowers hung from the ceiling around vintage windows suspended by wires. Soren continued into the area and stopped in front of a tall cabinet covered in little drawers with white porcelain knobs.

"There you are," he said. "The apothecary cabinet."

"Where is he?" I asked. The cabinet had at least a hundred drawers. How in the world were we supposed to know which one Easy was in?

Soren cocked an eyebrow at Iris. "You tell me."

Iris bit her lip and listened. Then she pointed and said, "That one."

I rolled my eyes. "That one" could've been any one of twenty. "Be more specific."

"Fifth row up, middle drawer. How's that?" Iris grinned, looking slightly superior.

"Are you sure he's in that one?"

"I'm sure," said Iris. "I can hear him breathing."

"Really?" I flew up and pressed my ear to the wood. I couldn't hear anything. Even if Easy had been screaming, I probably wouldn't have heard it through the wood. I was lucky to have Iris. Without her, Easy would be stuck in there, while I tried every single drawer.

Iris flew up next to me and knocked on the drawer. "Easy. It's us come to get you." She nodded at me. "He's okay, I think. He's just making those little chirps, not crying or anything."

We tugged on the porcelain knob. The drawer shifted but didn't open. We tried again, beating the air furiously with our wings. I stopped and wiped the sweat from my brow, wondering if there was a way to burn our way through.

Iris and I jetted sideways when a voice next to us said, "Here, let me."

I panted with my hands on my chest. "Don't do that."

"You scared me to death," said Iris.

The commander stood on the drawer below Easy's the same as if he were standing on the floor. He didn't have his shell on, but his smoking stick was clamped between his teeth.

"How'd you do that?" I asked. "Can you fly?"

"Not hardly. I am Spiderman." He showed us the palm of one hand.

I blinked. "What?"

"You should get out more often. I can't fly, but I can stick to things. I can stand on the ceiling if I want to."

"Why would you want to?" asked Iris.

"I don't. It's just an example. Come on. Let's get this kid out. I've got people to see and orders to give. I expect those spriggans to retaliate tonight at the latest."

The commander walked up to the drawer above Easy's and grasped the knob on Easy's drawer. Iris and I got handholds on bottom edges and together we pulled. The drawer scooted out a bit, but not enough to get Easy out. A little brown hand waved at us from the opening. I grasped it and kissed a finger. Tears flooded my eyes and I turned away.

"Time enough for that later," said the commander. "Let's get her done."

I got back into position and pulled with everything I had. I could hardly see through the tears, but that made me pull harder. The drawer inched open. We stopped pulling and peeked over the edge. Easy sat in the drawer, naked, with a pile of clothes next to him.

Iris and I lifted Easy out of the drawer and cradled him between us. Our cheeks rested on his dark curls and warm tears rolled from our eyes onto his plump cheeks. Our wings beat in time, floating on the warm air of the antique mall.

"You did it," said Iris.

"We did it. With a whole lot of help." I smiled at the commander and then down at Soren. "Let's get back to the mantel before another disaster strikes."

"Disaster's your middle name, ain't it?" asked the commander as he walked down the side of the cabinet. "You'd think you'd learn to prepare. You want his clothes?"

Iris wrinkled her nose. "They stink. We can get more from his house."

I nodded. I didn't know how we'd get the clothes anyway, since the commander was already headed to the floor. One of us might've been able to carry Easy alone, but I wasn't ready to try it. "Let's go down and thank them again."

We flew down and landed next to the commander's shell. He arrived a second later and popped it back on. Easy patted his mouth and chirped. The commander stood on his toes to get a better look at Easy and then looked pointedly at Soren, who gazed at Easy with a concerned expression.

"He's a good looking boy, no doubt, but there has to be more to it," said the commander.

"What do you mean?" I asked, shifting all of Easy's weight to my hip.

"The spriggans took a chance kidnapping him. They don't usually operate that way in the mall. They know Soren won't tolerate it." The commander tapped the unlit end of his stick against his chin. "I wonder what made him worth it."

"The spriggan baby said he was special," said Iris, stretching her arms.

"The spriggan baby?" Soren jerked his gaze from Easy to us. "Of course, they would've left you one of those treasures. I should've thought of it before. Do you want it?"

"No," Iris and I said, shaking our heads.

The commander laughed. "With Soren's permission, I'll take him off your hands and get him back where he belongs."

I agreed, but I felt a little queasy about it. The spriggan baby made it clear he didn't want to go back and I said I wouldn't trade him. But giving him to the commander to be taken back wasn't trading him, was it? He should be with other spriggans. I certainly wanted him to be with other spriggans.

"Can't stand around here all day dawdling. That's how you get in these fixes." The commander looked ready to race off.

"Wait a minute," I said. "What did you mean by that? It's not our fault the spriggans wanted Easy. We didn't know they'd take him."

I feared the commander would say it was my fault. That if I'd been a better babysitter or if I could hear better, Easy wouldn't have gotten stolen. Instead, he gave me a weary glance and shook his head.

"What?" I asked, not sure if I wanted an honest answer.

Soren took my hand. "It's not you Kukri's referring to. It's us."

The commander ran a hand over his face. "We should've protected you better. It's my duty, in particular."

"We all failed, Kukri," said Soren. "I should've put guards on you the moment I discovered you were here."

"You couldn't know," said the commander. "I'm looking at this boy and I can't figure out why the spriggans wanted him. It ain't obvious. That's for sure."

"Matilda." Iris yanked on my arm.

I ignored Iris and pulled my arm away. "Easy's just a wood fairy, like the rest of us."

"Matilda, listen to me," said Iris.

"Stop it, Iris." I hugged Easy tight to my chest and looked down at him. "Are you a kindler?"

Easy shook his head no. Both the commander and Soren looked at him thoughtfully.

"Matilda, Matilda!" yelled Iris.

"For God's sake, Iris. Stop it!"

"Gerald's screaming!"

"What?"

"Gerald's screaming. Something's happening to the mantel."

"Why didn't you tell me?" I shoved Easy into Soren's arms.

"Hey!" yelled the commander.

I flew upward and then in a circle. My heart thumped hard in my chest and then I recognized a cupboard with tin panels at the corner and remembered the way back to the mantel. I zipped by the cupboard, gaining speed with the mall's hot air rushing past my face. My skull felt empty, with only the one thought of getting back to Gerald rattling around in there.

Someone tugged my foot. Iris was huffing and puffing behind me. She shook her head and gasped something.

"What?" I asked.

Iris broke away and stopped. I pivoted in the air and flew back to her.

"Not that way." Iris clutched her chest and sunk down almost to the floor.

I floated down beside Iris. "Which way?"

Iris pointed to the left "Humans are taking the mantel away, but you'll never find Gerald without my ears."

"All right, but you've got to hurry."

We flew together around corners and through areas I hadn't seen before. We dodged around shopping humans and under dusty tables. When Iris slowed, I took her hand and pulled her. She spread her wings and glided along, catching her breath and resting. We came around a large bank of filing cabinets with me pulling and Iris resting. On the other side was the mantel. It sat, leaning back, on a wheeled metal contraption painted bright yellow. A man pulled the mantel toward an opening in the wall. Another man gave him directions and warned him to hurry up.

I let go of Iris's hand and zipped to the mantel. Gerald was at my bedroom window, a pretty fleur-de-lis. His little face peered out the opening. He pushed, but he couldn't get it fully open because of the weight.

"Matilda, Matilda!"

I landed on the mantel, balancing on a wooden flower petal next to my window. I stuck my fingers under the window and it popped open with much less effort than I expected. Gerald held his arms up to me and I pulled him through. The window slammed shut. The edge missed his feet by the tiniest margin. Gerald stared at the window and shivered in my arms for a second, his tears soaking me to the skin.

"I've got you," I said.

"I thought you weren't coming back."

"I told you I would," I said. "Come on. Iris is waiting."

The workman continued pulling the mantel toward the door. A cool wind blew in through the opening and chilled me as we flew off the mantel. Iris hovered by the filing cabinets. Her lower lip trembled as she watched the mantel.

"Where are they taking it?" she asked when we flew up to her.

"I don't know." I felt so sad watching our mantel being wheeled away. I wanted so badly to go with it, to stay within its solid walls. I didn't know if it was because it was my tree, as Soren would've said, or because it was home. I only knew I wanted to stay with it forever.

"We have to go with it. It's our home," said Iris. "How will Mom and Dad find us if we're not with the mantel?"

"If they follow the mantel, they'll come here and find us." I felt sure this was true, but it didn't make me want to stay and find out.

"I'd rather be out here than in there," said Gerald. "Nasty."

Iris wheeled around on him. Her hands were on her hips and her lip wasn't trembling anymore. She grimaced at him until he retreated behind me. "What do you mean our home is nasty? It's not nasty."

"Not the mantel," said Gerald, peeking out from behind my flapping wings. "That baby's completely gross. He's nasty."

Iris's eyes met mine. "Oh no!"

"What?" asked Gerald.

"The spriggan baby's still in there," I said.

"So what? Leave him. He stinks," said Gerald.

"We can't leave him," I said. "He's a baby. He'll die."

The workman pulled the mantel up a large hump in the opening. He groaned and yelled for help. Another workman came over and pulled with him. I landed on the mantel, looking frantically for an opening. All the windows and doors lay firmly closed. I pulled the hidden latch on the front door, but it didn't budge.

The mantel went up over the hump, driving me off the wood. The mantel began moving faster once it was outside the mall. The workmen joshed each other about being weak while practically breaking into a run. I landed back on the mantel, wobbling back and forth. I slid down the extreme angle and bumped into the threshold. The mantel jumped again and I cracked my head on the door. Strong arms wrapped around me and lifted me off the mantel. I didn't spread my wings. I let myself be carried, thinking somehow it must be Soren.

When I opened my eyes, I found Gerald supporting me on one side and Iris on the other. They strained to hold me up, their faces red and pinched.

"You got me," I said.

Gerald and Iris only nodded and floated down until we all landed on the cold grey concrete. The three of us staggered and sat down. The mantel continued to race away toward a white van with the words, "Things Past Antique Mall Jarvis Hornbuckle, Proprietor" painted on the side.

"It's not your fault," said Iris.

Gerald nodded. "Nobody could've done it. Not even my dad."

Nobody? I didn't think so. There had to be something. Maybe I wasn't strong enough, but there had to be another way.

Iris hugged me. "Gerald's right. Nobody could."

I pushed Iris away and stood up. I wasn't nobody. I was definitely a somebody. Somebody with fire.

Chapter 13

The workman bellowed and danced around in a circle. I grinned and formed another fireball, blue and crackling with heat. The workman stamped his foot, waving his arms and spitting curse words like watermelon seeds. The other one stared at him with a gaping mouth.

"Dude, what's your problem?" he asked, edging away while pushing the metal cart with the mantel on it.

"I'm going to kill you, man," said the hopping workman.

"What's wrong?"

"What's wrong? What's wrong? I'll show you what's wrong." The workman stopped dancing and thrust his left foot at his co-worker. "You set fire to my boot. You're going to pay for that."

The workman leaned over and eyed his partner's boot. A blackened area decorated the side. It smelled of burning leather and plastic. I watched them, ready with another blue fire ball poised in my hand. The human's shoe caught fire better than I expected. But three fire balls weren't enough. The men had stopped dragging the mantel toward the van, but the mantel was still tilted back. We couldn't get in unless it was upright.

The men argued. They yelled so loud they rained spit on each other and that only made them madder. The one with the scorched boot grabbed the one holding the mantel's cart. He held him by the neck and squeezed. The man's face turned purple. He flailed his free arm and the mantel rocked on the cart. It shifted a few inches to the right and teetered as the men's tussle became more intense.

Gerald flew up beside me. "Great plan, genius. They won't take the mantel away. They'll just break it into a million zillion pieces."

"Shut up, Gerald," I said.

"Don't tell me to shut up. I'm not the one who keeps screwing up."

"Well, I'm the one who keeps saving everybody, including you." My fireball grew larger.

"Don't throw that," said Gerald. "They'll break it."

"Throw it, Matilda," said Iris from behind Gerald.

Gerald turned on her. "You don't know. She's going to wreck everything."

"Throw it. You have to stop them. The more fire, the better," said Iris.

"If they drop the mantel, they'll kill the baby." Gerald crossed his arms and smiled triumphantly.

"If they take the mantel, he's dead for sure. Stop them." Iris stuck her tongue out at him.

The fire ball tickled my hand, begging me to throw it. And I wanted to. I wanted to set the workmen's pants on fire and watch them bark like madmen. What did they mean by taking our home? I'd teach them a lesson they wouldn't soon forget.

"You'll kill that baby," said Gerald again.

"We don't have Easy," said Iris with triumph in her eyes.

"What?" I said, almost dropping my fireball.

"We left Easy with Soren. You have to stop them long enough for us to get him and get in the mantel."

"We'll just get that spriggan baby out," said Gerald.

The men stopped fighting and examined the boot. "Man, just tell me how you did it."

"I'm telling you. I didn't do it," said the one without the burnt boot.

"Whatever. Let's get her done." He took a last look at his ruined boot, straightened the mantel on the cart and gave it a shove.

I threw the fireball. It arced through the air so bright even the humans could've seen it coming. It landed next to the previously burnt spot on the boot of the man pulling the mantel. The spot ignited and a wisp of smoke snaked up from the side.

"Do you smell that?"

"What?"

"Something's burning."

"Well, it's not me. Oh, dude, it's your freaking boot."

The man stared down at the bright yellow flame nipping at the edge of his jeans. The other one ran around in a circle, screaming for water. The first man thrust the cart handle away. The mantel lurched forward, threatening to tip over and crash on the cement. I caught my breath and charged forward. I hit the mantel's face full tilt. I pushed, bracing my cheek and chest against the wood. The mantel groaned and protested as it teetered on the edge of destruction. Then

Gerald and Iris were on either side of me. We pushed, all three of us together, without argument, without complaint.

"Harder," I gasped and we pushed even harder with strength we didn't know we had. Then the mantel creaked and fell forward. I reached out to Iris and Gerald to pull them from under, when a human's hand swooped in above us and pushed the mantel back into position on the cart.

"Look what you almost did, idiot," the human said. "Do you know how much this thing is worth?"

"My pants were on fire and look at my hands."

Iris, Gerald, and I lay against the mantel's face, shaking and gasping for breath. I patted Iris's quivering shoulder with a shaky hand.

"What about me?" asked Gerald.

"Can't reach you," I said.

Iris craned her neck to see the men. "Wow, you did a number on him, Matilda."

The man's hand was a riot of blisters. As we watched, the blisters grew and throbbed dark red.

"Dude, you need the first aid kit or something. Why'd you put it out with your hands?"

The man blew on his palms. "I don't know. I guess I panicked. Do you think I need to go to the emergency room?"

"Let's find the first aid kit first."

The man holding the metal cart pushed it upright. We spread our wings and glided down to the concrete. The men walked inside, leaving the mantel outside.

"That was close," said Gerald.

"We better go get Easy before they get back," said Iris.

"I'll get Easy and you get the spriggan." I rubbed my bruised knees and prepared to fly off.

"No way," said Gerald. "You're not leaving me again."

I pulled Gerald tight to my chest, resting my cheek on his brown hair. "Aren't you going to say something about my fire?"

"Well ..."

I pulled back. "You knew and you didn't tell?"

"My dad said it wasn't our secret to tell. If you hadn't burnt down Whipplethorn by the time we got there, you weren't going to."

I hugged him and kissed the top of his head. "I can't believe you knew all along."

Gerald struggled out of my arms. "You're still not leaving me here."

"I always come back."

"I don't care. I'm going with you. Things happen when you're gone."

Iris tapped him on the side of the head. "I suppose you think it's okay to leave me, though?"

"You can come," Gerald replied.

"That's big of you."

"Don't start, you two. Gerald can come with me because he got left last time. Okay, Iris?"

Iris nodded and poked Gerald in the shoulder.

"Stop it," he said.

"Iris, go try the door," I said.

Iris flew to our front door, and worked at the lock. The door swung open with no trouble. I waved good-bye, flew into the air, and through the opening back into the antique mall. Gerald followed me, never more than a wing length away. I smiled to see him so and wondered if he realized the impression he was giving. It was almost as if he liked me.

We flew down aisles, around fat old men arguing about World War II, and narrowly avoided a mother chasing a screaming toddler. When I looked over to check on Gerald, I found him smiling. Not a smile of triumph or sarcasm, but a smile of genuine joy. He caught me looking at him and the smile fell off his face, replaced by his usual resentful expression. I blew him a kiss. I don't know why I did it. I hadn't blown a kiss since I was five and heading out for the first day of kindergarten. It felt right though. Gerald gave me a puzzled look, but the smile crept back onto his face.

Then he waved frantically at me and we hovered.

"I heard Easy," he said.

"Are you sure?"

"I heard him. I thought he was ahead, but I think we passed him instead."

I thought about it and nodded. I decided to believe him. He deserved it. "Lead on."

Gerald led us back down the aisle past the mother and her still screaming son, past the old men who were now wiping tears from their eyes and looking at ball caps covered with commemorative pins. Then Gerald flew under a table. Green metal cartridge boxes sat in dusty rows next to foot lockers and a box filled with uniform hats.

"This is it," said Gerald after he landed.

I settled beside him and brushed the hair out of my face. I would've finger-combed it, in case Soren was there, but it was hopelessly tangled. "This must be where the phalanx live." It did seem appropriate, if a bit on the unfriendly side.

"Who? The commander? I heard someone call it headquarters."

"You could hear all that?" I asked.

Gerald blushed. "I can hear pretty well." He paused. "Not as good as Iris though."

"I couldn't have found this on my own. You did great." I ran my eyes over the boxes. "Any idea where the front door is?"

"No need. Easy's coming." Gerald shivered, but he held himself steady with only the tiniest flicker of fear. I could tell he was listening to something, and then I heard it. The scuttling sounds of dozens of phalanx fairies moving together. Funny how those sounds used to give me the creeps. Now they brought order to the world. A diamond formation of shiny black shells came around the hat box. Easy slid around on top of them, kicking up his plump legs and smiling. He wore a new diaper made of camouflage material. Soren and several dryads came out behind them.

The formation stopped in front of us. Easy pushed himself into a seated position and waved. One of the shells on the far right popped up, and the commander came forward. I expected him to be in the front, but then I realized he was always in different spots within the formation. I supposed this protected him in case of an attack. I wanted to ask him about it, but didn't have the nerve to question anything he did.

"That didn't take long," he said, popping off his shell and coming to Soren's side. "You made short work of Earl and Stanley."

"Earl and Stanley?" I asked.

"The workmen taking your mantel away," said Soren. "Are you all right?

"I'm fine," I said.

"You get more and more interesting every minute," said the commander. Then he looked at Gerald. "What can you do?"

Gerald opened his mouth, but then clamped it shut instead of telling the commander he was a certified genius like he normally would.

"Come on. Don't keep me in suspense. You Whipplethorns are an interesting crowd. The girl, Iris, has super hearing. And let me tell you, this baby is something and Matilda, well Matilda can throw fireballs the size of dimes. What can you do? Bend metal with your eyeballs?"

Gerald looked at his shoes. "I can't do anything."

"That's not true," I said. "Gerald is brilliant. He skipped two grades."

"Well, that's something. Maybe not as useful as the occasional fireball, but smarts are a gift. Never say they aren't, boy."

Gerald met the commander's eye and he stood a little taller. "Yes, sir."

I collected Easy off the shells. I gave him a squeeze as he patted my cheeks. "What did you mean about Easy?"

The commander rubbed his chin and looked at Gerald. "Don't tell me you got no clue."

Gerald paled. "I'm not supposed to say."

"So you know about Easy like you knew about me?" I asked.

He nodded and looked at Soren with pleading eyes.

"Shall I say, Easy?" asked Soren.

Easy chirped and waved his plump arms.

"Easy can read minds," said Soren.

"You can read minds?" I asked the baby.

Easy winked at me and I almost dropped him. Soren and the commander laughed. Several of the shells shook, but they were too well-trained to break formation.

"We've enjoyed having the little bugger around. I suspect he has a few more surprises in store for you," said the commander.

A shell scuttled up from behind me and reported something to Soren and the commander. Soren took a long look at us. "You better get going. Stanley's all bandaged up and headed back to the mantel."

"Is there anything you don't know about?" I asked.

"Well, I wouldn't know, would I?" Soren hugged me and then Gerald.

"Thanks for the new diaper and everything," I said, choking up.

"I'm happy to help you."

"Soren?"

"Yes."

"I'm not sure about what to do," I said.

"Should you go or should you stay. Is that it?"

"I just don't know what's best."

"Would you give the commander a light for old time's sake? He's always looking for a light."

I lit the commander's stick and watched him puff on it until he got a good ember glowing on the end. "You're saying we should go."

"I am," said Soren. "As much as I'd like you to stay, you're wood fairies. Stay with your mantel. It's where you belong."

"But what about our parents?" asked Gerald.

"If they can track you here, they'll make it to the next stop, too. Go quick before those dufuses make off with it. Good luck to you all." Soren held my hands. "I will see you again."

The commander took a long suck on his stick. "You're not out in the boonies anymore. You can get back if you want to. Better let us know the minute you arrive, though. Don't want any more incidents." The commander popped his shell on and disappeared back into the formation. It moved in one rippling motion away from us and zipped around a corner.

"Good-bye, Matilda," said Soren.

I kissed his cheek and rose into the air with Gerald. We headed back to the mantel, carrying Easy between us.

"The commander was pretty weird, but he didn't scare me," said Gerald, his forehead wrinkled in thought.

"At least he didn't eat any flies this time," I said.

"Gross."

"You have no idea. Let's go. We probably only have a few minutes. Even Soren won't be able to help us if we're late."

A.W. HARTOIN

Chapter 14

E asy got heavier by the second. Gerald and I were flying so low, my toes brushed the linoleum.

"We'll never make it." Gerald's face contorted and beads of sweat popped out on his forehead.

"Yes, we will. We just have to try harder." My words came out in short staccato bursts. My arms felt like they were being pulled out of their sockets.

"My shoulder hurts really bad," said Gerald.

Gerald's arm being pulled out of its socket seemed like a million years ago. "I forgot about that. I shouldn't have brought you."

Gerald scowled at me and beat his wings harder. "I can do it."

We rounded the last corner and flew out of the opening into the fall sunshine. Iris sat on the concrete just outside with a look of utter distaste on her pretty face. The spriggan baby toddled around, looking as gross as possible. He smelled so bad, his stench was nearly visible.

Gerald and I landed with duel grunts near my sister. Iris jumped to her feet and scooped up Easy. He chirped and nuzzled her cheeks. The spriggan baby plopped down on his butt and started bawling. I watched as fat tears rolled down his cheeks. The tears almost made him appealing. Almost.

"Aren't you going to go get him?" asked Gerald.

"You can go get him," I said.

"You're the babysitter."

The ultimate trump card. I was the babysitter. I grimaced and staggered to my feet. My muscles weren't happy that I was trying to use them again. The spriggan baby held up his arms, looking about as much like a baby as a rotting cabbage.

"Don't pretend you don't like me," he said. "I know the truth."

I gagged and picked him up. "You don't know anything."

"I know you threw fireballs to save me." He nuzzled my cheek in an approximation of Easy's affection.

"Well, I couldn't just let you die."

"You like me." He nuzzled me again, leaving a smear of gritty slime on my cheek.

"Wait a minute," I said. "You have a diaper on."

"Gerald put it on me. He said you deserve it," said Horc.

I looked closer at the diaper. It was made of a pale green fabric shot with brown threads. "Gerald!"

Gerald flushed and kept his eyes downcast.

"Gerald, so help me. Is this my skirt?"

He nodded slightly and a smile crept onto his lips.

I put Horc back on my hip and scowled. I glanced toward the opening. It wasn't too late. Soren would take the spriggan. Maybe I could get the baby to him and be back in time to go with the mantel. A few well-placed fireballs at Stanley's butt should do the trick.

The spriggan baby stopped nuzzling me and glared at Easy. "You don't know."

Easy chirped.

"You're so stupid. You can't even talk. She is not giving me back. She likes me."

Easy chirped, stuck out his tongue, and buried his face in Iris's neck.

"Not true! Not true!" shouted the spriggan baby.

Just then, Earl and Stanley came through the opening. Stanley held his bandaged hands out in front of him and Earl jabbed him in the shoulder, taunting him.

"I'm not a freaking wuss. I got like sixth degree burns here," said Stanley.

"You idiot. There's no such thing as a sixth degree burns. It only goes up to four."

"How come?"

"I don't know."

"It should go up to a hundred, 'cause this is really bad. I need some pain killers," said Stanley.

"You took some of that Motrin."

"That ain't enough. I need the good stuff. Take me to the doctor."

"I ain't taking you to no doctor. We're late. That happy housewife is gonna be pissed if she don't get her mantel on time," said Earl.

"She can wait. What's the difference?"

"The difference is we'll get fired, idiot." Earl grabbed the mantel's cart and pushed it towards the van.

I looked at Iris. "Can you carry Easy?"

"I'll help her," said Gerald, getting to his feet.

"We're going with the mantel?" asked Iris.

"Yes. Now get ready. Fly in the van when I say," I said.

Iris nodded and shifted Easy so Gerald could get a grip on him. Easy waved good-bye to the spriggan baby who wrapped his arms around my neck. A fresh wave of stink clogged my nose and I glanced toward the opening again. No time to find Soren, but he saw everything. I could leave the baby inside the opening. Soren was sure to find him. But when I glanced down at the spriggan, he gazed up at me with large eyes swimming with unshed tears.

"You like me," he said. "You saved me."

Stanley opened the van's back doors and stepped back. Earl wheeled up the cart. He got on one side of the mantel and prepared to lift. Stanley watched him, but made no move to help.

"Come on, dude," said Earl. "What are you waiting for?"

"I can't lift nothing."

"Suck it up. We got to go." Earl waved Stanley to the other side of the mantel. Stanley minced around, looking for a handhold and whining.

"Now!" I yelled as I flew into the air.

Iris and Gerald struggled to get the balance between them right and then flew up with Easy between them. The spriggan baby buried his face in my shoulder as we raced to the van's opening. We zipped past Stanley's face and into the back of the van. Earl and Stanley lifted the mantel and slid it in behind us. The mantel's top shelf brushed my feet as it passed under. I looked down at the mantel's intricate carvings in awe. Even in the musty interior of the van, it glowed with beauty and craftsmanship. My home. How could I ever have considered letting it go?

Earl shut the back doors and greyness enveloped the mantel. The smell of axel grease and furniture polish made my stomach flip. Two squares of light shone in through the grimy back window, making everything appear sad and dirty.

"What now?" asked Iris from between clenched teeth.

I spotted a black, flat shelf between the two seats in the front of the van. "Follow me."

Iris and Gerald landed on the shelf behind me with noises of disgust. I tried to turn around, but found my feet stuck in a puddle of sticky caramel-colored goo. I lost my balance and fell against a red metal cylinder lying on its side, almost dropping the spriggan baby. I pushed myself upright and read a list of ingredients on the side of the cylinder. Carbonated water, caramel color, aspartame, phosphoric acid.

"Weird," I said. "It almost sounds like food."

"Not weird. Delicious," said the spriggan baby.

Earl and Stanley sat in the seats on either side of us. Stanley plunked a square brown leather thing stuffed with papers down on the shelf, causing me to jerk away and fall over into the goo.

"Nice," said the spriggan.

"Quiet, spriggan," I said.

"My name is Horc, if you'll recall."

"Whatever."

"Not whatever. Horc."

"Fine." I touched the goo. A long string attached my finger to the shelf. The stuff looked gross, but I had to admit it smelled pretty good. So good that I briefly considered dunking Horc in it.

"Matilda, have you tasted this stuff?" asked Iris.

I turned to see Iris with a finger in her mouth and Gerald staring at her with an undisguised look of disgust. "Iris, are you crazy? Don't eat that stuff. We don't know what it is."

"It was an accident," said Iris. "I didn't mean to eat it."

"Yeah," said Gerald. "It was an accident that you placed your finger in your mouth."

"It smells great," Iris said.

"So does oleander. Don't eat it," I said.

Horc leaned over and tried to get a handful of goo. I jerked him away as the van lurched forward. If we hadn't been stuck to the shelf, we would've slid right off. I thrust Horc onto the brown leather square almost falling into the goo in the process. Horc starting jumping around saying he was hungry and he wanted the goo. I ignored him and dug my fingernails into the leather. I wiggled and pulled until I worked my way out of the goo. Horc patted my sweaty face as I lay panting on the leather.

"Hungry," he said. "Money makes me hungry."

"Uh huh." I closed my eyes and then popped them back open. "Wait, what money?"

Horc pointed down. "In the wallet."

Then I saw the bills sticking out of the side of the wallet. "Money makes you hungry?"

"I'm hungry now."

"I get it. Just give me a minute," I said.

I could've lain on that comfortable somewhat squishy spot all day, if Iris and Gerald hadn't started squawking about being stuck. "All right. All right. I'm coming."

"Don't leave," said Horc.

"I'm not leaving you. I have to go get them."

"No."

I rolled my eyes and took off for Gerald and Iris. I hovered upside down above them without thinking about it. Gerald's eyes widened and Iris grinned as they handed Easy to me. I flew him to the wallet, setting him next to Horc and then flew back to Gerald. I grabbed him by the forearms and pulled until my eyes felt like they'd pop out. The goo was thicker on his section of the shelf and he was in up to his ankles.

"Wiggle your feet," I said.

"I am," said Gerald.

Iris leaned over and yanked at his legs. "It's no good."

"Try to get out of your shoes," I said.

"No way. This is my only pair."

"You want to stay in the goo?"

Gerald's mouth turned down in irritation, but he worked his feet out. Once he was free, he flapped over to the wallet.

I took Iris by the arms, but almost let go when I saw Easy and Horc smacking each other. Gerald separated them, but they rolled into each other, grappling like a couple of crazed wrestlers.

"Gerald, do something!" I yelled as Iris slipped out of her shoes and into the air.

Gerald took a baby fist to the nose and stumbled backward, nearly tumbling off the square back into the goo. Iris caught him before he went off the edge.

"Good thing I got you," she said. "If you fell in again, you'd probably have to take off your clothes to get out and then we'd see your dirty underwear." Iris grinned at Gerald and ducked his swipe at her head.

"Not funny," he said.

I landed next to Horc. "It's kind of funny."

Horc looked me with something like a smile on his face. When he wasn't paying attention, Easy gave him an open-handed smack. Horc screeched and kicked Easy in the shin. I picked up Horc, trying not to breathe through my nose. Iris scooped up Easy and walked him to the other side of the square. Then the van went around a turn and we all stumbled to the right.

"Sit down before we fall off." I looked down at Horc. "Why'd you hit Easy? What's wrong with you?"

A better question might've been what was right. Horc snuggled me, getting more and more of his slime on my clothes. "His fault. He's as stupid as he looks."

"What are you fighting about?"

"Ask him," said Horc.

"I can't. He doesn't talk yet."

"See. Stupid."

I sighed. "Just tell me."

"He says you don't like me."

"What do you mean says?" I looked over at Easy, who stuck his tongue out at Horc and blew a huge raspberry.

"He says it in here." Horc tapped the side of his head.

"You can read minds, too?" I asked.

"No." Horc looked at me like I was completely brain-free. "He puts the words in my head."

"Easy can what?" asked Iris.

"How come you don't put thoughts in our heads?" I patted Iris's hand as she gaped at Easy.

Horc scowled. "Apparently, it wouldn't be polite to put thoughts in your heads."

Earl took another sharp turn and Stanley clunked his head on the window. "Dude, you almost like knocked off my head. I could have a compression."

"Shut up. We're almost there. Try to look professional," said Earl.

"Professional?" Stanley scratched his head and white flakes rained down on his shoulder. Iris inched away in case one of the flakes came her way.

"Everybody, get ready," I said. "We'll fly out when they unload the mantel.

Iris and Gerald nodded, their faces grim. The babies snarled at each other, apparently only worried about how soon they could get their hands on each other.

Earl took another sharp turn and slammed on the brakes. The mantel slid forward six inches and came to a halt. I thanked the heavens we weren't inside it. I squeezed Horc, and he squeezed back. His stench still bothered me, but I was getting used to it. Either that or I was losing my sense of smell.

Earl yelled at Stanley for trying to sneak a cigarette as they got out, and then they slammed the doors. The van became way too quiet. The waiting seemed to go on and on, but it was probably only a few minutes. Iris watched the back doors, biting her lip and quaking. Horc stroked my cheek in what I assumed was an attempt to soothe me.

"Can you hear anything, Iris?" I asked.

"Not really. I think the metal's blocking the sound," said Iris.

"Okay. I'm going to take a look." I peeled Horc off my chest. "Don't panic. I won't go far."

"I'm not worried. You like me," said Horc.

I gave him a weak smile and rose in the air until I could see over the door edge. Earl and Stanley stood in front of a blue house with a red door, arguing. I couldn't hear what they were saying, but it might've had something to do with the cigarettes Earl was waving around. The red door opened and a woman stepped out. Earl and Stanley stopped arguing and stood up a little straighter. The woman smiled and spoke. Something about her seemed familiar, although I was certain I'd never seen her before. She tossed her messy light brown hair back over her shoulder and sneezed into a tissue.

Her red-rimmed eyes accentuated her pale cheeks and green eyes. She wore grey pants and a top that looked out of place on her like she normally wore more attractive clothing rather than nondescript stuff two sizes too big. She nodded at Earl and followed him toward the van. I dropped to the shelf and gathered up Horc in one swift motion.

"They're coming," I said. "Get ready."

Iris and Gerald stood. They both got a good handhold on Easy and watched me with big eyes. Easy chirped while we waited, and Horc growled at him. Earl flung the back door open and presented the mantel with a flourish I wouldn't have thought him capable of.

"What do you think?" asked Earl.

"It's gorgeous." The woman touched a carving reverently, as though she might mar the wood with her fingers.

"So you want it?" asked Stanley, who flinched when Earl glared at him.

"I wanted it the minute I saw the first picture. Grandma knows best. Can you bring it in for me with those hands?" The woman gestured to Stanley's bandaged hands.

"Don't you worry about him, ma'am. Just show us where you want it," said Earl.

It was Stanley's turn to glare. "Easy for you to say."

"Stop your whining. This is our job, you jackass."

"I got sixth degree burns here. I should be at the doctors," said Stanley.

Earl turned to the woman who was staring at Stanley with a wrinkled brow. "Don't listen to him. Those ain't no more than fourth degree."

The woman hid a smile behind her tissue. "Well, if you think you can handle it. Bring it in the living room and place it on the hearth. It's all ready."

Earl and Stanley each grabbed a leg of the mantel and started pulling it out, much more gingerly than they'd pushed it in. The woman sneezed and watched, her red-rimmed eyes roving over the mantel. A smile flickered across her generous lips and she sneezed again.

"Let's go," I said.

We flew out of the van at a leisurely pace. No need to hurry when Earl and Stanley inched the mantel along so slowly. I could've walked out and still beat them.

We hovered near the woman's ear. She was sick, but she smelled a good deal better than Horc or Earl and Stanley.

"What now?" asked Iris.

The front door remained open and I inclined my head toward it "I guess we go in. That's where the mantel's going."

I led the way, flying up the walkway past enormous green-glazed pots filled with blood-red flowers that definitely didn't grow in the forest. Other flowers grew out of the ground in bushy clumps. Some were striped with purple and white. Others were solid pink or a purple so dark it appeared nearly black. Iris shouted something, but I couldn't hear her with the October wind whipping past my ears.

"She says the flowers are amazing," said Horc in my ear.

"Thanks." I wanted to tell him to be quiet. It depressed me to know that even a spriggan baby who'd known me for all of five minutes could see my defect so plainly. Mom always said it didn't matter; clearly it did and everybody knew it. I felt like the last to be brought in on a secret.

We flew up the steps to the door, past another pot with a weird pine tree in it twisting its way up to the sky like a spring. Warmth spilled out the open doorway. Warmth that made the antique mall feel like a January day. We slowed to a hover just outside. Iris's and Gerald's faces were crinkled in identical expressions of worry.

"It's hot in there," said Gerald. "Somebody should go in to check it out. We can't be too careful."

"It's weird, but it's not like it's on fire or anything," I said.

"There is a fire," said Iris.

I rolled my eyes. "Humans have fires in fireplaces. It's not on fire, is it? I mean, that woman was just in there."

"I'll check it out," said Gerald. "I should do it. I'm the man."

"Are you kidding?" I asked. "I'm the babysitter as you so recently reminded me. I'll go first."

"Well, somebody go," said Iris. "My wings are tired."

"This spriggan's no feather," I said. "But I'm going."

I flew over the threshold with Horc, past the red door into a dining room. At least I assumed it was a dining room. It had an oval table with shiny ornate chairs and a large cabinet filled with pretty dishes. I wanted to run my fingers over the gold-rimmed plates and study their pattern. I'd never seen an intact human dining room before and it was more beautiful than I imagined. Whipplethorn's dining room was empty, so I wasn't sure what made it a dining room, but that's what everyone called it.

"It's okay," I said, not bothering to shout. Iris and Gerald would hear me even if I whispered.

I fluttered over to the oval table and landed next to a flower pot filled with hot pink flowers that looked so light and delicate I wouldn't have been surprised if they'd floated right off their stems. Iris and Gerald landed beside me and collapsed into a heap with Easy. I set Horc beside them and touched a petal that drooped to the tabletop. The flower's brilliant color almost didn't seem real. When I touched it, I felt its warmth, its vibrancy flowing through the delicate veins.

"Is it real?" asked Iris, struggling to her feet.

"Of course it is," said Gerald.

We gave him stern looks and both touched the petal. The woman came through the doorway and picked up a mug off the end of the table. The sweet smell of chamomile caused a wave of homesickness to flood my chest. Mom loved chamomile. The woman turned to face Earl and Stanley. They argued at the door, trying to work out how to get the mantel over the threshold. The woman sipped and watched with a faint smile tickling the edges of her eyes

"Just give it a shove. It'll go all right," said Stanley.

"Look, dummy. It'll hit the frame," said Earl.

"Will not."

"Will too."

Gerald looked at me. "How long do you think it will take them to figure it out?"

"Considering Stanley thinks he's got sixth degree burns, it could be a while."

"I think they can do it," said Iris.

"You would," said Gerald.

The woman set her mug on the table and coughed. "Excuse me. I could be wrong, but perhaps you should set the mantel upright."

Earl and Stanley looked at each other and nodded. "We were just about to try that," said Earl.

The woman nodded. She sucked her lips into her mouth to conceal a smile and walked away deeper into the house, glancing back at the workmen. Earl and Stanley set the mantel upright and carried it through the doorway. They passed the table where we watched and followed the woman into another room. I waited until they'd passed and then picked up Horc. Iris and Gerald followed suit with Easy.

A chill wind blew in from the open door and I shivered. Amazing how just a few feet could make such a difference in temperature. "Let's go after them," I said.

I flew after Earl and Stanley, more and more aware of my aching arms and legs. Iris and Gerald lugged Easy along beside me. Both their faces were pinched. Gerald favored his injured arm and I felt bad for making him use it. We flew past a staircase, nothing like the one in Whipplethorn Manor. Fabric covered the steps and a plain railing led the way up to another floor.

When we got to the next room, I saw Iris's and Gerald's faces relax. They flew on a bit faster through a high archway into a room that had blood red walls with simple pretty woodwork. Its area was about the same as the mantel's room in Whipplethorn, and everything had a pleasant warmth about it.

Earl and Stanley pushed the mantel into place over a hearth with a lively fire going. Once it was up against the wall, the woman joined them to admire it. We crossed the room with a final burst of speed and landed on the mantel shelf. I staggered when my feet touched the wood and I almost dropped Horc instead of setting him down. My arms felt loose and empty like they'd been drained of blood. Iris toppled over beside me and Gerald had to hold Easy by himself. His thin legs shook, but he lowered Easy to the ground gently. Easy chirped and patted the spot next to him. Gerald sat down and watched the three humans.

"Wow. He gets heavy," Gerald said. "What's next do you think?"

"Nothing, I hope," I said.

Iris stretched out on the wood and covered her face with the crook of her arm. "I could go to sleep right here."

"Go ahead," I said. "I think we'll stay awhile."

"Says you. What if that woman decides she doesn't want the mantel?" Gerald asked.

"She'd be crazy not to want it."

I turned my attention back to the humans. Stanley rocked back and forth on the balls of his feet and Earl pulled a yellow slip of paper out of his pocket. "Here's your invoice. You want to look it over, just in case."

The woman came forward. Her head disappeared below the mantel shelf. Gerald scooted to the edge and looked over.

"Stay away from the edge," I said.

He stuck his tongue out at me. "Don't be such a worrywart."

"What was I thinking?" I asked. "Nothing ever happens to us."

Just then the woman's head came back up. Her hair grazed the shelf. I blinked and Gerald was gone.

"Gerald!" I yelled.

Iris and I ran to the edge and looked over. I hoped to see Gerald hovering just below, making faces at us, but he wasn't there.

"I don't see him," I said. "Do you hear anything?"

Iris jutted her chin out and concentrated. "I hear him, but he's hard to understand. This better not be a joke."

Behind them, Horc said, "It's not a joke."

"How do you know?" asked Iris.

"Say you like me," said Horc.

"There's no time for that silliness, Horc," I said. "Just tell us."

"Easy says you don't like me and I want to hear you to say you do." I knew from the set of his lumpy chin, there was no persuading him.

"Fine, I like you. Tell us," I said.

He's in the woman's hair."

"How do you know?" I asked.

"Easy told me." Horc rolled over and stretched. "Apparently, the woman's hair is strangling him, so perhaps you might want to hurry."

"Stay with the babies," I said to Iris. Then I dove off the edge of the mantel into the silence of the strange house.

The woman stood at the open front door, talking to Earl and Stanley. I darted to her right, looking for Gerald. The woman stepped away from the door and I bumped into her earlobe, scratching my ankle on the emerald earring dangling from it. I flew backward as Earl pumped the woman's hand until her whole body shook. The woman pulled back, flexing her fingers. She ushered Earl and Stanley out the door, then closed it and leaned against wood.

I circled the woman's head until I found Gerald tangled in a nest of soft brown curls. A strand encircled his neck. His face was turning from bright red to a hideous blue. He tugged at it, straining and kicking. I forced my hands under the strand. Its fine texture bit into my palms as I pulled at it.

Gerald's arms flayed about. He kicked me in the stomach. I clung to the strand, trying to get my breath back.

"Stop struggling," I gasped.

But Gerald was too terrified to hear. He kicked and grabbed at me. I positioned my feet beside Gerald's torso and yanked on the strand. My hands burned, but I closed my eyes and pulled harder. The strand gave a bit and I opened my eyes in time to see an enormous hand coming toward us. The woman stuck her fingers under her thick hair and fluffed it. Gerald rocketed up, dragging me with him. The woman's pinkie grazed Gerald's head and he fell limp. The strand stretched and broke. We tumbled down, landing on the woman's shoulder. Gerald started sliding over the edge, his face slack and mouth open. I scrambled over the edge after him and managed to snag his hand before he fell. I heaved him back up onto the woman's shoulder and held him around the middle.

"Gerald," I said. "Wake up."

Gerald groaned, but didn't open his eyes.

"Iris!" I dug my nails into the fabric, but we kept sliding.

Gerald lifted. Iris had him by the arm. Her wings flapped frantically, blowing my hair out of my face. The woman turned and stepped away, leaving us hovering with Gerald suspended between us.

"Get to the mantel," said Iris between clenched teeth.

When we reached the mantel, Gerald's body hit the side of the shelf. The pain jolted him to consciousness. He caterwauled as we pulled him up and over the edge.

"Are you trying to kill me?" he asked as the three of us collapsed on the mantel shelf.

"Maybe later," I said.

Horc picked up one of my bloodied hands and examined it. "Why didn't you leave him? You hurt yourself." His forehead furrowed and he looked genuinely puzzled.

"Wood fairies aren't like that," I said.

"I want to be a wood fairy," said Horc.

"What do you want me to do? Wave a magic wand or something?"

"Give me a bath. Wood fairies don't stink," said Horc.

"I'll get right on that." I rolled over and saw Iris with Easy looking over the edge of the shelf.

"Get back!" I yelled. "Haven't you learned anything?"

"Come look," she said.

"Every time you say that it's a bad thing."

"Please come look, Matilda," said Iris, her eyes big and pleading.

"Fine, but if I get attacked by hair, it's on you."

I stood up and looked at the room spread out before me, still and quiet. Warm sunshine slanted in from a row of windows to my right. The red walls changed color in the sun and took on an orange tint. I'd never seen that color before, so rich and inviting. The mantel's mahogany looked well against it as if the woman had known and painted the walls just to suit it.

Next to the mantel, a set of black shelves piled with candlesticks and books clung to the wall. Titles like *The Poems of Robert Service, Dinosaurs, Gone with the Wind*, and *Phrase and Fable* called out to me. In the room, a short table was stacked with more books and papers. Next to the table were dark brown chairs, thickly padded and shiny. A large cream-colored chair sat in the middle, too big to be a chair and could've seated three humans at least. Under the table and chairs lay a thick oriental rug, swirling with intricate designs and exotic shapes. Grandma Vi told me rugs like that used to be in Whipplethorn Manor when she was young. The rug lay on a gleaming hardwood floor much like the one in the formal dining room, although the planks weren't nearly so wide.

Past all these things, I saw a small dining table in a room just beyond. Maybe it was a kitchen with cabinets enclosing the room on three sides. The cabinets were honey-colored oak, not especially carved, but interesting just the same. The bottom cabinets had a shiny top on them that looked like granite. Another table sat in the middle of the room with more granite on top. It shone like ice in winter. On two of the walls, big metal boxes sat huge and equally shiny. I couldn't imagine what they contained. If we stayed awhile, maybe we'd get to find out.

Then I checked myself. I wanted the mantel to go back to Whipplethorn. Even as I thought this, a little niggling thought emerged in the back of my mind. The house was quite pleasant and warm. There were books and rugs and who knew what. Whipplethorn Manor seemed rather stark in comparison. I forced the thought out of my mind. No place could be better than Whipplethorn. No place had anything better to offer.

"Matilda, you have to look. Come on." Iris's face glowed with excitement and I began to get curious.

I crept over to the side, where Iris was crouching, and looked over, a little afraid that a mass of hair might sweep us away. Looking up at me was the strangest pair of animals I'd ever seen.

"Aren't they adorable?" Iris clapped her hands.

"I don't know what they are." I stared the animals. Were they some kind of miniature bear? If I hadn't seen their sides moving, I might've thought they were stuffed.

"They're dogs," said Gerald as he looked over.

"Dogs?" I asked. "Dogs don't look like that. Where are their eyes?"

Iris pointed. "That one has eyes."

True enough. The one on the left did have eyes, although they were exceptionally small compared to the head. Furrows of skin covered the body and two tiny ears were perched on either side of the head. Long droopy lips concealed the mouth and short bristly whiskers poked out of its snout. As weird as it was, it made the other one look ridiculous. Its fur was longer and the wrinkles were so heavy, they covered the eyes completely. The ears were even smaller. I stared at it. How could that be a dog? It couldn't hunt or dig anything up.

"I think they know we're up here," said Iris.

"They don't look smart enough to know anything," said Gerald.

"It's not about smart," said Iris. "They can smell us."

"If they can smell us, they might want to eat us." Gerald jumped up and down, waving his arms. "Go away. We're not lunch."

Both animals jumped to their feet and wagged their curly tails.

"They are dogs," said Iris.

Easy clapped his hands and even Gerald looked pleased. I wasn't so sure. Being in a house with ginormous dogs didn't seem like the best idea.

Iris looked over at me, her face flushed and shiny. "Can you believe it? We have pets."

"They're not our pets." Gerald's eyes bugged out of his head. "They're monster dogs. You could fit in one of their nostrils easy."

Iris ignored him. "I always wanted a pet. Can I touch them?"

I opened my mouth to shout no, but Iris had already shoved Easy into my arms. She dove off the mantel towards the monster dogs that now had their mouths open in anticipation.

Chapter 15

This is insane." Gerald dangled his feet off the edge of the mantel's shelf next to Easy. They both looked down with covert longing.

For once, I agreed with him. The situation screamed insanity, but at the same time I couldn't help feeling happy about it. Below us, Iris lay draped across a dog's snout, giving it a good scratch. Both dogs' tails wagged in unison and they didn't seem to be a threat. I probably should've gone down there and dragged Iris back to safety. That's what my parents would've expected, but I couldn't do it. Iris just looked so happy.

"What kind of dogs are they?" I asked Gerald.

"I don't know, but they're pretty fancy. I wish I had my dad's books."

"Your dad has a lot of books?"

"Dozens. And he lets me read any one I want." Gerald straightened and threw back his shoulders.

"So that's how you know so much," I said.

Gerald slumped and picked at a hang nail on his thumb. "It hasn't done us much good, has it?"

"What do you mean?"

"You heard the commander. I can't do anything."

"That's not what he said."

"Well, that's what he meant," said Gerald.

A faint stink rolled over us as Horc toddled up. Gerald coughed and scooted away. Easy tried to take advantage of the opportunity and attempted to leap off the mantel to the dogs. I snagged his diaper and pulled him away from the edge.

"Hungry," said Horc.

I divided our last fruit leather between the babies and Gerald. Horc finished his piece in two bites and held out his hand for more. I'd have to go inside the mantel and see what food we had left and I didn't want to. The damage had to be worse after the last move and it pained me to think about it.

Easy started chirping at Horc. Horc crossed his arms and turned up the lump he called a nose.

"What's Easy saying?" I asked.

"I'm hungry," said Horc.

"He still has his fruit leather."

"No," said Horc, pointing to himself. "I'm hungry."

"I know. I'll find you something. Now what's Easy going on about?"

"I want lots."

"Fine."

"He says he smells something," said Horc.

I sniffed and caught the scent of something not entirely unfamiliar. "What's that?"

Gerald smiled as wide as his narrow face would allow. "Smells kind of like my mom's flatbread, but different."

"I'll go check it out. Bread would be awesome."

"No, wait," said Gerald. "I hear someone. I think the woman's back and she's not alone."

All my good feelings disappeared. What if the woman sold the mantel? Stranger things had happened. We might be on the move again.

"Iris! Come back up!"

Iris shook her head and continued to scratch the dog.

"Gerald, go get her and don't take no for an answer," I said.

Gerald plunged off the mantel out of sight. I carried Easy back away from the edge and told Horc to sit beside him. Gerald returned with Iris, who carried a dog hair twice her height.

"I'm sorry," said Iris, brandishing the hair like a sword. "I wasn't paying attention. I didn't hear."

"Well, it's a good thing we have Gerald." I gave Iris a wink.

"They're coming in the front door, I think," said Gerald.

The dogs jumped up and shot out of the room, slipping on the hardwood. The woman came around the corner carrying fabric bags with the dogs following close at her heels. She yelled over her shoulder "We're behind. I don't want to hear any whining."

Two children dashed into the room, lugging backpacks and shoving each other. I sat up straighter when I saw them. Children. I never considered that there might be children living in the house. The boy looked about my age. He wore baggy pants and a black shirt with a skull and crossbones on it. The girl was much smaller, maybe seven or eight. Her features mirrored the woman's, delicate and pretty, but the expression on her face was anything but delicate as the boy bolted past her, knocking her into a wall.

"It's not my fault. Dufus forgot his algebra book." The girl rummaged around in her backpack.

The boy brushed a fringe of light brown hair out of his eyes and scowled at his sister.

"Mom, I got an A on my spelling test," she said, thrusting the paper at her mother.

"Excellent," said her mom.

The boy pulled a piece of paper out of his backpack. "So what? I got one hundred plus two bonus words."

"It's not my fault Miss Cortier doesn't give us bonus words," said the girl.

"I still have a higher percentage."

"Okay," said their mom as she dumped one of the bags on the stone table. "You both got As. One A isn't better than the other." She eyed the boy until he looked away.

"Here's my test," he said.

His mom waved it away. "Judd, give me second, will you?"

Judd shrugged. "I'm hungry. What's to eat?"

"Dirt," said his mother, wrinkling her nose and smiling. "And lots of it, mostly dragged in by you."

"Mom," whined Judd. "I'm starving."

"Have a yogurt."

"How many?"

"One, Judd. One yogurt," said his mother.

"Yeah," said the girl. "Stop eating everything."

"Quiet, Tess." Their mother stood up and began putting away the rest of the stuff from the bag into the cabinets I noticed earlier.

Judd opened the tall metal box and got a couple of small containers. He tossed one to his sister. She placed it on the table without looking at it. Instead, she looked in the direction of the mantel. For a second, I thought Tess saw us until I realized that Tess couldn't possibly see us all the way across the room even if she was capable of seeing fairies.

"Mom, what's that?" Tess asked, pointing at the mantel.

"The new mantel I just bought. What do you think?"

Tess walked across the room, her eyes roving over the mantel's many details. "It's really pretty. And big."

"I know. It's bigger than I expected, but fits perfectly," said the mom.

Tess disappeared from view and I crept to the edge, peering over to see her. She ran her fingers over the mantel's carvings, tracing the fleur de lis, oak leaves, and columns made so long ago. She looked up and caught me in her pale blue gaze that mirrored my own. She raised a finger to the mantel's shelf and I jumped back.

"What's she doing?" asked Gerald.

"Just looking," I said.

Tess's voice came from below the shelf. "Are we keeping it, Mom?"

"Of course. Now hurry up and eat your snack. We have to go to your brother's practice," said her mom.

She turned around, opened a white box and pulled out a metal container. A wonderful smell drifted across the room to the mantel and I groaned.

"That smells so good," said Iris.

"No kidding." Gerald licked his lips and rubbed his hands together.

The mom turned the metal container upside down and a brown rectangle popped out. "I'll just let the bread cool while we're gone. Judd, grab your cleats."

"I don't want to go," said Tess, still next to the mantel. "Can't I go to Great Grandma's?"

"Not today." Their mom herded her kids out of the red room, both protesting, Tess because she didn't want to go and Judd because he was still hungry. When they were gone, the silence surprised me. Humans really fill up a room. The dogs trotted back to the mantel, sat, and tilted their muzzles up, waiting for another scratch. Iris waved her dog hair at them.

"Stay here," I said. "I'll see if I can get some of that bread.

Gerald spread his wings. "No way. I want to go."

"Me, too," said Iris, dropping the hair.

"I'm going," said Horc.

Easy chirped and stared at Horc. Horc crossed his arms. "Apparently, I am now that baby's translator. He says he wants to go, too."

My mouth watered and I could hardly stop myself from flying to the bread straight away. "Fine. Gerald, come here and help carry Easy."

"I can help you with Horc, if you want," said Gerald.

"You'd rather carry Horc than Easy?"

"No. I just thought I'd help you." Gerald fidgeted and avoided looking at me.

"Gerald Whipplethorn offering to help. You're like a new person."

"It's no big deal."

"I think it is," I said. "But I don't need any help. Iris does."

Easy gazed up at Gerald and held up his hands. Gerald scooped him up and Iris got a good handhold on him. I led the way across the red room with Horc clasped to my chest. I flew low over the brown chairs and tried to read the titles of the books on the short table. Kipling's *The Jungle Book* and *His Majesty's Dragon* were the only ones I caught. Gerald nodded to the kitchen. He and Iris zipped off with Easy before I could utter a word. The dogs trotted after them, sniffing and wagging.

When I caught up, they already stood next to the bread loaf on a granite-covered table that swirled with a multitude of colors: orange, black, white and grey. I shivered as the granite's cold crept up my feet into my ankles. How it stayed so frigid in such a warm room was a mystery. I looked over the edge. The dogs spied me and began whimpering. I waved at them and turned away. Iris and Gerald moved into a ring of warm moisture around the bread. The bread was enormous up close; bigger than our entire home in the mantel. Iris gazed up at it, holding Easy, who strained towards the loaf with his arms outstretched. Gerald pounded on the side of the bread.

"I can't get any," he said. "It's hard as a rock."

The smell filled the air around me so thick I felt like I could open my mouth, take a bite, and be satisfied. I set Horc on the stone. He swiped his hand through the bread's moisture and licked his fingers.

"Oh, Horc," I said. "Don't do that."

"Why not?" He licked his other glistening hand.

"It might be dirty."

"Look at me," said Horc. "Do I look concerned with dirt? Spriggans can live on anything and frequently do."

I shrugged and leaned against the bread. Warmth radiated off it and drool almost slipped down my chin before I caught it with my finger.

"Do something," said Gerald. He looked about ready to cry. "I'm so hungry."

I knocked on the side of the loaf. Gerald was right. The bread was hard as a rock. I craned my neck back and looked at the top. It appeared shattered and broken at the top. I flew up and grabbed a jagged edge. A piece the size of my head broke free and I dropped it on the table next to Horc. He snatched it up and stuffed the whole thing in his mouth before anyone else could react. I tore off more chunks and only stopped when the pile next to Horc teetered taller than him. Then I fluttered down and watched the rest eat their fill before taking my first bite.

We lay down on the cold granite when we finished, bloated and sleepy. Horc snored and began farting. The rest of us scooted away to a safe distance. Once we were out of firing range, Horc seemed to sense our absence and woke up.

He sat up, rubbing his eyes and glancing around until he'd spotted each one of us. I crawled over and patted his lumpy head. "We're still here."

"I need a bath," he said.

"Yeah, you do," said Gerald. "There's water over there. I can smell it."

Once Gerald pointed it out, I could smell the water, too. I patted Horc again, and then flew straight up, spinning slowly in the air. The water lay in a deep hole like a gigantic bowl. I swiveled again and made sure no humans were coming. I knew Iris or Gerald would warn me, but I felt better looking just the same. Then I floated down beside Horc and picked him up.

"Are you sure you really want a bath?" I asked. "All the stink your mother put on you will be gone."

"I don't need her stink. I've got you," said Horc.

That's when I knew I was stuck with Horc for life. I cringed when I thought about Mom and Dad's faces when they saw him, all lumpy and weird. Still, it didn't matter. Horc belonged with us.

"All right. If you're sure," I said, flying back up. I turned to tell Iris I'd be back, but Iris was on her feet, facing the other direction. She sniffed the air like one of the dogs and walked towards the container that the boy, Judd, had taken out of the metal box. The container had dozens of words written on the side, but I didn't know what most of them meant. What in the world was L. Acidophilus or gluten?

"Where are you going?" I asked.

Iris didn't answer. At least, I didn't hear one, but that didn't mean much. Iris flew up over the container and hovered above it. She spun around, said something, and clapped her hands. Then she lowered herself to land on a long metal stick that poked out of the top of the container. Her feet touched the metal. It wobbled for a second, and then the whole thing flipped over. The metal stick clattered against the stone and a spray of pink goo shot across the tabletop. I expected Iris to fly up with her hands over her mouth like she did when she was trouble, but she didn't. I didn't see her anywhere.

Chapter 16

The container lay on its side. Pink gelatinous goo flowed out of the opening. Before I could react, Gerald made it to the container, he slipped and fell in the mess, his arms flailing. I plopped Horc on the stone and darted over, grabbing Gerald's pink-coated arm. My hand slipped off and I tumbled backwards into the container, tripping over the metal stick that turned out to be a giant spoon. I stumbled back out, slipping and sliding, and found Gerald standing. He wiped the goo from his eyes and shook it from his fingertips.

"Where's Iris?" he asked.

I whirled around until I spotted a tiny foot sticking out of a glob of jiggling pink goo. I shot to the foot, wrapped my hands around it, and yanked. Iris's leg emerged, but the rest of her remained in the glob.

"Help me!"

Gerald fell beside me, face down in the goo. When he came up, he yelled, "I've got her dress. Pull!"

We hauled Iris out together. Gerald leapt to her face and cleared the pink stuff from her mouth. She gasped and he fell back with his hands over his eyes.

"What happened?" Iris asked.

"The container fell over and you got trapped in the mess," I said.

Iris sat up. She held her dripping hands in front of her. "This is disgusting, but it tastes great."

I bit my lip, but I couldn't hold it in. Laughter bubbled up, overflowing my lips. Soon we both lay back in the goo, holding our aching stomachs and letting the laughter gush out of us.

Gerald stood up. He clenched and unclenched his fists. "Stop laughing. It's not funny."

Iris howled again. I contained myself for a moment, but the look of outrage on Gerald's face wound me up and I couldn't help myself. I laughed. I laughed until I thought my stomach would split right open. It felt wonderful, like flying without having to leave the ground.

"It's not funny!" Gerald yelled. "Iris could've died!"

Iris sat up and hurled a glob of goo at Gerald. It struck him square in the chest. He stumbled back, mouth open in astonishment. For a second, I thought Iris had gone too far. Gerald might just lose it. Instead, he scooped up some goo of his own and slammed Iris in the face with it.

"Hey!" she yelled.

"You deserve it," he said. "You scared me to death."

"Oh, yeah?"

"Yeah!"

Iris and Gerald dove at each other and fell into the goo. From the yelling, I suspected some biting might've been going on. I considered separating them, but it seemed easier, not to mention cleaner, to let them have it out. Horc sat down beside me, scooped up some pink stuff with both hands and shoved it in his mouth. His eyes glazed over and he shoveled it in.

"Slow down. You'll make yourself sick," I said.

Horc grunted and kept on shoveling. He ate so much his stomach expanded to previously unimagined proportions. I grabbed his hands and held them until he stopped struggling.

"Delicious," he said.

"Better than stink bugs?" I asked.

"Better. But it doesn't have that stink bug piquant aftertaste."

"Bummer."

"I want more."

I stood up and put him on my hip. "No more. You might pop and that would be a worse mess than this."

Horc smoothed his ecstatic expression and tried to look dignified. Pink goo ringed his mouth and there were splatters of the stuff all over him. I stifled a laugh and wondered what the other spriggans would think if they could see him now. Especially since the pink goo almost made him smell good, like strawberries.

Horc licked the back of his hand. "Easy wants you."

I retrieved Easy from beside the bread and let him eat some of the pink stuff. He shoveled it in as fast as Horc.

"He wants to know what this stuff is," said Horc.

I went to the other side of the container and read out loud "Low Fat Strawberry Yogurt." Closer inspection of the ingredients revealed that yogurt was made of milk. Grandma Vi told me that humans drank cow's milk and I'd been totally disgusted with the notion. But after having a taste of the yogurt, I had to admit they might be on to something.

"Yogurt." Horc lay on his back while trying to lick his foot clean.

Easy chirped at Iris and Gerald, now crumpled in a heap next to him. They panted and occasionally poked at each other, but otherwise seemed spent. He slurped some of the yogurt off his hand and let out a chorus of chirps at me.

"Horc, what's Easy going on about?" I asked.

"Yogurt. He says his mom knows how to make it," said Horc.

I pushed a curl off Easy's forehead and thought about his mother, the beautiful Mrs. Zamora. I couldn't picture her doing anything as mundane as cooking. "Wait," I said. "Your mother, Easy. Where's your mother? I saw the blood. Did she fall out the window?"

Easy chirped at Horc, who looked bored while licking his other foot.

"Horc, what did he say?"

"I want some more yogurt. My foot tastes bad."

"Well, stop licking it. Get back to Easy."

"More yogurt," Horc said.

"No more yogurt," I said, pulling his foot away from his mouth. "I told you it will make you sick."

"You don't want me to be sick."

"Of course not."

Horc seemed to mull this information over, and then turned to look at Easy. "Easy says his mother didn't want him to be sick either."

"Why would she?"

"I don't think my mother cared one way or the other," said Horc.

I didn't know what to say to that. It made sense. His mother gave him away. She probably didn't care about him one way or the other.

"I suppose your mother cares if you're sick?" asked Horc.

"Yes, she does," I said. "Mom's wonderful when we're sick. She makes soup."

"Interesting." Horc pushed himself upright and touched my hand lightly. "Easy says his mother hit her head and fell out the window when the humans came."

I gathered Easy in my arms and rocked him. I wished Mom had taught me how to make soup. Horc wormed his way into my arms. The babies glared at each other. Easy kicked Horc in the ribs and Horc returned the favor by yanking one of Easy's curls.

"Enough, you two. Like we don't have enough problems," I said.

"He's sticky," said Horc with a scowl.

"You should talk," I said. "You're almost completely pink."

"Easy says he wants a bath, please," said Horc.

I set Easy down and stood up, struggling to keep a grip on the slimy Horc.

"Where are you going?" asked Iris.

"Horc and Easy want baths."

"I would love a bath," said Iris.

"Me, too," said Gerald.

"There's no escaping them," said Horc.

"Or you," I said, smiling.

I waited for Iris and Gerald to scrape some of the yogurt off their wings. Once they were able to fly, they picked up Easy and took off. They flew over the big bowl, wobbling and almost out of control with the extra weight on their wings. We floated down into the bowl, our eyes roving over the shiny white surface walls. Water dripped out of a silver spout positioned over the bowl and pooled at the bottom of a grey basin. The pool rippled with every drop and spread out onto the white surface of the bottom the way I imagined ocean waves did. I dipped my toe in the water and smiled.

"How is it?" Gerald stared up at the tall white walls, his eyes jumping all around as if expecting something to squash them flat.

"Not as cold as I would've expected." I gave Horc a stern look. "You're not going to pee or poop in the water, are you?"

Horc crossed his arms and turned up his nose. "I am not an animal."

"You pooped on my mattress," said Iris.

"That was to make a point."

"What point was it?" asked Gerald. "That you're gross?"

"Grossness is what makes a spriggan a spriggan," said Horc.

"So you were just being gross?" I asked.

"I was being a spriggan."

I dangled him over the water, letting his toes brush the surface. "So why wouldn't you poop in the water? You're still a spriggan."

"I've decided not to be a spriggan anymore. That's the difference. Now I'm ready for my bath."

Gerald frowned. "That doesn't make any sense. It doesn't matter what you decide. You're still a spriggan."

"Not true. I can be whatever I want, and I want to be a wood fairy. Bath, please."

I held Horc up to eye level. "Did you say please?"

"Wood fairies say please," he said.

"But you're not a wood fairy," said Gerald.

I took my favorite skirt off Horc's bottom and turned to Gerald "I suspect a lot of us aren't exactly what we say we are. Let's face it. I'm not a real babysitter. Horc isn't a wood fairy and you're not a Whipplethorn. Who cares? It doesn't matter."

Gerald clamped his mouth shut and stepped into the water with Iris. They held Easy by the arms and let him kick and splash. I put Horc in the water, keeping a close eye in case he let something nasty fly. But he didn't and I let him sit next to Easy.

I waded in hip-deep, trailing my hands in the cool water. I splashed some on my face and slicked my hair back. I wondered what Mom and Dad were doing right then. Were they headed to the antique mall? An unwanted thought crept in. Could they possibly be waiting at Whipplethorn, hoping we'd find our way back? I didn't think Mom and Dad would be so complaisant about us, especially Mom. She'd bite the head off a spriggan, if it stood between her and us. Still, they could be hurt like Mrs. Zamora.

Wherever Mom was, whatever she was doing, she'd want me to keep up her standards. She'd hate it if she knew what a mess we all were. I dipped my hair in the water and swished it around. The yogurt wasn't coming off.

"Humans must have soap," I said.

Iris splashed Gerald, who kicked a wave of water at her. She stood, gasping and dripping. Then she ran for him and chased him around the edge of the water. I reached out and grabbed her sleeve as she passed.

"Watch the babies," I said.

I flew up to the top of the bowl and found a bottle with an iridescent orange drop on the tip of its spout. An experimental sniff confirmed that it was soap. It smelled like three dozen flowers were crammed into that small drop. Definitely not like any soap Mom made. I scooped some of the soap off the spout and floated down next to Horc.

"What's that?" he asked.

"Soap."

He opened his mouth and waited. Iris and Gerald giggled. Horc closed his mouth and then spat at Easy.

"Hey," I said. "We don't spit."

"He said I'm stupid. Can I bite him? Do wood fairies bite?"

"No biting and Easy stop calling Horc stupid."

Iris picked Easy up and he buried his face in her neck.

"You hurt his feelings," said Iris.

"Oh, for goodness sake." I rolled my eyes and said to Horc, "This is soap. You wash with it. It'll take your stink off."

Horc took a deep breath. "I'm ready."

I washed him from top to bottom. When I was done, I sat him in a dry area and stepped back to get a look at the new Horc. He surprised me by being a totally different color. He wasn't pretty by any means, but his new greenish-grey color reminded me of moss in the forest.

Iris got some soap, washed Easy, and then put him next to Horc with a reminder to be nice. Then Iris, Gerald, and I dove into the center of the pool. We flipped in the water, doing handstands with only our toes above the surface. Soon a layer of pink scum floated on the top of the water. Gerald retrieved some soap, the last bit on the spout, and shared it with me and Iris. We scrubbed our skin pink as the yogurt. Then we swam to the opposite edge of the pool to rinse ourselves in the only clear water left.

When I finished, I wrung out my clothes the best I could. The wood pattern painted on by the dryads became dull and muddied. The beautiful decorations that had once identified me as Soren Maple's friend went too easily.

"I guess we better get back to the mantel and start cleaning up," I said.

"No kidding," said Gerald, cocking his head to the side. "The humans are back and there are more of them this time."

I looked up, half expecting to see a crowd of humans around the bowl. But there wasn't and for all I knew they were in another room or even outside. I turned to Iris for confirmation.

Iris's brow furrowed. She spread her wings, drops of water flung off the tips, and she scooped up Easy. "They're already in. I'm sorry I wasn't paying attention again."

Gerald shifted some of Easy's weight over to himself. "That's okay. I was."

I picked up Horc and led the way out of the bowl. When we emerged, we found a human, a man, standing above us. His hand shot out toward the spout, grazing me and Horc. We tumbled down into the bowl as a torrent of water rushed in.

A wave covered my head. I slammed against the side of the bowl and realized my arms were empty. I'd lost Horc. I kicked and got my head above the water. The spout above me poured a waterfall into the bowl.

"Horc!" I screamed.

The man's hand came down into the bowl. It pulled the grey metal basin out of the bowl's bottom. The second he lifted the basin, the water started draining out. A brown lump bobbed in the water on the opposite side of the bowl. I kicked off the wall and swam toward Horc. Dad's hated swimming tips bounced around in my head. I didn't get far before the current swept me away. I didn't fight it. I swam toward Horc. His back floated above the water as he bobbed around in a quiet corner.

The current drew me toward the center of the bowl. The water was going down into a vortex. The sight spurred me on, my legs pumping madly. The current caught Horc and thrust him into the same stream as me. Instinct kicked in. I spread my wings and used them to propel me through the water, but the extra boost gave me too much momentum. I rushed past Horc, grabbing his arm at the last second. I pulled him to my chest and his arms went around my neck. I changed my trajectory to the edge of the current. The far reaches of the bowl's bottom were already dry. If I could swim through the current, we might have a chance.

My wings seemed to be made for swimming and I went with it. I gave up using my free arm and put everything I had into my wings. My foot brushed the bottom, but the current kept at me. I was tiring. The vortex got closer as my wings beat the water slower. I couldn't do it. I tucked myself around Horc. Maybe we had a chance to get down the hole in one piece.

Something yanked my head backwards. My body began to drag in the current. I opened my eyes. I saw nothing but the swirling vortex, gaping and hungry for us. We didn't move away from the hole, but stayed in place. The water rushed past and in a massive, quick movement it vanished down the hole and was gone.

I dropped to the bottom of the bowl, landing painfully on my rear. I gasped and fell over. Horc clutched my neck, let go, and then clutched it again like he was having some sort of spasm.

"Matilda, can you hear me? Matilda!" Iris's voice seemed far away, but I could feel her breath on my ear.

Iris rolled me over and pulled the tangled hair out of my face. "Matilda, say something."

"You pulled my hair."

Tears burst from Iris's eyes. She covered her face and rocked backwards. Gerald came into view. "We both pulled your hair. There wasn't anything else to grab. Your wings were too slick."

"Thanks," I said.

"You're welcome," said Gerald.

"I've never heard you say that before."

Gerald peeled my arms off Horc and lifted him off my chest. "What?"

"You're welcome."

Gerald shrugged and peered into Horc's face.

"I'm okay," said Horc. "We wood fairies are sturdy."

"Yeah," said Gerald. "I've heard that about wood fairies. We better get out of here before that man decides to douse us again."

I got my feet under me and tried to stand. My legs shook. They wobbled so violently, I fell back. "I don't think I can."

"Let her rest," said Iris.

"No way," said Gerald. "This place is swarming with humans."

He grabbed my arm and pulled me to my feet. Now my whole body shook and my teeth chattered. The wall swam in front of my eyes, looking like white liquid, dripping and oozing.

Iris put her arm around my shoulders and said something in my ear. I could hear her. I just couldn't understand the words.

Gerald and Iris hooked my arms over their shoulders. I watched the bowl bottom sink away from under my feet. They flew me onto a shelf inset into the wall with a window behind it. My body convulsed when it touched the chilly granite surface.

"She's too cold," said Gerald. "We have to get her into the sun."

They pulled me into a patch of warm sunlight and I stopped convulsing.

"What's wrong with her?" asked Iris.

"I think she's in shock," said Gerald. "We'll never be able to carry her to the mantel. I'm going to get some blankets. You stay here and keep her awake."

"How?"

"Do whatever you have to. Pinch her. Shake her. I'll be right back."

Iris lay down next to me, pressing her warm body against my cold one.

"I'm okay," I said, then everything went black.

When I woke up, the patch of sun was huge and almost hot. A pile of blankets covered me up to my chin. I could hardly move under their weight. Iris sat next to me combing her hair. It bounced and coiled into ringlets with each stroke. I worked my arm out and touched her arm.

"You're awake," she said.

"How long have I been out?" I asked.

"All night. It's morning," said Iris.

"Is everybody okay?"

Iris tucked her comb into her pocket and said, "We're all fine. I found some of our old diapers for Horc and Easy. I made them some shirts and pants from some of Mom's fabric."

"You've been busy," I said.

"It was easy."

I patted Iris's hand. I didn't trust myself to speak. My throat felt all hot and twisty. A headache bloomed in my forehead and my stomach flipped around like I'd swallowed a fish.

"Do you want something to eat?" asked Iris.

I wasn't sure I could eat anything, but I nodded anyway.

Iris jumped up and clapped her hands. She flitted away, past the mom with her mug and landed on the granite-covered table in the center of the kitchen. She strode across the table with her shoulders thrown back and lightness in her step that I'd never seen before. She went to a spot of brown, and then flew back to me with a thick flake.

I sniffed and took a small bite. It tasted like Mom's flatbread, except crispy and sweeter. "What is it?"

"Bran flake. It's good, isn't it?"

I nodded and nibbled on the flake.

"Matilda?" Iris's happy expression vanished like it'd never been there at all.

"What's wrong?" I asked.

"When do you think Mom and Dad will get here?"

"I don't know. Shouldn't be much longer."

"What if it is? What if they don't come?" Iris asked.

"They'll come. It hasn't been that long."

"What if they're not looking for us?"

"Of course they're looking for us," I said. "Don't be ridiculous."

"It's not ridiculous. Easy cried last night for his mom. He thinks she's never coming. Gerald doesn't say it, but he's worried, too."

I didn't say anything. I was worried, too, but I didn't want it to show.

"What if they're hurt and waiting for us to help them?" asked Iris.

I watched the mom pour a brown liquid into the bowl and sneeze. I couldn't lie to Iris. Something could've happened to them when the humans came to take our mantel. Something definitely happened to Easy's mom.

"We could ask the humans for help," said Iris.

I heaved the blankets off my legs and stood. The mom left the kitchen, but Judd remained slurping what looked like bran flakes out of a bowl with a spoon. I pointed at him. "Ask the humans? They can't see us. Remember?"

"We could make them see us and they could take us back to Whipplethorn to find Mom and Dad."

"How, Iris?" I asked. "When's the last time a human saw any wood fairy? Six generations ago. Even Dad can't do it."

Gerald landed on the shelf with a frown on his face. "You could do it."

I crossed my arms and leaned against what had to be a piece of yellow fruit. It felt hard and silky under my hand. The smell was glorious, sweet, and exotic.

Gerald frowned deeper. "You could do it, Matilda."

"I've never done it before, and believe me, I've tried," I said.

"You didn't want it bad enough," said Gerald.

"That's what Dad said."

"See. You want it more now and so you'll do it."

"Why me?" I asked. "You want it just as badly."

"You're bigger. Size matters."

"Now that's ridiculous. We're so tiny to them. My being a bit taller won't make any difference."

Gerald went to Iris's side. "It's you that will make the difference. Humans would want to see you."

"What makes you say that?"

"Humans love fairies. They write books about us, draw pictures, and make fairy toys for their children. If a human could meet a fairy, they'd want to meet one like you. You're …" Gerald swallowed and his usual resentful expression came over his face. "You're perfect. You're just what a fairy should be. Not me, and not Iris."

"You think I'm perfect?"

"I think a human would find you perfect. It's not the same."

"You do think I'm perfect." I grinned and punched him in the arm. "You like me."

Gerald rubbed his arm. "I like you the way you like Horc."

"That's good enough for me," I said.

"What about me?" asked Iris.

Gerald raised an eyebrow at her.

"Do you like me?"

"You're all right when you're not annoying me," he said.

Iris smiled and linked her arm with his. "I'll take it."

I looked over at Judd, wondering if I could make him see me. What would happen if he did? I'd never made contact with a human before. What would he do? As I watched him, Judd dropped his spoon on the table, glanced around, and drank out of his bowl. He plunked his bowl down on the table, splattering white stuff across the gleaming surface.

"Nice," I said.

"Just because he's a slob doesn't mean he won't help us," said Iris.

"What is it with you and asking for help?" I asked.

"Help is good. What would we have done without Soren?"

"You're right about Soren, but that's different. He's a wood fairy. These are humans."

Gerald paced back and forth on the edge of the shelf, muttering to himself. I took the opportunity to look around.

Beyond the yellow fruit was a basket filled with huge spoons and spatulas. They had to be at least one hundred foot lengths long. On the other side of the shelf, a three-tiered metal basket hung from the ceiling. The top level contained yellow ovals with pitted skin. The middle held round blackish-purple things and the bottom was filled with apples. I smiled at the apples. At least something was familiar. The smells of the fruit drifted around together, creating a sweet invisible fog that made my mouth water. Mixed in with the fruit smell was a more pungent scent. I looked until I spotted a conical tree, standing in the corner of the shelf.

"Gerald, do you know what all these things are?" I asked.

Gerald jumped when I spoke. He looked surprised to see us still standing there.

"I was thinking," he said. "Maybe we could get the humans to drive us to Whipplethorn. It took vehicles to get us so far away. It'll take a car to get us back."

"Maybe we should wait for our parents to come here," I said.

"Do you know how long it would take to fly the distances we've been driven? Are you willing to wait when we don't know what's happened to them?"

Iris shook her head no and turned to me.

"I'm not getting these humans to see me until I know more about them," I said.

"That's prudent," Gerald agreed.

"And slow," said Iris.

"For once, I'd like things to happen slowly. It would be a nice change. Now, Gerald, do you know what these fruits are or what?"

Gerald smiled and pointed to each one. "Those are bananas. Those are lemons, plums, and apples."

"What about the tree? I didn't know trees could smell so strong," I said.

"It's not a tree. It's rosemary. An herb."

"Can we eat it?" asked Iris.

"I think humans cook with it, but I don't think they eat it straight. Horc probably would though. He'll eat anything."

I spun around. "Wait a minute. Where are the babies?"

"They're sleeping," said Gerald.

"Still, they probably shouldn't be alone."

"Easy's mom left him alone."

Iris crossed her arms. "Don't start that. She didn't do it on purpose."

"I don't know that. Maybe that's just the way they are," he said.

I fluttered up and landed on the banana. Gerald's words bounced around in my brain. I couldn't quite figure out what he was getting at. I walked the length of the banana, trying to find a way in through the thick peel, so I could taste it. The fruit appeared to be well protected. I kicked it as Iris and Gerald landed beside me.

"You won't get in like that. We'll have to wait for one of the humans to open it," said Gerald.

I turned to him and said, "What did you mean by 'that's just the way they are'?"

Gerald stared out into the kitchen and ignored me.

"Yeah," said Iris. "No wood fairy would ever abandon their baby."

"Well, they're not exactly regular wood fairies, are they?" Gerald met my surprised gaze.

"Of course they're wood fairies," said Iris. "What else would they be?"

"They're not like us. Just look at them and you can tell," said Gerald.

"Mrs. Zamora is beautiful," I said, thinking of how Mom kept looking in the mirror after Mrs. Zamora moved in. She would fluff her wings and rub berry juice on her lips.

"I'm not talking about being beautiful. They don't look anything like us," he said.

"So what?" Iris frowned fiercely. "Neither do you. You're wings aren't iridescent at all."

"Right and I'm not a real Whipplethorn. We've established that. Now, what are they? Think about it. They avoid us. Stay inside. Never come to council meetings. Easy can read minds. Come on, girls."

I looked out of the kitchen toward the stairs. I didn't really care what the Zamoras were as long as they didn't care what I was. I felt better and was itching to explore. We were in a real human house. A human house filled with human stuff. I wanted to see the rest of it "Okay. So I think I'll take a look around and check things out."

"Don't you even want to know?" asked Gerald.

"Gerald, I already know. They're different. So are you and so am I. Who cares?"

"They're mindbenders. All of them. Jeez, you two are dense," said Gerald.

Chapter 17

I flew up the stairs with Iris close at my heels. Gerald's information rattled around in my head. I didn't know which was more surprising, that the Zamoras were mindbenders or that Gerald's family had known and kept it quiet. A few days before I never would've imagined them staying quiet to protect someone. Gerald's father irritated my dad with his haughty ways and sly insinuations about intelligence. They had all those books and they never shared them. Gerald's family always seemed to be trying to get an advantage over everyone else, but when they had the chance to out the Zamoras, they didn't take it. I couldn't wrap my mind around it.

Iris and I reached the top of the stairs and hovered on a landing area. Four doors hung open inviting us in four different directions. I turned to Iris to get her opinion and found my sister watching with sad eyes and a downturned mouth.

"What's wrong?" I asked.

"I don't know what to think," Iris said.

"About Gerald?"

Iris's brow wrinkled. "No. About Easy. He's a you-know-what."

"The Zamoras never did anything to us," I said.

"How do we know? Dad said mindbenders can read your mind, put ideas in your head and make you do things you shouldn't. What if they had something to do with the humans coming and taking our mantel?"

"Mindbenders are just another type of wood fairy. Just like how I'm a kindler. It's just how we are and I don't believe they knew anything about the humans coming. Mrs. Zamora loves Easy. I know that for sure. What do you want to do? Toss Easy out because of who he is?"

"No."

"Good. Now let's do some exploring while Gerald watches the babies. Which door?"

Iris gestured to the door that opened up directly in front of the stairs. I rubbed my hands together and zipped in. The room was somewhat of a disappointment. It was a small square, smaller than any room in Whipplethorn. A length of fabric imprinted with monkeys concealed one side. A couple of shiny white things sat on the other side. They looked like they were made of the same material as the bowl in the kitchen. My shoulders slumped. I expected something majestic. I reminded myself to stop expecting, since I was always wrong.

"What's this?" asked Iris as she pointed to the squat white seat to their right.

The seat had a rectangular white box attached to the wall behind it. We landed on a silver lever on the front of the box.

"There's water in it," said Iris.

I wrinkled my nose. "It smells like …"

"Wee," said Iris with a look of disgust. "Do you think it's a chamber pot?"

"If it is, it's really big even for a chamber pot for humans," I said. "Let's check out the other one."

We flew up onto the other white thing and discovered it was just another bowl like downstairs in the kitchen.

"Let's go through another door. You pick," said Iris.

I picked the door to the far left and wasn't disappointed. The room was quite large and furnished with walnut furniture with pleasing lines but few carvings. I went straight to the bed and landed in the middle of a blanket that looked soft as cattail fluff. Iris plopped down next to me, lying on the bed and sighing. I watched my sister's sweet face smiling with growing enjoyment.

"I could go to sleep right here," Iris said.

"Me, too."

"Gerald will be mad if we don't come back soon."

"He'll be mad either way," I said. "He's good at it."

"Gerald's not so bad." Iris flipped over and nestled her head in the crook of her arm.

"He's not a stink fairy underneath it all."

Iris closed her eyes. "I could lay here forever."

"I couldn't." I poked Iris in the shoulder. "Look."

"What is it?"

"Books. Look at all the books."

Iris sat up and her mouth fell open. Bookcases covered the wall next to the door from floor to ceiling. I couldn't believe I hadn't noticed them the second we came in. I flitted over and touched the spine of an old book with gold lettering, *The Red Badge of Courage*. Iris flew around in a frenzy, clapping her hands and counting.

"There are fifty books on this shelf alone," said Iris, pointing to the shelf I stood on. "Can you believe it?"

I shook my head, mute with wonder. Books were so rare. And human books, fairies hardly ever got a chance to read them. I wished one would fall off the shelf and open so we might read a page and see what humans liked to read.

We spent an hour reading titles and guessing what might be inside those dusty covers. I kept coming back to *The Red Badge of Courage*. It spoke to me. It must be more thrilling than the one Iris liked, *Versailles: A Biography of a Palace*, no matter how decorative the spine.

I ran my hand over the peeling gold lettering once more and turned to Iris. "We better go if we want to look at the other rooms."

Iris left her favorite book alone on the shelf. She kept glancing back as we flew away out into the hall. Iris picked the next room and stopped short as soon as she flew through the door. I bumped into her and rubbed my nose where it had whacked the back of Iris's head.

"Hey," I said. "Why'd you stop?"

Iris turned, her face screwed up so that she resembled a dried up old apple. "Boy room."

Definitely a boy room. No mistaking that. It smelled of dirty socks and sweat. Half the bedding hung on the floor off a set of bunk beds. Clothing lay in heaps all over the place. A bookshelf called to me from across the room, but I fought off the invitation. I didn't want to fly through the sour boy stink despite the intriguing titles on the shelves. *Diary of a Wimpy Kid* and *City of Ember* might be interesting, but not enough to tempt me.

"Let's try the last room," said Iris.

I shook my head. "I don't think so. I smell a cat in there."

Iris made a face at me and started to fly into the room. I grabbed her hand and pulled her back. "I said no."

Iris yanked her hand away and flew into a pink room. I zipped in behind her. My eyes darting around the room for a sign of the cat, but didn't find one. The room was much better than the boy's next door. No stink, no clothing on the floor. Lace drooped down from a canopy and hung over a small bed, a waterfall of pretty. The bed was nicely made. My eyes ran down the length of the bed and I found myself staring into a pair of slanted pale blue eyes. I lunged for Iris.

"No, Iris!"

Iris shook me off while yelling, "Kitty!"

Before I could catch her, Iris landed on the bed. The cat saw her. No doubt about that. Its eyes followed my tiny sister as she advanced across the bed towards it. Its long, skinny tail lashed the air and the tip of a very pink tongue poked out from between its furry lips. I rocketed across the room, my arms outstretched to snatch her up. But before I reached Iris, the cat lifted a paw with curved white talons and batted her. She tumbled through the air and disappeared over the side of the bed. The cat leapt after her.

I shot over the bed and bumped into the window on the other side before I could stop myself. I shook my head and looked down, expecting the absolute worst. I only hoped I wouldn't have to pry my sister's mangled body out of the cat's jaws.

The cat sat hunched over and pawed at the floor. I darted forward to see Iris dancing between the creature's paws.

"Iris! What are you doing?"

She waved and dodged a white paw as it slammed down on the very spot where she'd been standing. The cat wiggled its fuzzy butt and pounced. Iris dashed away and dodged the next paw while throwing her head back in laughter.

"Get away from that thing or I'm going to have to come get you," I shouted.

A cat. It had to be a cat. How many killer cat stories had Grandma Vi told us over the years? Now Iris was down there trying her best to get eaten. It was too much. I'd flown out into a strange antique mall to save Gerald, battled spriggans to find Easy and risked getting flattened by the mantel to rescue Horc, but a cat was too much.

I hovered for a moment watching Iris risk her neck with the ultimate monster and then swallowed the hot bile bubbling up in my throat. I waited for the right moment. The cat meowed and Iris ran between the cat's forelegs. She emerged from underneath its side and flew over its head. The cat stared up at her, eyes cold and unblinking. Iris flitted back and forth. The cat opened its mouth. I dashed in, snatching Iris from between its jaws. The cat's hot breath engulfed us, smelling of fish and rotting grass. It leapt up behind us, snapping its jaws shut just as I got Iris over the edge of the bed.

I shook as I flew us across the room to a book shelf and landed next to a stack of books five deep. "What's wrong with you?"

Iris broke out of my grasp. "What's wrong with me? What's wrong with you? Why'd you drag me away?"

I stared at her open-mouthed.

"Hello," said Iris.

"Iris, come on. Do you want to get eaten?" I asked.

"She wasn't going to eat me. We were playing."

"Yeah, right."

The cat stalked across the floor, sat next to the bookcase and stared up at us, lashing its tail.

Iris pointed. "See. She misses me."

"She misses the chance to eat you. Where's your sense?"

"She's a pet. Pets don't eat people."

"They do if they're cats. Grandma Vi would have a heart attack if she saw what you were doing," I said.

"No, she wouldn't. She liked cats. You heard her stories."

"A cat ate her uncle."

"He was an idiot," said Iris, screwing up her face into a look of ultimate stubbornness. "It's not the same at all."

"You mean he was such an idiot he played with a cat?"

"Are you calling me an idiot?"

"Well …" I couldn't quite figure out what I wanted to say. Clearly, Iris was an idiot, but it didn't seem like the right time to point that out. "Let's just go."

"I'm not going until you apologize to me and Powder Puff," said Iris.

"Powder Puff?"

Iris gestured to the cat that was now licking its paws. To me, it looked a lot like washing up for dinner.

"Forget it," I said.

Iris cocked her head to the side and gave me a sly little smile. "If you don't apologize I won't tell you what's happening downstairs."

Startled, I glanced toward the door. "What is it?"

"I'm not telling," said Iris.

"Fine. You can go feed yourself to the cat while I go check it out alone."

Iris's face lost her angry expression. "But you need me to hear for you."

"I can still see, Iris. I'm not a total invalid."

"I never said you were an invalid."

"And I didn't mean to call you an idiot, but look at that thing. It's a cat, Iris. Carnivore. Get it?"

"She was just playing."

I rubbed my forehead and watched the cat eyeing us. A pet. Only Iris would find that monster appealing. "Please tell me what's going on downstairs."

"A party."

"Really?"

"Yep."

I flew out the door and smiled to find Iris close at my heels. Unfortunately, the cat wasn't far behind, padding along and watching us with an intensity that made my pits sweat.

At the bottom of the stairs, the mom leaned on the newel post, chatting into a silver rectangle. A young man with eagles tattooed on his bicep stomped past her carrying a rack filled with glassware. I hovered next to her and watched the man place the rack on the floor. He went back outside and returned with another rack. A young woman in an apron bustled in, ordering him to be careful. He didn't answer, but I saw him roll his eyes when he put the rack on top of the other one. The young woman crossed her arms and tapped her foot as he ferried more racks and then flat silver containers.

The mom took the rectangle away from her ear and punched a few buttons on the face. "Mom," she said into the rectangle. "This is ridiculous. They're bringing glasses and chairs. We have chairs."

She listened and then said, "I know, but I don't need this. Fine. I'll see you in a couple hours."

I looked at Iris. "I thought you said it was a party."

"I meant they're planning a party." Iris pointed at the mom. "She's graduating from something."

The mom made a low noise in the back of her throat. The man with the tattoos heard and grinned at her as he carried a plastic container filled with bunches of flowers by. I gazed through the archway into the kitchen as the sour young woman scrubbed her hands and started laying vegetables on a cutting board.

The little girl, Tess, ran in the front door and stopped short when she saw the piles of stuff the man brought in. "What's all this, Mom?"

"I told you Gram is throwing a party for my graduation today," her mom said.

"That's a lot of stuff."

"You know how Gram loves a party."

"Who's coming?"

The mom pulled a tissue out of her sleeve and blew her nose. "Everybody."

"Who's everybody?" Tess's eyes wandered over the piles of vegetables and a newly uncovered box of chocolate on the kitchen table.

"Please, Tess," said her mom. "Go play for a bit, and then you can get dressed. I'm going to lie down."

The mom turned and went up the stairs. Iris and I followed Tess into the kitchen Tess propped her elbows on the granite tabletop and watched the young woman chopping carrots.

"What are you making?" Tess asked.

"Amuse bouche," said the woman with a sneer.

"Does it have chocolate?"

"Certainly not."

Tess lowered her eyes to the carrots and then fixed them on the woman. "What is it then?"

The woman sighed. "Amuse bouche means to amuse the mouth. It is a one bite appetizer, if you must know."

Tess grinned and twirled one of her extremely long ponytails. "I must." Then she flounced out the door, leaving the woman frowning in her wake.

I turned to Iris. "I like her."

Iris pursed her lips while looking at the woman. "Her? I don't like her at all."

"Not her," I said. "Tess. Did you know what an amuse bouche was?"

"No, and I bet Gerald doesn't either," said Iris. "Let's test him."

I spun around and flew past the man with the tattoos who was now pushing furniture out of the way. We fluttered above stacks of chairs and bouquets of flowers to the mantel. I headed for our front door when I caught sight of Gerald walking on the mantel shelf. I turned to Iris, but she'd already spotted him. We lit on the shelf a dozen steps away and watched. Gerald's back was to us. He stood next to a pair of crystal candlesticks that hadn't been there before we went upstairs.

"We've been decorated," I said.

"Look at the pictures." Iris pointed at several frames containing pictures of fat drooling babies. "They look so real. Not like paintings at all."

I nodded. The pictures were incredible, like real babies were pressed in the frames. "I wonder how they do that."

"Check out Horc," said Iris.

Horc toddled to one of the candlesticks, heaved himself over the bottom lip and began climbing the steep slope. When he reached the summit, he sat on his wide butt and slid down with his arms raised. Easy sat a distance away with a severe pout on his face. He chortled something at Gerald.

Gerald shook his head and turned around. His face revealed relief with just a touch of guilt. He rushed over to us, tripping on one of Iris's teddy bears and bumping his knee.

"You've been gone forever," he said.

"Have not," said Iris. "Why won't you help Easy go on the slide?"

He groaned. "I already did. About a million times. It's not as thrilling as you'd think."

"Why didn't you stay inside?"

"There's something in there." He gestured to the other side of the mantel, Easy's home.

"I don't hear anything," said Iris.

"Me neither," said Gerald.

I walked towards the babies with Gerald and Iris at my side. "If you didn't hear anything, how do you know something's there?"

Gerald's old resentful look came back to roost on his face. "Ask Easy."

"Easy?" I asked.

"He's a mindbender."

Iris gasped and I bit back a sharp retort. Easy made a sad chirp, his eyes brimming. I scooped him up. "Don't call Easy that, Gerald. I'm serious."

"What are you going to do?" Two red spots appeared high on Gerald's cheeks.

I stepped closer to him and lowered my face until we were nose to nose. "I don't know, but you won't like it."

"All right. All right." Gerald backed up.

Horc slid down the candlestick again, faster than before and ended up rolling head over heels to rest at our feet. "That was an intense experience. You should try it," he said, wobbling and greener than usual.

"I'll pass," I said. "Did Easy tell you something's in his house?"

Horc jutted his chin out at me. "Hungry."

"Not that again. Why do you always get hungry when we need information?" I asked.

"Best time to negotiate."

"You don't need to negotiate for food," I said. "We'll feed you no matter what."

"Excellent. I'm ready." Horc opened his mouth and waited.

I handed Easy to Iris. "Not this minute. Is something in the mantel or not?"

Horc shut his mouth reluctantly. "Easy said there is."

Easy nodded and buried his face in Iris's shoulder.

"What is it?" I asked.

"He doesn't know. He just knows it's there. He feels the presence of more minds," said Horc, yawning.

"I take it you're not worried."

"What's to worry about? You'll take care of it. Now about lunch."

I turned to Easy. "How many things are in there?"

Easy concentrated and then looked at Horc.

"Several," said Horc.

"Great," I said. "I guess I'll go check it out."

"You can't go in there alone. It's crazy," said Gerald.

"Glad you think so, because you're coming with me."

"No, I'm not," he said. "I say we just leave whatever's in there alone. Maybe they'll go away."

"If there's one thing I've learned, it's that things don't just go away. Come on, Gerald. It's your turn," I said.

Gerald opened his mouth and then shut it. Iris stuck her tongue out at him and then asked, "Do you know what an amuse bouche is?"

Gerald wrinkled his forehead. "It's a small bite of food, like an appetizer. Why?"

Iris's mouth dropped open, but she recovered quickly. "Never mind. Easy, you want to go on the slide?"

Easy chirped happily as I took off and hovered above the mantel. "I'm waiting, Gerald."

He followed as slowly as possible. For once, I was glad I couldn't hear the complaints that were surely aimed at me. We flew down to Easy's front door and lit on the ledge in front of it.

"Do you hear anything?" I asked.

Gerald shook his head. That fact didn't seem to make him feel any better though. I rubbed his back and pulled open the door. The hall lay dark and deserted. Debris littered the floor, but there weren't any glowing red eyes or anything.

"Do you smell that?" asked Gerald.

"I sure do," I said.

Subtle smells, moss, lemongrass, and cattails wafted around us. Gerald wrinkled his nose and stepped back.

"It's okay," I said. "I know what it is."

"Are you sure?"

I lit a sweet little flame in the palm of my hand and held it aloft, casting soft yellow shadows on the walls. "Pretty sure," I said as I advanced down the darkened hall.

Chapter 18

I leaned on the living room doorway, watching Gerald circling the room. He kept his eyes fixed on a pile of brown fur. Several arms and legs twitched, but no heads were visible. The pile emitted a low wheezing sound every few seconds, or so Gerald claimed.

"Don't worry," I said. "They won't wake up."

Gerald poked at the pile, even going so far as to pick up a hand and let it drop.

"Are you sure?" he asked.

I watched a flame dance across my hand, separate into five little flames and flow out to the tips of my fingers. "That's what Soren said. Trow are nocturnal."

"Are they dangerous?"

"Soren didn't seem to think so."

"But you don't know."

I willed the flames to reform into one and looked at Gerald. "No, I'm not sure, but I feel fine about them. You do too, don't you? We'd feel it if they were dangerous."

"Maybe. I wonder why they sleep like this. It almost looks like one creature instead of a bunch." Gerald brushed his hand across the brown fur. It sprung back into place as though nothing had disturbed it.

"You can ask them at dusk," I said. "Soren says that's when they wake up."

Gerald stopped and listened. "More humans are here."

"Maybe the party's starting," I said. "Let's look."

"Should we lock the trow in?"

"We'd just have to let them out. Why bother?"

Gerald opened his mouth to say something, but shut it without the expected protest. I went to the front door, peeked out, and watched as a new woman arranged flowers on a long table where the sofa used to be. The regular furniture framed the edge of the room that now had a multitude of humans in it. Judd and Tess dodged adults carrying platters and flowers. They stole several things off a tray on the kitchen table. They popped them in their mouths and chewed. Judd gagged and spit his out into his hand. Tess was daintier. She swallowed, but not without an expression of agony on her face. Judd tossed his bite into a vase and went back for seconds.

"Oh, no you don't." An elderly woman came around the corner by the stairs and shook her finger at Judd. Her voice sounded stern, but her face gleamed with pleasure at the boy.

I grabbed Gerald's arm. "Look who it is."

"Who?" asked Gerald as he pulled his arm away and rubbed it.

I looked at him incredulously until I remembered that I'd been alone in the antique mall when I'd run into the old ladies.

"Sarah. I saw her in the antique mall."

Gerald shrugged, pushed past me, and tried to take off. I grabbed his arm and yanked him back.

"Hey!"

"She believes in fairies."

Gerald regarded Sarah with more interest. He leaned on the door frame. "If she already believes, maybe she'll see you."

"Just what I was thinking."

"So you could ask her for help?"

I watched Sarah hug Judd and then cuddle Tess. Sarah said something to Judd while gesturing to his smudged chin. Judd grimaced. The kids ran up the stairs and out of sight. Sarah surveyed the room. She wore an emerald green dress with a dozen strands of pearls looped around her neck. The green made her silver hair shine and I hoped I'd look as good when I was old. Sarah's scent reached through the smells of flowers and food to make me smile. Lavender and cookies. Just like in the mall.

"It's worth a try," I said.

Gerald clapped his hands together and rubbed them vigorously. "Excellent. Let's tell Iris. She was pretty worried about our parents."

"You and Iris have a lot to say to each other."

"When you forget she's fat, she's not so bad," he said.

I punched him in the shoulder. "Shut up, Gerald."

He flushed and he looked ready to spout anger at me, but when he saw I was smiling at him, he hung his head. "I'm sorry. I shouldn't have said that."

"Apology accepted."

We flew out and closed the door behind us. The red room buzzed with activity. The mom watched it all, leaning on the newel post with a tissue in hand. She now wore a strapless black and white dress with red high heels. Her hair flowed back from her face into a sleek chignon, emphasizing her wide mouth. Tess rushed down the stairs to join her mother. She danced on tiptoes and twirled. Her blue party dress spun out, revealing black netting under the skirt. Her hair was braided and coiled around her head, making her exceptionally pretty, much prettier than her mother.

"Rebecca," said Sarah to the mom. "You look like a dream."

Rebecca kissed Sarah's pale cheek. "Thank you, Gram. This party is amazing."

"You deserve it. I can't wait to show you your present. Don't look outside."

"That's too much," said Rebecca. "You shouldn't have gotten me a present, too."

"Do I get a present? Do I get a present?" Tess hopped up and down, her skirt popping open like an umbrella.

"When you graduate," said Sarah.

Tess pouted, but hugged her great-grandmother anyway. They turned to spy Judd thumping down the stairs, looking marginally better than before. His thick hair was brushed back from his face, which appeared freshly scrubbed. Sarah kissed him and he wiped his cheek with the back of his hand.

Gerald and I flew to our side of the mantel and landed on the shelf near Iris. She caught Easy after he slid down the candlestick. When Easy saw me, he tapped his mouth.

"He's hungry, too. Can we eat yet?" Horc asked.

"In a minute," said Iris. "What did you find? Was Easy right?"

"We found trow." Gerald straightened up to his full insubstantial height and tried to look like an expert. "They're harmless."

"I wouldn't say that exactly. I just know that Soren wasn't afraid of them," I said.

"What do we do?" asked Iris.

I shrugged. "There's nothing to do until they wake up."

"I'll get some food," said Gerald.

"All right," I said. "Get a carrying bag first and make sure you get enough for everyone."

Gerald blushed a furious pink to the tips of his ears. "You mean by myself?"

"Sure. If you can handle it?"

Gerald spread his wings slightly. "I'll do it."

"Call out if you need anything and be careful. There's a lot of activity going on out there."

"Don't worry about me." Gerald hovered above us for a second and then flitted over the edge of the mantel.

"Do you think that was a good idea?" asked Iris.

"Gerald needs to feel important. Just keep a sharp ear out for problems."

We took the babies inside the mantel. I opened the windows, letting light and delicious smells from the party waft in. With that goodness around me, the disaster didn't seem so bad. My precious things were shattered, but everything important could be mended. Seeing Sarah made me think that anything was possible. Sarah believed in fairies. It wouldn't be very hard for her to believe in me. Sarah would take us to Whipplethorn and we would find our parents.

I found Mom's broom and swept a clean spot in Iris's room. It remained the least messy. "Iris, let's put the babies in here."

Iris found a clean blanket and laid Easy on it. He yawned and rolled over. I sat Horc down and he pinched his nose. "Stink."

"Smell that, do you?" asked Iris. "That's my mattress you ruined."

Horc blinked at her as though he had no idea what she was talking about. I found the mattress on the other side of the room folded in half.

"We have to get rid of it," I gasped.

Iris nodded and pointed to the window. We dragged the mattress over to the window and tried to stuff it through. The mattress wouldn't begin to fit, so I got one of dad's saws and cut it in half. That didn't work either, but cutting it into quarters did. When we pushed the last bit out of the window, I leaned out to see where the pieces had fallen just in time to see one of the dogs suck them up his left nostril.

"Gross," I said.

"What happened?" Iris pushed past me and looked.

"You don't want to know."

"One of the dogs is sneezing. I wonder if dogs get colds," said Iris as Gerald returned carrying two bags and glowing with pride.

"I got so much. You won't believe it," he said.

We ate cheese and fruit and a type of dark pungent bread none of us recognized. The babies went to sleep on a pallet in Iris's room and I started cleaning in earnest. By the time I got the kitchen in order, the party outside was in full swing. Iris stopped working every few minutes to peek out and admire the dresses or the food. I hardly got any work out of her after I told her about Sarah. Iris gave me reports on Sarah's movements every five minutes.

"It's getting dark outside, Matilda. The sun must be going down," said Iris.

"Okay. I think we should just take all the broken furniture down to Dad's workshop to get it out of the way until he can fix it," I said.

"Sarah is really old. She might go home. You better go out there and talk to her."

"She's never going to notice me in all that excitement. I'll wait until people start going home."

"But it might be too late then."

Iris had a point, but I didn't think it could be helped. It was really hard for a human to see a fairy. If there were distractions around, it would be impossible.

Iris leaned out the window. "Come and look, Matilda." Iris's dress hiked up and revealed her dimpled thighs. She looked just the way she had the morning the humans came to Whipplethorn.

"They just rolled in this huge desk with a bow," Iris said.

The desk was the one Sarah purchased at the antique mall. Now it shone with fresh lemon oil and had a red bow on top. Rebecca hugged Sarah and wiped tears from her eyes.

Iris turned to me. "Rebecca said it's just like Grandpa's fairy desk, isn't it? What does that mean?"

"Sarah's husband used to tell stories about fairies living in his father's desk," I said.

"What happened to that desk?"

"The family sold it when they lost all their money." I smoothed back my hair. "Help me find my yellow dress. It's the brightest."

"Are you going to talk to her now?"

"As soon as I get ready."

Iris found my dress wadded up under my dresser. I shook the broken glass off and slipped it on. Iris combed my hair, and rubbed some of Mom's favorite scent on my wrists for good measure. Gerald stopped his trash hauling to check out my new look. He nodded his approval and went back to work. Iris led me to the front door and then hugged me.

"I just know you'll do it. Gerald is right. You can do anything."

Iris's face shone with her belief in me. I kissed her forehead to hide my own expression. One second I was sure I could do it and the next I felt I was inadequate to the task. What made me think I could do it, when six generations said I couldn't?

I flew out the door and wove my way through the crowded room past adults and children. They were carrying plates of food with such delightful smells they almost distracted me from my mission. I glanced back at the mantel. It gleamed with two dozen candles lit on top and Iris waving at me from the front door. Her smiling face was all the inspiration I needed.

Sarah sat alone upstairs, dozing in a cushioned chair in the big bedroom. I fluttered around the room, trying to work up a plan. Trying was so scary. If I failed, who knew when I'd get another opportunity. I could wait around all night, but it was clear no plan was going to form in my brain. There was nothing for it but to go ahead.

I circled Sarah's head twice, looking for a place to land. Sarah's hands lay folded in her lap. Her thumb looked like the best, most-stable spot. I hovered over it for a second and then landed. My feet touched the wrinkled warm skin and I looked up at Sarah's face. Nothing. No reaction at all.

"Sarah. Wake up!" I shouted.

Sarah didn't move. I shouted until my voice grew hoarse and tears ran down my face. It wasn't working. How would I tell Iris and Gerald and the babies? They were so sure I could do it. I yelled again, my voice cracking and strained. I spread my wings and stomped as hard as I could, driving my heels into Sarah's tender skin. I teetered and almost fell off. But I managed steady myself and look up at Sarah once more. A sigh escaped Sarah's faded lips and her eyes opened. Just a glimpse of blue at first and then before I could think, those eyes looked right at me.

I held my breath. Sarah shook her head. Her soft silver hair caressed her cheeks. Those blue eyes stayed on me, but drooped toward sleep. I waved my arms over my head. I stomped. I shouted. I was so close. Sarah blinked and her gaze grew more intense. A little thrill of satisfaction shivered through my body.

"Gram?" Rebecca's voice came from behind me.

Sarah's eyes popped open and she sat up straight. "Yes, dear?"

"No!" I screamed, waving more frantically than ever.

"Are you ready to go? Evan will drive you," said Rebecca.

"I'm ready. Give me a hand up, will you?"

I spread my wings and drove my heels into Sarah's knuckle. "No! See me. You have to see me."

Sarah's eyes stayed on Rebecca's face. I jumped up and down, but I couldn't get Sarah to look at me again.

Rebecca patted her grandmother's shoulder. "You had the funniest look in your eyes when I came in. Were you daydreaming?"

Sarah smiled up at her. "I certainly hope so."

Rebecca lifted Sarah to her feet and I tumbled off her thumb. I didn't try to break my fall. I let myself roll down the length of Sarah's body and land on the cushy carpet.

Sarah took a careful step. She wavered on her feet. Rebecca held her arm and put another around her waist.

"Why do you hope you were dreaming?" asked Rebecca.

I watched the women with tears rolling down my chin.

"Because I thought I saw something that couldn't possibly be there. It had to be a dream since I'm not senile yet. I hope to avoid that particular indignity."

Rebecca led Sarah away from me. "I wouldn't worry about that. You're sharper than most people I know."

Their voices faded from my ears as soon as they crossed the room. I sat with my legs splayed, just the way Mom taught me not to. It wasn't dignified for a girl, but I didn't feel like pretending to be dignified. I was a big failure. Sitting nicely wouldn't change that. My wings drooped on the carpet and my black hair concealed my lap as I slumped, trying to think of a way to tell the others what happened without causing them give up hope. I stared out the doorway, wondering what to do next, when a brilliant flash of blue made me sit up. Tess danced past the door, followed by her brother, who wasn't dancing so much as fighting, his imagination in full flight. He swung an imaginary sword and pretended to get bashed on the head.

A flicker of hope alighted in my mind.

Children.

Dad once said that children were more likely to see fairies. They were more open to possibilities. I'd never been able to test the theory since children didn't often hike in the national forest next to Whipplethorn, just grizzled men smelling of stale sweat and mosquito repellent.

I jumped to my feet and fluttered to the doorway. Both Tess's and Judd's doors were open. They were getting ready for bed, undressing and apparently not shy about it. They stripped to their underpants and slipped on pajamas. Judd resumed his sword fight and Tess danced in a circle, flapping her arms. I never considered Judd given his sweaty boy stink and went straight into the girl's room. Tess flapped over to her bookcase and chose a book called *Pippi Longstocking*. Two legs with miss-matched stockings and enormous shoes decorated the cover. Tess dashed to her bed, flung herself on it, bounced twice, and burrowed under the covers.

I waited as Tess settled herself on her fluffy pillows. She pulled multiple pins out of her hair and unwound the long braids from around her head. She ran her fingers through her hair until it lay shimmering in soft waves down over the covers. She picked up her book and opened it, propping it on her chest. Then I flew over and landed on Tess's pillow. But the pillow was so soft I couldn't keep my footing and slid down the slick fabric until I landed on Tess's shoulder. Tess didn't notice, but at that moment I didn't care. The book, the human book, was open to me. Its large black letters decorated the page just like in fairy books.

Tess's lips mouthed the words. I settled on her shoulder and read along. Every page or so Tess giggled. I considered getting Iris so she could read the book, too, but I couldn't make myself miss a second. The story enchanted me. A little girl all alone in the world having adventures and longing for her lost parent. The book could've been written for me personally.

"Tess," said her mom, Rebecca, from the doorway. "Ten minutes until lights out."

"Okay. Night, Mom," said Tess, not bothering to look up from the page.

Ten minutes. It wasn't much time. I tore my eyes away from the story and flew to the top of the book. I landed on the spine and watched Tess's face for signs that something unusual had occurred. Tess's eyes moved back and forth, not noticing me at all.

I waved a little wave. I wanted Tess to see me, but I didn't know how Tess would react. With Sarah I was reasonably sure there would be joy and fascination, but Tess was young. She might scream and freak out.

"Hello!" I yelled.

Tess kept reading.

I grew bolder with Tess's lack of response. I stomped on the book, screamed, and pounded the paper with my fists. My voice broke and still Tess's eyes never left the page. When I couldn't croak out another word, I slid down the page to Tess's chest. Sadness welled up. If Tess wouldn't see me, what hope was there? Maybe our parents would come and maybe they wouldn't. Tess was our last chance for human help. The parents didn't believe in fairies and any shot at Judd was doomed to failure. He wouldn't notice me if I was on fire.

Fire. Why hadn't I thought of it before?

I flew back up to the spine. With the book so close, I feared an accident, so I formed a teeny flame in my palm. Tess didn't notice what must've been a pinprick of light to her. It wasn't enough. So I left the book and hovered above it. I grew my flame until it was the size of my head and tinged with blue. Tess's eyes still flitted across the page, but hesitated when she changed from the left page to the right. I concentrated. My flame grew again and began crackling with short snaps of energy. I stared at Tess's face, willing her to see. Dad said I had to want it very badly to make a human see me. Very badly didn't come close to what I was feeling. This wasn't just for me. It wasn't about me. This was for everyone I loved.

Tess's head tilted forward. She stared right at my flame. Then she gasped and jerked her head back, dropping her book onto her lap. I flew to Tess's eye level and spread my wings as wide as they could go.

"Tess!" I cried. "See me!"

"Oh," whispered Tess.

"Tess! Do you see me?"

"Um …" Tess's eyes darted around the room and I knew. She saw me, but she didn't know whether or not to believe.

"I'm here. Really I am. Sarah believes in fairies. It's okay."

"Sarah?" Tess blinked and a line appeared between her eyes.

"Your great-grandmother. She believes in fairies."

"Why are you yelling?"

That stopped me. I pulled back and considered. Then I spoke in my normal voice, sure that Tess would never hear. "I thought you wouldn't hear me if I didn't yell."

"I can hear you," said Tess, looking fearful. "I'm not crazy, am I?"

I doused my flame. "Not a bit."

"So you're a fairy?"

"A wood fairy. My name is Matilda."

"How come I'm seeing you?"

I fluttered closer. "Because I wanted you to. I wanted you to see me so very badly."

"Why?"

The room was suddenly bathed in semi-darkness. Tess screeched and I tumbled backwards from the burst of air she emitted.

"Lights out, Tess," said Rebecca, silhouetted by the hall light shining into Tess's room. "Night night."

"Mom," said Tess in a small voice.

"Yes?"

"Do you see anything unusual in here?" Tess stared at me hovering in front of her face, my wings glowing faintly in the dark with their Whipplethorn luminescence.

"Like what?" asked her mother.

"Um … nothing I guess. Night," said Tess.

Rebecca shook her head and left.

"Your wings are beautiful," said Tess. "They glow a little."

"It's because I'm a Whipplethorn." I turned so Tess could see my wings from the back, my best angle.

"What's a Whipplethorn?"

"It just means where I'm from. Whipplethorn Manor. Have you heard of it?"

"No. Are you the only one?"

"No. There are lots of fairies."

Tess relaxed on her pillow. "My dad says fairies aren't real and neither are trolls or goblins or anything like that."

"He's wrong. I've heard about trolls. I'm not sure about goblins, but I've seen spriggans and they're probably worse."

"So you're really real and I can see you." Tess held out her finger and I landed on it. I walked to the tip of the fingernail and examined the pale pink paint on it.

"Can you feel my weight?" I asked.

Tess screwed up her face. "Kind of. It's like a mosquito landed on me. I might not notice if I wasn't seeing you there."

"Tess!" yelled her mother. "I can hear you talking. Now go to sleep."

"Okay," called Tess.

"I need your help," I said. "But I'd better go before I get you in trouble."

"Help? What can I do? I'm only eight." Tess lowered her voice to a whisper.

"You'd be surprised what you can do. I'm thirteen and I've fought spriggans and saved babies."

"Wow."

"We're living in your new mantel on the right side. Come see me tomorrow." I flew forward and touched Tess on the tip of the nose.

"You live in our mantel?"

"Yes. On the right side. Don't forget. Tomorrow."

"I won't forget. There's no way I could ever forget you."

I smiled and flew towards the door. I looked back and Tess waved. Her excitement shone strong and beautiful even in the dim lighting.

"I did it," I said to myself and flew out the door.

Chapter 19

I flew down the stairs toward the man with the tattoos. He clomped past the stairs carrying a dirty rack of glasses that dripped a sweet smelling sludge across the floor. I flew past him into the kitchen. A snack would go well with my good news. The young woman was still there, looking crabbier than ever. She muttered to herself as she stacked bowls in a bin. Every bowl she picked up scattered more crumbs across the granite table. I landed and sniffed a pale brown chunk. I didn't know what it was, but it smelled sweet and delicious. I tucked the chunk under my arm and walked among the crumbs, picking up the ones that would fit in my pockets. I popped a couple of the smaller crumbs in my mouth. One was an odd salty bread and the other a spongy sweet cake.

The woman swept her hand across the surface of the table. The crumbs disappeared under her lemon-scented hand. I watched the woman dump all that food into the bowl I'd almost drowned in before. All that food. It was such a waste, but I didn't have a way to carry it anyway. I left the kitchen and went into the red room where several adult humans remained, talking in low tones and sipping red liquid out of goblets. I flitted over the back of the sofa between two men. One had a stick clamped in his teeth, except his stick had a little bowl attached at the end. I sniffed and discovered that his stick wasn't lit. I wondered if he was waiting for a way to light it the way the commander always seemed to be.

"Jarvis, either light that thing or put it away," said the other man with a frown.

"I don't need to light it to enjoy the feeling it evokes in me," said Jarvis.

"This is why Lynn won't go out with you."

"Why?" Jarvis clamped his teeth hard on the stick.

"You're a pretentious jackass. That's why. Ditch the pipe."

"Evan, you never did have a sense of style."

"And yet I'm married," said Evan, brushing a wave of light brown hair out of his smiling eyes. Jarvis noticed and scowled. He rubbed his bald head and pulled at the wispy beard perched at the tip of his chin.

"Then again," said Evan. "Maybe that's not it. But seriously, ditch the pipe. It's just embarrassing."

"Forget it. The pipe is cool."

I hovered nearer to Jarvis. He was kind of pretentious. He reminded me of Gerald actually. I decided, like Gerald, he could use a little excitement to knock him out of his funk, so I formed a large orange flame on my palm. I zipped over and dropped it in Jarvis's pipe. A flash of movement caught my eye as I darted away. Tess peeked at me from the staircase with her hand over her mouth. Her eyes crinkled in laughter and her body quaked.

The smell of burning leaves reached my nose and I spun around. A thin line of smoke rose from Jarvis's pipe. Neither man noticed. They continued to argue about pipes and pretentiousness. I looked back at Tess who nodded. I grinned at her and dashed over to the pipe. I blew in it and flew backwards just as a flame leapt over the lip.

Jarvis made a screechy noise and tossed the pipe away. It clattered across the wood floor, spewing flames and ashes.

"Jarvis, you idiot!" Evan scooped up the pipe, tossed it on a dirty plate, and stomped on the ashes.

"It was on fire."

"It's supposed to be on fire. It's a pipe."

"Well, I didn't light it."

"Then how was it on fire?"

"How should I know?"

"It was in your mouth," said Evan, blowing on his hands.

I giggled and looked for my ally. Tess had both hands over her mouth and was bright pink. Just then Rebecca came out of the kitchen and glared at Tess. Tess winked at me and vanished up the stairs. Evan and Jarvis sat on the sofa and examined the pipe, arguing over whether Jarvis had lit it or not. I fought off the urge to light the pipe again, just to really freak them out.

Evan and Jarvis hadn't seen me, but Tess had and more than once. That cinched it. I flew to the mantel with visions of triumph in my head. I imagined Iris's joyful clapping and Gerald's wary smile. No other living Whipplethorn fairy had ever made contact with a human, but I, Matilda

Whipplethorn, had done it. Before my feet touched the doorsill, I did some spins and twists.

I reached for the door pull, but the door swung open before I touched it. Iris and Gerald stood crowded together in the doorway. Both their faces puckered into frowns. They must've been worried about me. I opened my mouth to say I'd done the undoable, but before I could get the words out, Gerald and Iris spoke simultaneously in quick staccato sentences.

"Slow down," I said. "I can't understand you."

Iris blew a deep breath out from between her pursed pink lips. "They're awake."

"We didn't know what to do," said Gerald.

"Should we leave or not?" asked Iris.

I held up my hands. "What are you talking about? Who's awake?"

"The trow," said Gerald and Iris together.

"How can you tell?"

"I hear them," said Iris.

"Me, too," said Gerald.

"Well, what are they doing?" I asked.

The two of them looked around confused.

"They're awake," said Iris.

"We've established that." Gerald gave Iris a fierce look and turned to walk down the hall.

We followed him into the kitchen, where Horc chewed on a wooden spoon and Easy banged two pots together. Gerald stopped on the far side of the room with his arms crossed. Iris sat down at the table.

"Don't you want to hear what happened upstairs?" I asked.

"Upstairs?" Iris asked.

"Yes, upstairs," I said, raising my hands in exasperation. "Don't tell me you forgot about Sarah."

"You did it," said Gerald, without a trace of doubt.

"You did?" Iris clapped her hands. "You really did?"

"I did." I smiled, enjoying the looks on their faces. "But it wasn't Sarah who saw me."

"Who was it?" asked Iris, picking up the plate and wiping it with a cloth.

"Tess."

"Oh, no," said Gerald.

"What's wrong with that?" I asked. "She's a human."

"She's a kid."

"You're missing the point, genius." I put my hands on my hips. "She saw me. We talked."

"She won't be able to do anything," said Gerald.

"She can help us. I know she can," said Iris.

Gerald shrugged. "Maybe you're right. She could get the adults to help us. She is a girl."

"What does being a girl have to do with it?" asked Iris.

"Everything," he said. "Who do you think would be more persuasive, Tess or Judd?"

"Tess," said Iris. "But not because she's a girl. She's just nicer."

"You think that because she's a girl."

Iris scowled at him and I laughed. "I don't care why she can help us, as long as she does."

"What about the trow?" said Iris.

"Why are you so scared?" I asked. "Soren would've said if they were dangerous."

"Easy's worried," said Iris.

Easy didn't look worried to me unless he was worried about whether he could whack a pan hard enough to crack it.

"He seems fine to me," I said.

"He's not worried," said Horc, still gumming the spoon. "Iris and Gerald are worried. Nonsense, really."

"Why is it nonsense?" I asked.

"Because dangerous fairies don't play music."

"I don't know if that's true."

"I do." Horc bit the end of the spoon so hard it splintered. He chewed for a minute, then turned his head and spit out the fragments. "Name one species of fairy that makes music and is violent."

I couldn't, but only because I couldn't think of any musical fairies. "So they're doing what? Singing?"

Gerald and Iris looked embarrassed. Horc rolled his eyes and bit the end of the spoon clean off.

"Don't do that," I said. "You'll hurt your mouth."

"I'm teething," he said with another chomp. "And they're not singing. They're playing instruments."

Easy chirped and kicked his legs. He held his arms out and I picked him up.

"He says he wants to go visit," said Horc.

"Why?"

"He wants to play, too. It's what mindbenders do."

At the word mindbender, everyone gasped. Horc looked at us, blinking slowly and totally disinterested in our astonishment. Easy tucked his head against my shoulder. I tried to interest Easy in a nibble of cake, but he wouldn't look up.

"Don't say that, Horc," said Iris.

"What?" He eyed the piece of cake in my hand until I tossed it to him.

"You know, don't say the M word."

"I certainly do not know." Horc popped the cake in his mouth and looked for more.

"It's not nice to say it," I said.

"Why not? It's just a type of wood fairy."

"Nobody wants to be called that. It's an insult."

"Did Easy say he didn't want to be a mindbender?"

Easy shook his head and I looked at Horc.

"He wants to be a mindbender, but he doesn't like that you don't like it," said Horc.

I touched Easy's chin. "We like you and if you like being called a mindbender, that's what we'll call you."

"He still wants to go over there," said Horc.

"I can't take you until I know it's safe."

"He says music makes it better. He wants the music."

"Makes what better?"

"It drowns out others' thoughts. That's why mindbenders play."

"Oh," said Iris. "That's nice."

"I wish music were playing right now," said Gerald, looking disgruntled.

"I haven't got anything to hide," I said. "So I don't mind."

"Well, I do." Gerald stomped across the room and left.

"Well?" I asked Easy.

Horc spit out more splinters. "He says mindbenders don't tell and please go visit the trow."

"Don't tell what?" asked Iris.

"Mindbenders don't tell what others are thinking," said Horc. "It isn't polite, but I don't know what polite has to do with it."

"You wouldn't." I ran my fingers across Easy's brow. His large eyes watched me, their expression flickering between fear and hope. "Iris and I understand. We won't ask what you don't want to tell."

Easy placed his hand on my cheek. The warmth of it imprinted on my skin and I realized I loved him. When I told the spriggans that he was our baby it became true. I wasn't just the babysitter anymore. "I'll go next door and see the trow."

Easy chirped and held his arms out to Iris.

"I'd say be careful, but I'm not worried," said Iris.

"Why not?"

"Easy wouldn't ask to go if there were something to worry about." Iris sat Easy on the floor next to Horc, who promptly whacked him on the head with the remains of his spoon.

"Horc!" Iris and I exclaimed.

"He says I still stink," said Horc as Easy blew a raspberry at him.

I bit my lip to keep from laughing. "Easy, that's not nice to say."

Easy looked up, his big eyes moist and mournful.

"Don't give me those weepy eyes," I said. "If Horc has to be nice to you, then you have to be nice to him."

Easy snatched the spoon out of Horc's hand swung it over his head like a mace and cracked Horc on the top of the head. Horc yelped and lunged for Easy. Iris whisked him away, trying to wrestle the spoon out of his hand.

"Do you need help?" I asked.

"No," said Iris, still struggling with a wiggly Easy. "I can handle it."

"Good luck," I said. "I'll be back in a bit."

Iris didn't answer because Horc was stealing all of Easy's pots and Easy wasn't happy about it. She just nodded and looked pained. I left the kitchen and went room to room until I found Gerald sitting on a window sill, staring out into the human's living room.

"What's your problem?" I asked.

"I don't have a problem," Gerald answered, without looking at me.

"Could've fooled me."

"That's not hard."

I touched his arm. "Seriously. Why don't you like Easy?"

"I like Easy. I don't like him listening to my thoughts. Doesn't it bother you?"

"It did at first, but really my thoughts aren't that interesting," I said.

"You're not worried about people finding out you're a kindler?"

"Easy wouldn't tell. Besides, I couldn't hide it now, even if I wanted to."

"If anyone finds out about Easy being a mindbender, it will be bad."

I hugged him and rested my cheek on his soft brown hair. "Soren and the commander were okay with it, maybe the rest of Whipplethorn will too. Come with me. I'm going next door."

"I'll stay here," he said.

"Gerald, come on," I said. "In case you haven't noticed, I don't hear so well."

Gerald slid off the sill and eyed me, his eyes throwing a challenge. "Are you saying you need me?"

"Yes, Gerald. I need you."

"Because I'm really really smart."

"No, idiot, because you can hear. The smarts don't hurt though," I said.

"All right then."

I rolled my eyes at him, went to the front door, and flew out without waiting. Gerald followed and landed on Easy's front doorstep a second behind me. I knocked on the door and waited. Nothing happened, so I knocked again.

"What are they doing?" I asked Gerald.

"Nothing," he said. "They stopped playing."

"Are they coming to the door?"

"I don't think so."

I pushed on the door to see if it was latched and it creaked open, casting a rectangle of light into the hallway.

"Check it out," said Gerald, gesturing behind us.

The dogs sat in front of the mantel, pointing their snouts at us. "I have to admit they're kind of growing on me. They're better than the cat anyway."

"Iris said the cat was nice. She played with it."

"It tried to eat her."

"Oh," said Gerald. "Should we go in?"

"Why not? What could happen?"

"Don't say that," said Gerald.

"Why not?"

"Because it's us. Anything could happen and probably will."

I grinned at him and lit my palm with a bright cheery blaze. "Come on, Gerald Whipplethorn. Let's go check out 'anything.'"

Chapter 20

They're not here," said Gerald, nervously sidling out of the parlor and bumping into me.

"Don't be ridiculous," I said. "They're here. You just heard them. They must be hiding."

"I say we let them hide. I mean, we're kind of breaking and entering."

"We are not. This isn't their house." I looked around the room, which had been organized and swept. "Do you smell something?"

"We're not leaving, are we?" Gerald slumped and walked into the hall, dragging his feet.

"No," I said. "We've only looked on the first floor so far. Do you smell glue?"

"Wood glue to be precise," said Gerald.

"Right. Wood glue. What do you think they're doing?" I went into the hall and grabbed Gerald's hand. "Let's go find out."

Gerald protested, but I pulled him along behind me to the staircase. "It's stronger here. They must be upstairs in Grandma Vi's sitting room."

We climbed the stairs to the next floor landing. My flames cast flickering shadows on the walls and Gerald's hand felt slippery in mine. He jerked out of my grasp, but I managed to snatch a hold of his sleeve before he ran back down the stairs.

"Do you hear anything?" I asked.

Gerald groaned and pointed to the closed door. "They're in there."

"What are they doing?"

"Breathing."

I opened the door and the smell of fresh wood glue socked me in the face like a stinky wet fog. "Whoa. That's really strong." I coughed, letting go of Gerald's sleeve. He turned around and ran down three steps before I called out after him. "Get back here unless you'd like all of Whipplethorn to know you ran away in the face of glue."

Gerald tromped back up the stairs with his arms crossed. I walked into what used to be Grandma Vi's sitting room, keeping my palm lit, though I hardly needed it. Light shone in from the human's party through the sitting room's open windows, soft and diffused. The room didn't look like Grandma Vi had ever lived there, but, for the first time, it didn't bother me.

"Look, Gerald," I whispered. "They fixed everything."

When I rescued Easy, the room was filled with smashed instruments. Now the floor was clean of debris and the instruments were sitting neatly on tables, held together with woodworker's clamps. Some weren't put together yet, their parts spread on felt pads, ready for reassembly.

"Hello," I called. "We won't hurt you."

"Please don't hurt us," said Gerald.

"I'm Matilda and this is Gerald. We heard your music." I paused. "Well, that's not true. I didn't hear it, but Gerald did. Please come out."

Slowly, a dozen dark brown furry heads appeared from around corners, behind tables or cabinets. Their fur rippled when they moved. It concealed most features except for their eyes.

Gerald grabbed my hand and squeezed it white. "Oh, Matilda. Please let's go."

"It's okay. Can't you feel it?"

"I feel sick."

"They're friendly," I said.

"I'm going to throw up."

"Stop it, Gerald. Horc was right, wasn't he? Musical fairies aren't violent."

"There's always a first time."

"Well, it's not this time." I smiled and waved at the nearest one.

The trow lowered its gaze and peeked at me from underneath long thick lashes. Its eyes were dark brown with no white at all. The trow shrank back as I picked up a violin. The neck had been broken off, but was beautifully repaired. A light coat of wax made the repair almost invisible. I wouldn't have noticed it if I hadn't been looking for a break.

"You do beautiful work," I said, placing the violin back on the table.

The trow nodded and I suspected a smile on its concealed lips.

"Can you talk to me?"

I saw the trow's lips move under the curtain of fur, but I couldn't hear anything.

"What?"

Gerald stepped forward, puffing out his chest. "He whispered, 'We are trow.'"

"I know you are," I said. "Soren Maple told me about you."

At the mention of Soren, the rest of the trow crept forward out of their hiding places. I felt like they'd taken a huge sigh of relief.

"You know Soren?"

All dozen trow nodded. The one closest to me held out its hand. The palm looked like black leather. Calluses tipped the fingers and decorated the palm in hard ridges. Gerald grabbed my arm, but I took the trow's hand anyway. It regarded me shyly and then patted my hand.

"We're wood fairies," I said.

Gerald relaxed and let go of my arm. "He says that Soren told them about a wood fairy with black hair in the antique mall. He told them not to scare you."

I stifled a giggle. The thought that the trow could frighten anyone seemed a ridiculous notion. "You did well. I'm not frightened. You're musicians?"

The trow picked up the violin and the bow next to it. He placed the instrument on his shoulder and played a quick tune so lovely and intricate I stopped breathing for a second it was so beautiful.

"Wow," said Gerald.

"Wow, indeed," I said. "Would you play some more?"

The trow all picked up instruments and assembled themselves in the middle of the room. Three played violins, one a harp, two had cellos, two more had guitars and the rest situated various drums. Once they were assembled, I had a hard time telling them apart. If it hadn't been for the violin, I wouldn't have known the one whose hand I'd held. I started to ask their names, but they began playing a slow melodious tune that made me feel like I was in a boat, rising and falling with gentle waves.

The trow played the song for several minutes. When they stopped they leaned forward, their eyes searching my face. I almost couldn't react, the song was so wonderful. "That was the most beautiful thing I've ever heard."

The trow murmured something.

"They said thank you and would you like to hear more," said Gerald.

"Yes, definitely, but would you mind more visitors? I know a little mindbender who can't wait to meet you." I smiled, although the word mindbender stuck in my throat a little.

The trow nodded.

"Gerald, please go get the others," I said.

"Why do I have to go?" he asked. "I want to stay with them."

I glanced over at him. "Really?"

Gerald ducked his head. "I like the music. Okay?"

"Okay. I'll get them.

I left Gerald there listening to a sonata. It was hard to tear myself away once the trow began playing. I skipped down the stairs, buoyed by the music and feeling as light as I did when flipping around in the warm air outside the mantel.

The dogs waited outside, their noses still tipped up. They wagged at me, probably hoping for a scratch, but I wasn't quite ready to risk being eaten yet. I retrieved Iris,

Horc, and Easy and brought them to Grandma Vi's sitting room. As soon as we walked in the door the babies stopped squabbling and stared at the trow who ignored them and played a jolly tune worthy of a parade.

I sat next to Iris on the floor and blew out my flame. The dim light from the party lent itself to the music. Iris heaved a sigh and sank back against the wall as one of the trow gave Easy a lyre. His plump fingers skipped across the strings. In a second, the trow picked up his melody and accompanied him in a song that spoke of longing. My eyes burned with unshed tears. I'd known Easy's family played, but never heard them. I'd missed an essential part of life in the months the mindbenders lived in Grandma Vi's house.

I whispered to Iris, "Is this what Easy's family sounded like?"

"Pretty close, but there were only three of them. Mom really liked their playing," said Iris.

"How come nobody ever told me what they sounded like?"

Iris cast a sad look at me. "Because you couldn't hear it."

I turned back to the music, determined to enjoy it. With all those musicians in the same room, I was having nearly the same experience as everyone else.

We stayed for hours. When the humans turned off their lights, darkness overtook the music room and I relit my palm. "We have to go, but we'll visit again, if you'll allow it."

The trow nodded vigorously and kept on playing. They continued even after we left and took my light with us.

"Are they still playing?" I asked when we got to the front door.

"Yes," said Iris. "I guess they don't need light."

I asked again when we were all getting ready for bed and Iris nodded yes. The expression on her face told me that the music was still beautiful and I felt a pang of sorrow. Easy tapped his foot and Horc swayed back and forth. Only I sat in silence.

I made us pallets for the night, all except Gerald, who said he was too big to sleep with us. He went to my parents' room. I lay down next to Horc, watched his breathing, and ignored the faint spriggan scent that remained in spite of the scrubbing I'd given him. I ran the songs I'd heard through my head, delighting in the rhythms, but also with a great sadness settling around my heart. I didn't know how much I'd been missing and I wanted to go back to a time when I didn't know. Back to when the mantel was on the wall of Whipplethorn and my worst problem was babysitting for Gerald.

I woke early, crept out of the bedroom and left by the front door. The red room lay dark and empty before me. Tess wouldn't be up for some time. I yawned and considered going back to bed before seeing a flash of movement. The dogs dashed out from behind the sofa and ran up to the mantel. They sat their furry butts down and pointed their fat snouts at me.

"Nothing gets by you, does it?" I waved at them.

The dogs wagged, then jumped up and ran back across the room to the stairs. A few moments later, the man I'd seen at the party, Evan, tromped down the stairs in a blue bathrobe. The dogs followed him into the kitchen and sat wagging furiously until he patted their heads. He was talking, but he was so far away I couldn't make out the words or see his lips.

I closed my eyes to concentrate and then popped them back open. Evan was still in the kitchen with the dogs, but when I closed my eyes it was like they ceased to exist. What little I thought I could hear went away. I watched him opening cabinet doors, pulling out pans and containers. I would've sworn I heard it, a little clinking far in the distance. When I covered my eyes, the clinking disappeared. Evan poured water in a black and silver contraption. Then he spooned dark brown chunks in the top and pressed a button. A little orange light appeared on the front of the contraption and the man turned around, leaning on the cabinet. The dogs sat in front of him and I was able to read his lips.

"What are you doing, you worthless animals?"

The dogs wagged harder.

"How can I love creatures so ridiculous?"

I covered my eyes and sat in silence. I thought about all the things I'd taken for granted as normal. Iris edging in front of me to talk. Mom always telling me to face Dad when he spoke. My teacher, Miss Penrose Whipplethorn, giving all her lectures directly in front of my seat. I'd always wondered why she did that. I wanted her to go lecture in front of someone else so I could relax. Maybe I didn't have the exceptional hearing that was expected of wood fairies, but I thought I could hear well enough.

That day watching Evan, I realized how bad it was. I couldn't hear. I really couldn't hear. No wonder Grandma Vi insisted I learned to lip read. I'd thought it was pointless, since I only needed it at a distance. But it wasn't about distance or direction or the tone of the speaker's voice. I needed it all the time.

I dropped my hands. Evan moved about the kitchen, pouring ingredients in a big bowl and it seemed like I could hear it. But I couldn't. I was just filling in the blanks. I jumped off the edge of the mantel and flew towards the kitchen. It wasn't all my imagination, not Mom's voice, not the trow's music. How much could I hear? I landed on the counter near to Evan's bowl and closed my eyes.

"You dogs stink," he said.

I definitely heard that. Then I flew farther away and tried again. I heard his words, but they were fainter. Another small flight and they were fainter still. One more and nothing. I flew back a little and turned around. As soon as I turned Evan's voice almost disappeared. It was better if I faced him.

Evan poured a black liquid out of the contraption into a misshapen mug that said "Tess" on the side. He took a drink and went to sit at the table. A fresh flowered tablecloth covered the expanse. Candles and a bunch of flowers were arranged in the center. He opened a flat, skinny box lying at the end of the table and stared at a shiny blue screen while sipping the liquid. The dogs didn't follow him, but sat looking at me.

"I think I can hear humans better than fairies," I told them and they wagged their answer. "I wish it were the other way around, but I suppose it can't be. Humans are probably pretty loud in comparison."

Evan began tapping his fingers on the box and I flew over to see what he was up to. The dogs followed me and sat next to his chair. He looked down at them and said, "You two have been acting kind of weird lately."

I hovered over the box and saw rows of grey buttons with black numbers and letters on them. When Evan pressed a button the corresponding letter appeared on the screen.

"That's pretty cool," I said as I dropped closer to get a better look. Some of the buttons had words on them like "Caps Lock" or "End." "I wonder what that's about."

"What are you doing over there?" Evan asked.

I jerked away and saw him, not looking at me as I'd hoped, but at Tess who was standing on the mantel's hearth. Her nose brushed against the mantel's shining wood and she ran her fingers over the curves and ridges of the intricately carved wood. She must've said something in response, but she was too far away and I couldn't see her lips.

"What are you looking for?" he asked.

Tess turned around. "Just looking, Daddy."

"I'm going to make pancakes. How many do you want?" he asked.

But Tess had turned back to the mantel, and her answer was lost to me.

"Get away from there," he said. "I haven't fixed it to the wall yet."

Tess jumped off the fireplace hearth and skipped across the room to the kitchen table. She skidded to a halt when she saw me hovering above her father's hands.

"Daddy," Tess said.

"Yeah, sweetheart."

Tess placed her small hand on her father's large shoulder. "Do you believe in fairies?"

Dimples appeared on his cheeks and a smile danced on the edges of his mouth. "Why do you ask?"

"Do you, Daddy?"

"Not really, no."

Tess winked at me. Then she burrowed under her father's arm and perched on his lap. My palms started sweating and I couldn't have started the meekest of blazes. This could be it.

Any minute Tess's father could turn his head and see me. I flew closer to make sure he couldn't possibly miss me, if he was willing to see.

"Daddy, if I told you I saw a fairy and that she was here right now, would you believe me?" Tess gazed up at her father with wide, hopeful eyes. I didn't know how he could resist such a face. Tess's cheeks were flushed with excitement. Her tangled hair cascaded over her shoulders and made her look a bit like a magical creature herself. She looked so young, she almost made me feel old.

"A fairy," he said. "Right here, right now?"

"Yes. She's flying there." Tess pointed at me and I spread my wings wide and waved.

"I don't see anything."

"Come on, Daddy. She has long black hair and beautiful shiny wings."

"Nope. Now let me finish this e-mail, will you?"

"Daddy," Tess pleaded.

Evan shifted his focus to the glowing screen again and began pushing the letter buttons. I landed on the broad area behind the buttons. Tess looked at me with her trembling bottom lip sticking out.

"It's fine," I said.

I wiped my hands on my shirt and lit my palms. Blue blazes erupted. Their heat stung my face and I stared intently up at Evan. He looked past me at the screen, punching buttons. My flames grew higher, turning white hot.

"Daddy," said Tess. "Try harder. She's standing on your keyboard holding balls of fire."

He shook his head. "Your imagination has always been a wonder."

"It's not my imagination."

Evan reached above the keyboard. His hand went over my head, grabbed the edge of the box, and swung it down towards me. I jetted off the box and flew over the letters, but I wasn't fast enough. The top of the box hit me, driving me down between A and S. The last thing I heard before the box closed completely was Tess screaming, "No!"

Chapter 21

I opened my eyes in time to see an enormous pair of fingernails coming at me. I shrieked and struggled, but my shirt was caught on the letter S. The fingernails pinched my shirt and I shrieked again.

"Hold still." Tess's face hovered over me. "I'll get you out."

"Wait." I worked my hand underneath the S, found the caught material and released it. "Pull, Tess."

Tess lifted me from between letters A and S and placed me on table. "Are you okay? I thought Daddy squashed you."

"I'm fine. What happened?" I asked.

"My dad closed his laptop on you. He didn't mean to. He just didn't see you there."

I rubbed my forehead where it had struck a letter. Evan's head appeared next to his daughter's and he grabbed Tess around the middle. She laughed and tried to get away, but he tickled her until she shrieked.

"Talking to your fairy?" he asked when he tired of the game.

"Yes," said Tess.

"Say hello for me." He returned to the stove where he poured something in a skillet.

Tess waited until he'd turned his back, and then leaned over me. "That's my dad. He says hi."

"I heard."

"Last night you said you needed help. What's wrong? What can I do?"

"Pull up a chair," I said.

Tess sat in her father's chair and held out her finger. I stretched my wings and, finding nothing amiss, I flew onto Tess's finger. "I do have a problem and a story. Do you want to hear it?"

"I do," said Tess, her cheeks turning even brighter pink.

I sat on Tess's finger and told her everything about the humans taking our mantel. I told her about Gerald running away, Soren Maple, and the spriggans. I explained about being a kindler, keeping Horc, and meeting the commander. I told her all of it and Tess listened with her entire being. She gasped when the spriggans attacked and got teary-eyed about Easy's lost mother. When I finished she leaned back in her chair and let out a tensely held breath.

"So your parents could be anywhere," said Tess.

"We have to get back and see if anyone's left at Whipplethorn. Will you help us?"

Tess sat up straight. "I will."

Before I could say more, Judd came up to Tess and shoved her shoulder hard. "What are you doing, dufus?"

"Ow, Judd. That hurt," said Tess as I flew off her finger.

Evan walked over with a plate stacked high with flat cakes. "What are you doing, Judd?"

"Tess is talking to her finger."

He shot Judd a warning look. "So what's it to you? She can talk to her foot for all I care. Leave your sister alone."

Judd bent over his sister's ear. "Weirdo."

"Daddy, Judd called me a weirdo."

"What's wrong with being a weirdo? It's a sight better than being average." Tess's father put down the plate. "Eat your pancakes. I have to call Grandpa about the mantel. Judd, go wake your mother for breakfast."

Rebecca walked in the kitchen, slinging a traveling bag over her shoulder. "No need."

"Where are you going?" asked Evan.

"To that tea at the botanical garden," Rebecca said.

"You're really going to that?"

"I said I would, Evan. I'll be back after four."

Evan shrugged and went back to the stove. Tess eyed her mother as she rummaged around in her traveling bag and then smeared some red stuff on her lips.

Judd sat down and piled his plate with cakes. He cut them into large chunks and poured a sweet-smelling liquid over them. My mouth watered and I was about to fly down and swipe a crumb when I saw Tess tug on her mother's sleeve.

"Mom, can I talk to you in private?" Tess asked.

Judd looked up, his mouth half full. "She wants you to talk to her finger."

"Shut up, Judd," said Tess.

"Don't say that, Tess," said Rebecca. "I don't have time right now. I have to go. I'll see you tonight."

"Mom, please. It's really important."

"Yeah," said Judd. "Fingers are really important. I've got ten, but I don't talk to them."

"You've got eight fingers and two thumbs," said Tess. "Thumbs aren't fingers."

"Says who?" asked Judd.

"Everybody." Tess stuck her tongue out at him and then turned to her mother. "Mom, please."

Rebecca kissed Tess on the forehead. "Tell, Dad. I have to go. Be good."

Rebecca left and the remaining humans sat at the table eating. I sat with them, nibbling on a pancake crumb and considering my options. There weren't many. Evan refused to see me. Tess was eight. Rebecca didn't have time and Judd was obnoxious. I could probably get Sarah to see me with Tess's help, but it needed it to happen quickly. It'd been days since we'd been taken from Whipplethorn. Anything could've happened in that time.

Evan stood up and cleared his place. Then he went upstairs, leaving Tess and Judd at the table alone. Judd continued to stuff his face and Tess picked at her pancake. Her forehead puckered and she kept stealing glances at her brother. Judd ignored her and took the last cake.

I flew up and hovered over Tess's plate. "Don't bother with him. We'll think of something. When will you see Sarah again?"

Tess shrugged. That wasn't good news. We needed to see Sarah soon.

"Judd?" Tess set down her fork.

"Yeah."

"Do you still want that new video game you've been talking about?" asked Tess.

Judd looked up, his eyes narrowed. "Yeah."

"How much money do you need?"

"Twenty bucks. Why?"

"I have twenty bucks."

"So what? Are you going to like give it to me or something?"

"I might." Tess smiled. She put her elbows on the table and steepled her fingers.

"What do I have to do?"

"Believe," said Tess. "Just believe."

Judd stuffed a huge bite in his mouth. "I believe you're a weirdo." Crumbs sprayed out of his mouth, raining down on the table. I suddenly lost my appetite and dropped my crumb.

"You have to believe in fairies," said Tess.

I flew in front of Tess's face. "Don't do it. He'll just take your money."

"No, he won't." Tess smiled at her brother. "Mom says Judd is a lot of things, but he's not a liar. Besides, he won't be able to lie."

"I can lie my head off," he said. "I believe in fairies. See?"

"Nope. You have to describe her. Then I'll give you the money."

"Describe who?"

Tess gestured to the candles on the table. "Light one, Matilda. Make him see."

I darted to the candle nearest Judd and formed white hot flames. They snapped and jumped into the air. "Now?"

"Just a second," said Tess.

"What exactly am I supposed to be seeing?" asked Judd.

"Remember when I told you I saw Jason Applegate stealing your model plane?"

"Yeah."

"After you found it at his house, you said you should've believed me."

Judd's cynical expression softened. "Okay."

"Believe me now," said Tess. "Light it, Matilda."

I put my hands together around the wick. The cotton material sizzled to life and threw up a flame as tall as Gerald. Judd sat bolt upright, his eyes fixed on the candle.

"Whoa. Did you see that?" He stood with his hands on the table and leaned forward, his nose very close to me.

"Yes," said Tess. "And so did you."

"I don't see any fairy."

"Look harder."

Judd glanced at his sister. When his gaze came back to the flame, he sucked in a breath, hard enough to make the flame flicker in his direction. His eyes fixed above the candle on me and my flaming palms. I waved, letting the fire dance along my fingertips. Judd ran his fingers through his hair, lifting the heavy bangs off his forehead. And it was my turn to be surprised. Judd's face with its pale freckles, square chin, and mischievous eyes was captivating. I blushed at having his eyes being trained on me and I wished I'd bothered to comb my hair.

Tess moved in close to Judd, putting her cheek up close to his. "You see her, don't you?"

"Uh, huh."

"For twenty bucks, describe her for me."

"I don't want the money," said Judd.

Tess raised one of her eyebrows and dropped it as the edges of her mouth curled up.

"He sees me. I can tell," I said as hot tingles raced up and down my body.

"Describe her, Judd," said Tess.

"She's really tiny. Maybe a half an inch tall with long black hair to her waist. And she's holding white fire. Good enough?"

"Is she pretty?"

Judd dropped his hands. His hair flopped down over his face and he fell back into his chair. A pink tinge crept up his neck from his collar.

"Tell me if she's pretty," said Tess. "That's how I'll know for sure."

"Yes, she's pretty. Happy?"

Tess flung her arms around her brother and squeezed. "I'm so happy."

Judd pushed her off and crossed his arms as I doused my flames and landed on the table. I walked to the edge and sat next to one of his juicy crumbs.

"What are you exactly?" he asked.

"I'm a wood fairy," I said, trying not to show how flustered I felt about being called pretty by a human.

Judd frowned. "A wood fairy that makes fire. Isn't that kind of a problem?"

"It's a paradox, I admit."

"What's a paradox?"

"A contradiction."

"Like how I don't believe in fairies, but I'm seeing you?"

"Exactly."

Tess pulled her chair over next to Judd's and perched on the edge. "Matilda needs our help."

"What kind of help?"

"Go ahead, Matilda," said Tess.

I tried to tell Judd the story of the mantel, but Tess cut me off so many times, I gave up and let Tess tell it. Tess was a better storyteller anyway. Everything sounded more fantastic, more amazing, when it came from her lips. When Tess finished, Judd looked willing to do just about anything.

"So you want to get out to Whipplethorn today?" he asked.

"Can you do it?" I asked, absolutely certain that he'd find a way.

Judd threw back his shoulders. "Sure. No problem."

Chapter 22

Judd collapsed onto the sofa and heaved a sigh. His thick hair concealed most of his face and he seemed to be growing larger every minute I knew him, larger and more capable. I left Gerald and Iris on the sofa table and fluttered over to Judd, landing on his knee. I peeked up under the curtain of hair to see his dark eyes looking back intently.

"What happened?" I asked.

"I can't do it," he said.

"Yes, you can. You can do anything." I patted Judd's leg. Warmth radiated from under the dark blue material. Heat was just one of the many ways Judd differed from his little sister. Tess was positively cool to the touch. Judd pulsed with energy where Tess stood calm in the face of his storm.

We'd watched as Judd threw himself into our problem. He asked a million questions and answered half himself. He found Whipplethorn Manor's location on something called the Internet. He called cousins and friends looking for a ride. He discouraged easily, but managed to overcome the disappointments and find another avenue. He reminded me of a saying Dad often used: "If the door is closed, find a window."

"We just need a window," I said.

Judd jerked his head up and peered at me through breaks in his heavy bangs. "What?"

"Nothing. Just something my dad says."

Iris darted in front of Judd's face. "Dad says, 'If the door is closed, find a window.'"

"I can't think of any more windows," he said. "When do I get to meet the babies?"

"Yeah," said Tess from her spot on the floor beside the sofa table. "I want to see them, too."

"Why?" Gerald sat on the table with his arms and legs crossed. Since I'd brought Tess and Judd to the mantel for introductions, he'd been quiet. He wasn't overjoyed as I expected. He watched the humans like a science experiment. His face had a closed expression with small creases of worry holding firm on his forehead.

"Why what?" asked Tess.

"Why do you want to meet them?" asked Gerald.

"They're baby fairies. They'll be so cute."

Gerald thrust his chin out at Tess. "They are not cute."

"I'm not into cute or anything, but I want to see them," said Judd.

Gerald jumped to his feet. "I'm telling you. They are not cute and one is a mindbender."

"Mindbender?" asked Tess.

"Easy can read minds. So there," said Gerald.

"Cool," said Judd.

"It is not cool. It's weird."

"Why is it weird?" asked Tess. "It just means he's special, right?"

"Especially strange," said Gerald.

"I'd like to know what Cecily Jenkins is thinking about," said Judd.

"Don't you get it?" Gerald jumped up and down to emphasize each word. "He's a freak. He can put thoughts in people's heads, too."

"That is really cool. I wonder if he could tell Dad to give us ride."

"I don't think it works with humans," I said.

Tess sighed. "It wouldn't work with Dad anyway. He'd never listen to a fairy voice in his head. He'd just think we'd finally driven him crazy. He always says we're going to drive him crazy."

"I guess you're right. I don't know what to do next," said Judd.

"Somebody has to give us a ride," said Tess. "What about Buddy?"

"He's going to Sunday dinner with his girlfriend," said Judd.

"Buddy has a girlfriend?"

"Who's Buddy?" asked Iris, still hovering near Judd. Since they'd been introduced, Iris stayed near Judd whenever possible, blushing and fiddling with her hair.

"He's our cousin," said Judd. "He's a geek."

Tess frowned at him. "Mom says he's socially-challenged."

"That's what I said. He's a geek. Anyway, he's busy."

"What about Sarah?" I asked.

"She's at church," said Judd.

Gerald flew to Tess and landed on her shoulder. "Maybe," said Gerald, "we should just stay here and wait."

"You want to wait?" asked Iris. "You're the one who ran off to find your parents. You said we had to get back."

I left Judd's knee and landed next to Gerald. "What's wrong with you? Since when don't you want to find our parents? It's practically all you've talked about."

"My parents are brilliant. They'll figure out where we are. We should stay here where it's safe."

"What about our parents and Easy's just a baby. He needs his mother."

"Fine. Whatever." Gerald turned away.

I spun him around. His forehead creased even more deeply and he had tears in his eyes. I hugged him, but he didn't hug me back. His arms stayed limp at his side.

"Gerald, what's wrong?"

"Do you like me?" he asked.

I pulled back in surprise. "Of course I like you."

"You didn't used to. Nobody did."

I wanted to lie, to say some words of comfort, but they died on my lips. We'd been through too much to start lying now. "I didn't use to like you, Gerald. That's true. But I like you now."

"That will all change when we get back. I'll have no friends again."

Iris came and wrapped her arms around him, too. "That won't happen."

"Yes, it will. You won't want people to know you ever liked me."

"Gerald, you'll just have to trust us," I said.

Gerald's forehead smoothed and his expression became resigned. I hugged him again, and this time he hugged me back. Then he pulled away and flew down to the table.

"It's one o'clock," said Gerald. "Too late for church."

"Right," said Tess. "Church is over."

Judd leaned forward, putting his elbows on his knees. "It doesn't matter. Gram can't drive."

"Oh, right." Tess held out a finger for me to land on. "I don't think we're being much help."

Gerald took a bite of a banana slice Tess had put out for us. "How'd she get to the antique mall then?"

"Her friend must've driven her," said Tess.

Everyone stared at one another.

"Which one? Marie?" I asked.

Tess shrugged. "Maybe?"

"Don't look at me," said Judd. "They're old ladies. I can't tell the difference."

"Oh, you can too," said Tess. "Marie's the one with the pregnant granddaughter. I heard Mom talking about it. She said it was a scandal."

Judd brightened at the word "scandal." "What happened?"

"I don't know. Mom saw me and stopped talking."

"You have to be stealthier," said Judd.

"I know, but anyway, Marie can drive. Call Great Grandma, Judd."

Judd picked up the telephone, dialed, and began talking eagerly into the receiver. I couldn't read his lips, but he was smiling and nodding. After a few minutes he put the phone down, but before he could tell us what Sarah said, Evan came into the room. "What are you two doing?"

A.W. HARTOIN

"Nothing," Judd and Tess said.

"Nothing?" Evan frowned at his children. "You two are sitting together voluntarily and doing nothing?"

"Yeah, Daddy. Nothing," said Tess.

"Well," said Judd. "We were thinking of visiting Gram today."

Evan's frown deepened and one eyebrow lifted. "That's weirder than nothing. What are you up to? You're not going to ask her buy that video game for you, are you?"

"No way, Dad," said Judd.

"So you just want to visit a bunch of ninety-year-old ladies for fun?" Evan walked over to the mantel and began taking the candlesticks and pictures off the top.

"A bunch?" asked Tess.

"It's her sewing circle day."

"Oh," said Judd. "I, um, like sewing."

"Now that's just insanity." Evan grasped the mantel.

"What are you doing?" asked Tess.

"I have to look at the back of the mantel."

"What for?"

Evan didn't answer. He pulled the mantel away from the wall and leaned it forward in one swift motion. Tess and Judd rocketed to their feet and everyone, human and fairy alike screamed, "No!"

Tess and Judd eased the mantel back against the wall. Evan leaned on the wall and rested his arm on the mantel. "Somebody better tell me what's going on right now. And don't say nothing."

I darted past him but saw our front door was blocked by his elbow. "Iris, do you hear the babies?"

"They're crying," said Iris. "Really loud."

"I checked the side door," said Gerald. "It's locked."

I flew to Judd and Tess. They stood with their hands in their pockets, looking at the floor. I fluttered under Judd's face and said, "We can't get in. Make him move."

"Answer me," Evan's voice boomed.

"Dad, we were…" Judd's voice trailed off.

I went to join Iris, who was tugging on Evan's sleeve. He didn't so much as blink in our direction.

"We thought you might break it," said Tess with her hands clasped.

Judd looked at her like she might be a genius. "Yeah. We didn't want it to get broken."

"You two were worried about something being broken?" asked Evan in his normal volume. "You break at least two things a week around here. What's really going on?"

"Really, Dad. Mom said the mantel is seriously delicate. We're not even supposed to touch it," said Tess.

"That I believe." Evan let Tess pull him away from the mantel.

Iris and I rushed through the front door. Horc sat in the hall with an enormous bump on his head and a bloody nose. He wasn't crying anymore, but had a look of fury on his face that I recognized. The adult spriggans gave that look to the phalanx fairies before they attacked.

"I'll find Easy," said Iris, running past Horc.

"Don't bite me." I scooped Horc up and felt over his arms and legs. Except for some bruises and scratches, he seemed fine.

"You are the worst babysitter in the history of babysitting," said Horc. When he opened his mouth a dribble of red spit slipped down his chin.

I wiped it with my sleeve. "How many babysitters have you had?"

"You are the first and the worst."

"What did the spriggans do with you when they went somewhere?"

"They usually put me in a drawer," said Horc, his expression not softening one bit.

"I'm better than that. Home is better than a drawer."

"Nobody ever flipped the drawer over."

"You've got me there," I said. "I didn't expect this to happen."

"You're not big on expecting, are you?" Horc's lip trembled and he buried his face in my shoulder.

I patted his back and walked down the hall after Iris. I found her in our parents' room. Iris held a sobbing Easy tight to her chest and murmured in his ear. I couldn't see her lips clearly enough to make out what she was saying.

"Is he okay?" I asked.

Iris pulled Easy away from her so I could see his face. He looked like he'd been whacked with a big stick right down the center of his face. Tears dripped off the tip of his swollen nose and he wailed when he saw me.

"I think he hit Mom's bedpost when he rolled off his pallet." Iris dabbed at his nose with one of Dad's old shirts.

"He wants to know if we're under attack," said Horc.

"No," I said. "But we'd better get out of here before Evan decides to move the mantel again."

When we got to the front door, I peeked out to find Evan gone. Tess sat on the floor. She watched the mantel with intense eyes. Behind her, Judd talked into what I now knew was the phone. As soon as Tess saw us, she jumped to her feet.

"Are they okay?" she asked.

"They're a little banged up, but they'll be fine," I said.

"You better get out of there. Dad's getting his tools."

We landed on the sofa table next to Gerald, who sat munching on the banana slice. "Why didn't you come help us with the babies?" I asked.

"I checked on the trow. Besides, you don't need my help."

"Yeah. I never need any help." I rolled my eyes and smiled at Gerald until he let a grin slip onto his face. "Are the trow okay?"

"Still asleep. I don't think they even noticed," he said still grinning.

Iris and I sat the babies next to him and he frowned at their supposed cuteness.

"They are so cute," said Tess.

"You think they're both cute?" asked Gerald. "Even that one?" He pointed at Horc.

Tess paid him no mind. "They're so teeny. Can I hold one?"

"I don't know how you can hold one. They don't fly and they're pretty little," I said.

Horc held up his arms. "She may hold me. I am extremely holdable."

Easy saw Horc raise his arms and held up his own.

"She can't hold you both at the same time," said Iris.

"I'm first," said Horc.

Easy reached over and cracked Horc on the side of the head. Horc wobbled for a second and then lunged for Easy's foot. I grabbed him before he could connect, but his jaws stayed in biting mode, opening and closing, as he looked around for something to chomp on.

"They're fighting," said Tess.

Evan came up behind Tess. I shook my head at her, but Tess didn't notice. She reached her hand toward Horc. "I'll take the biter."

"Biter?" Evan bent over Tess. He had a tool box in one hand and a cup in the other.

Tess froze and blushed.

Judd plopped down on the sofa with the phone still in his hand. "She's nuts, Dad. She thinks this place is crawling with fairies. So do your fairies bite, weirdo?"

Tess assumed an imperious look and put her nose in the air. "Some do. I hope one bites you."

"I'd pay to see that," said Evan.

"I'd pay for you to see that, too," muttered Judd.

"What was that?"

"Nothing, Dad."

"What are you going to do with the tools?" asked Tess.

"Not sure. I have to find a way to attach the mantel to the wall." Evan set down his tools and rubbed his chin. "Maybe a lightweight adhesive would do the trick. Help me lay the mantel down, so I can get a better look at the back, Judd."

Judd stood up and went to the mantel. "Okay."

"What? No protests?" asked Evan.

"It's cool," said Judd.

They laid the mantel down on the rug and Evan ran his hands over the back.

Gerald turned to me. "Anything that wasn't broken before is now."

"This stinks," said Iris. "We were just getting everything back in order."

"We cleaned it before. We can do it again," I said.

"I like the mess," said Horc. "Doesn't smell quite right though."

"You mean, it doesn't smell bad enough," said Iris.

"Exactly."

Judd knelt beside his father and touched the backside of the mantel with a soft fingertip. The dull unfinished wood had a rosy hue that lured me over from the sofa table. I landed next to Judd's hand, squatted, and touched the raw wood. A little thrill went through me. I'd never touched my home in its original state before. Humans shaped, stained, and varnished the outside and my ancestors did the same to the inside. I didn't know why they bothered. I liked the warmth, the softness of the grain without the gilding. My fingers slipped across its silky face and I knew I'd made the right decision to stay. I'd never leave my wood, even if it meant Whipplethorn Manor was lost to me forever. I had no doubt my parents felt the same way.

Judd bent close over me. He breathed out and a breeze smelling of syrup ruffled my dress. He held out his finger to me and I touched the tip.

"Check this out." Tess pointed to something on the other side of the mantel near the top.

Evan and Judd crowded around her. I darted to the area and hovered. Large loopy letters decorated the upper right hand corner. The words were written in pencil and faded with time but still legible.

"Nathaniel Whipplethorn for Susannah Whipplethorn November 1882," said Tess.

"That cinches it," said Evan.

"What?" asked Tess.

"This piece is signed by the maker. There's no way your mom is going to let me glue it to the wall."

"Probably not," said Judd as the doorbell rang.

"Expecting someone?" asked Evan.

Judd jumped up and ran to the front door, followed closely by Tess, me, and Iris. Judd flung open the door and found two old ladies standing on the front stoop, clutching square black purses and wearing tiny hats covered with netting.

"Good morning, Judd," said Sarah. "You remember Marie."

"Gram, I didn't expect you so soon."

"Why ever not? You said it was urgent on the phone."

Judd glanced over his shoulder toward the mantel room. Two fierce red spots surfaced on his cheeks.

"Judd?" Sarah's forehead puckered and she began to look very suspicious.

Evan came through the archway into the dining room. "Guys, we have to go to Wood Crazy." Evan stopped short when he saw the open door.

"Evan," said Sarah. "Shouldn't you be lying down?"

"What for?" asked Evan.

Tess clamped her hands over her mouth and Judd sputtered, trying to speak but coming up with nothing. Sarah eyed them both before returning her warm gaze back to Evan.

"Never mind, dear. I misunderstood something Judd said this morning."

"Well," said Evan. "Come on in."

The ladies walked into the dining room and handed their purses to Judd who looked quite confused. Tess pointed to the table and he set them down like old was contagious. Sarah led us through the archway into the mantel room and she perched on the sofa, flanked by Marie.

"Not that I'm not glad to see you, Gram, but what are you doing here?" asked Evan.

Tess stepped up and took a deep breath. "We, I mean Judd and I, asked them to come for a visit."

"A visit?" said Evan. "Gram was just here last night."

"Right and, um, I have a report. A report on the Great Depression, because we're having a depression right now and I have to do a report." Tess sucked in another breath, but then bit her lip and held it.

"Let me guess. This report is due tomorrow and you expect Gram to drop everything to help you out."

Tess hung her head. "Sorry."

"Think nothing of it, Evan," said Sarah. "We're happy to help."

Marie humphed but didn't say anything.

"Well, I still have to go to Wood Crazy," said Evan. "Would you mind watching them?"

"I'm thirteen. I don't need to be watched," said Judd.

Tess elbowed him in the ribs and he said, "Well, maybe I do."

"Then we're all set. We'll watch the children and you go to the wood place," said Sarah.

Evan didn't move. He stood next to the mantel lying on the floor and furrowed his brow. The two old ladies sat serene, waiting for him to go. Their lavender and cookies scent filled the room, soothing us all.

"I guess I'll just be going," Evan finally said.

"Bye, dear," said Sarah. "Take your time."

Evan left by the back door, but not before he glanced over his shoulder three or four times. No one moved. We just watched him go. When at last the door closed behind his father, Judd let out a rush of held breath.

"All right, you rascals," said Marie. "What are you up to?"

Sarah leaned forward and her hat fell over her eyes. She stuck it back in place with a wicked hat pin longer than our living room. "You don't know they're up to something, Marie. They're just children."

"Just children. Bah. They have the same look my granddaughter had before she dropped her little baby bomb on us. Mark my words. They are up to something, and we aren't going to like it."

"That's not true," said Tess. "You are going to like it."

"Don't contradict me, big eyes. You might be cute as button, but you don't fool me."

"I'm not trying to fool you."

Sarah watched the exchange with a neutral expression.

She kept glancing at Judd who was smiling faintly at the sofa table where Easy and Horc were battling again. "What are you looking at, Judd?"

Judd jumped. "Nothing, Gram."

"You brought us here under false pretenses. Now it's high time you fess up," she said.

Judd looked to Tess and said, "You tell them."

"Why me?"

"Why do you think? Dad says you could sell ice to Eskimos."

"I'm not buying," said Marie.

"Hush, Marie," said Sarah. "Go on now, Tess. Let's have it."

"Somebody told me you believe in fairies," blurted out Tess.

Marie laughed a soft laugh like she hadn't the energy to make a more raucous noise. She relaxed back onto the cushions of the sofa, but Sarah sat bolt upright, her eyes trained on Tess. "Who told you that?" Sarah asked.

"A fairy."

"Would this be Tinkerbell or Rumpelstiltskin?" asked Marie.

"Rumpelstiltskin was a dwarf," said Tess.

"Same thing."

"No, it isn't, and Great Grandma Sarah knows it."

Marie straightened her hat and tried to stand. Judd rushed over to help her, only to be snorted at and pushed away. Marie clung on to the sofa arm and pulled herself up, panting like a marathon runner.

"I have known your Gram for seventy-two years, little girl, and she does not believe in fairies. Enough of this nonsense. We have quilting to do."

"Please sit down, Marie. I'd like to hear what my Tess has to say," said Sarah.

"I just stood up."

"Consider it good exercise."

Marie sat. She made grumpy noises as I gathered my little tribe on the sofa table in front of them. It wasn't easy, but I even got Easy and Horc to stop smacking each other for no reason.

"Great Grandpa believed his father when he said there were fairies living in his old roll top desk, and you believed Great Grandpa, didn't you?" asked Tess.

"Yes, I did," said Sarah.

"If you believed him then, there's no reason why you can't believe us now."

Sarah shook her head. A silver strand of hair fell across her cheek. Her faded blue eyes grew moist and her wrinkles seemed to deepen with sadness.

"It's more complicated than that, dear. Grandpa was a little boy when his father told him those stories. He would've believed the sky was orange, if his father told him so. I believed that my husband believed. Can you understand what I'm telling you?"

Marie nodded and huddled closer to Sarah, a barely perceivable movement, but I saw it. Tess knelt on the floor by the sofa table and pointed at us. "Don't you see them, Gram? They're right there."

"I'm sorry. I don't see anything," said Sarah.

"She needs proof." I fluttered to Tess's shoulder and whispered in her ear.

"Gram, when you were at the antique mall the other day, did you talk about Miss Marie's great-granddaughter getting pregnant?"

"Yes," said Sarah slowly. "How did you know that?"

"Matilda, the fairy, was there. She heard you."

"That proves nothing," said Marie. "Everyone knows about that."

I whispered in Tess's ear again.

Tess smiled. "You said the boy who did it was a carhop and Gram corrected you. He's a bellhop."

"You were there. You heard us saying that," said Marie.

"I was at school. You can ask my mom, if you don't believe me."

Sarah reached out to Tess. Tess leaned forward and Sarah cupped her great-granddaughter's cheek in her soft, withered hand. "I believe you, dear. I just can't figure out how you know what we said."

"I told you. Matilda was there."

"Stuff and nonsense," said Marie.

"Is it nonsense that Gram bought that desk for Mom's graduation because she loved Great Grandpa's stories?"

"She probably told her why when she gave it to your mother," said Marie.

I tugged on Tess's earlobe and whispered one last fact. Our last chance to convince the ladies that they should try to see.

"If I tell you one more thing, Gram, one more thing I couldn't possibly know without being there, would you try to believe there are fairies sitting on the sofa table?" asked Tess.

"I'll believe there's a flock of pink elephants sitting on the table, if you can tell me something only a fairy could know." Marie crossed her arms. Her bottom lip protruded, and she looked more stubborn then Gerald at his worst.

"You saw a string of pretty beads in a jewelry bin on the desk you bought for Mom. You said they looked like the ones Marie's mother wore every day. You bought them for her. They cost $1.99. Gran said, 'Two memories to purchase and it would be her pleasure.'"

Sarah gasped. "That's exactly what happened."

Marie touched the string of beads around her neck. They glinted pearlescent and pretty with their dreamy colors against Marie's pale skin. Sarah rested her hand on Marie's knee. None of them looked very old anymore. I saw the girls they once were and still were in their hearts. Pretty girls both of them. Ready to believe.

"Look. Right there on the table," said Tess. "They're not so very hard to see once you know how to look."

Both Sarah and Marie leaned forward in one fluid motion. I zipped from Tess's shoulder to land behind the babies, who were waving frantically instead of clobbering each other. Iris jumped up and down, clapping and waving. Only Gerald stood still, his intense eyes trained on Sarah. Flames erupted from my palms. They snapped and tickled, jumping joyfully into the air. I could've juggled them had I wished to.

"See them." Tess pointed at me. "See them and know everything Grandpa believed was true."

The light of my flames danced in Sarah's eyes as they searched the tabletop. I willed Sarah to see, not only for my own benefit but for Sarah's too. Then the old lady's gaze settled on me. Her eyes widened and her mouth formed an O.

"Thomas," Sarah said.

Marie threw her hands in the air, shouting hallelujahs.

Next to her, Sarah's eyes rolled back in her head and she fainted dead away, falling off the sofa and landing softly on the floor.

Chapter 23

I rolled across the car seat and smacked into Sarah's silk-covered leg. Gerald hit her a second later and Iris a second after that. Another swerve sent us tumbling back the other direction.

"For goodness sake, Marie," said Sarah. "Slow down."

Marie gripped one side of the steering wheel. "No time for that."

"I'm certain their parents wouldn't want them to get killed on the way back to Whipplethorn." Sarah scooped all of us up and cradled us in her cupped hands.

"They'll be fine. They're tough. Aren't you tough?" asked Marie.

"I feel sick," said Iris.

"I'm tough," said Gerald, turning a violent shade of green and falling over.

"Please slow down." I flew off of Sarah's hand and hovered between the two old ladies. "We're not used to driving."

"Sorry. You wanted to go home and I only have two speeds. Stop and fast," said Marie.

Gerald struggled to the edge of Sarah's palm. "Stop is not a speed."

Marie gave him a flinty look. "Smart aleck, are we?" She grabbed a long black lever next to her right knee and shoved it with a violent thrust.

Sarah started looking a bit green herself. "I knew I never should've let you buy this car. It's like giving a rocket to a pyromaniac."

"Let me? Let me?" Marie wrenched the wheel to the right and I bounced off her cheek. "Since when does anyone let me do anything? This is my dream car. Why shouldn't I have it?"

"I thought that Jaguar was your dream car," said Sarah.

"I thought so, too, but it was a mite stodgy for me. This is more my speed."

"Don't all cars go fast?" I asked, landing on the flat area in front of the wheel.

"Not fast like this one. This is a Shelby Cobra. It does zero to sixty in four seconds."

Marie's right leg pressed down and we shot forward. I almost fell off the edge of the ledge.

"How are the babies back there?" I yelled.

Tess's head peeked up over the back of Sarah's black leather seat. She held up a small white box filled with cotton batting. The babies lazed on the batting and nibbled on a raisin. "They're fine. It's a good thing Gram thought of this box, though."

Tess's head disappeared and Judd's popped up from the other side of the back seat. "This Mustang is awesome. Miss Marie, can I drive it when I get old enough?"

"I'll teach you to drive." Marie grinned. Despite the silver hair and glasses she looked positively wicked.

"Oh, yes," said Sarah. "That's just what we need."

"Glad you agree," said Marie.

"How is it that they took away my license," said Sarah, "and you still have yours?"

"Because I was smart enough to get mine in Arizona. It doesn't expire for another eleven years," said Marie.

"Heaven help us."

"Hold on!" shouted Marie. "Gravel road."

I managed to grab the edge of the shelf before Marie hit the brakes. For a second all I could hear was the humans screaming as we skidded to a halt. Grey billowing dust surrounded the car and then everyone became quiet.

"Are we there?" asked Judd.

I staggered to my feet and pressed my face to the glass. The dust cleared, revealing a narrow road winding away from us through a dense forest. "Almost."

Sarah set Gerald and Iris on her lap and looked at a flat grey box. "It says we have to drive up this road for two miles."

"That didn't take as long as I thought," said Marie.

"No kidding," said Gerald. "We must've been going a hundred miles an hour."

"One hundred five, smarty pants," said Marie. "Hold on to your hats."

"Saints preserve us," shouted Sarah.

"Calm down, old lady."

"Old lady? You're an old lady, too, or have you forgotten? You should be driving an Oldsmobile."

"Oldsmobile? Car and Driver said they stink," said Marie.

"You rock, Miss Marie," said Judd.

"I do indeed rock, young man. And I will teach you to drive."

"Awesome."

Sarah dropped the flat box. "Please, Marie. Rebecca will never forgive me if something happens to these kids."

"Nothing's going to happen. Not on the gravel anyway. Do you really think I'd risk dinging my paint job?"

"I wish it were gravel all the way then," said Iris.

Marie winked at Iris and drove onto the gravel road. I watched as the trees went by and admired the fall colors that had come out strongly in the days since we'd been gone. Yellows shone more brightly than I remembered. The burnished reds deeper and more beautiful.

I waved to Iris and Gerald. Iris waved back, but Gerald stared straight ahead. I watched him for a moment and then turned back to the road, holding my breath and waiting for Whipplethorn Manor to come into view. But it didn't. Marie drove up into a little clearing and parked next to an enormous bare spot surrounded by piles of scrap wood and a scattering of slate tiles.

"Oh, no," said Sarah.

Iris flew up. "What is it?" She spun around frantically, looking out the windows. "Where is it?"

"It's gone," said Sarah. "We're too late."

Gerald buried his face in his hands. Iris hovered above Gerald, her face blank. "What do you mean 'gone'?"

I held out my arms to Iris, but my little sister darted past me. She ran over the shelf and put her hands against the glass. My face got all tingly and hot. Whipplethorn Manor was gone. Nothing was left except a few moldy scraps of wood and rubble.

It made sense. The humans were taking all the beautiful woodwork, everything of value. Of course they would knock down the old, decrepit building. Despite the logic of it, I expected Whipplethorn to still be there, standing stately against the pines of the dark forest. Now nothing would be the same ever again.

Iris turned. Tears streamed down her face, rivers of pain. "What happened to Mom and Dad?"

"Out looking for us, I expect." I gathered Iris into my arms and let her sob against my shoulder.

"May as well get out," said Marie. "Someone might be left."

Sarah opened her door and waved us out. Iris went first. Her wing beats slow. I expected her to drop to the ground immediately, but instead she fluttered over to the bare spot and landed in the dirt. I followed, dimly aware of the humans coming up behind us. The air teased me with its familiar smells. The pine trees somehow managed to smell both sticky and green. A blustery wind kicked up the dirt. It pelted against Iris, but she didn't acknowledge it. She stood in the bare patch with shaking shoulders.

"I'm so sorry," I said.

"Did you know?" asked Iris.

"No, but it makes sense that they were going to tear it down."

"Maybe if we got back sooner."

"It wouldn't have made any difference. We just would've seen it happening. I'm glad we weren't here."

"Me, too, I guess."

Tess walked past them, holding the little white box. "Fairies. Are you still here? We have your kids. Come out."

Iris lifted her head. "Don't bother. If they were here, they would already have heard us and come out."

"Why don't you listen and see if you can hear them?" said Sarah.

Iris and Gerald closed their eyes and listened. After a few minutes, a tear slipped down Iris's cheek.

"No one's here," she said.

Gerald nodded and put his arm around Iris's shoulder. "We'll find them."

"We may as well go." Marie straightened her hat as she glanced at the bare spot. "No use crying over spilt milk. We'll find your parents. They're just not here is all."

"Does that mean you'll drive at a reasonable speed on the way home?" asked Sarah.

"Not hardly." Marie snorted.

We stood together, huddling in the middle of the bare spot. Tess's face was fixed in a furious pout. At first, I thought she was angry, but then I saw Tess trembling. Sarah had her arm around her great-granddaughter, her face ashen, her red lips a slash of color in a dreary portrait.

"Don't look so upset," said Gerald. "This only means they've gone looking for us. Isn't that right, Matilda?"

"Absolutely," I said.

"That's the spirit," said Marie. "Speaking of spirits, I could use a drink. Let's go find a liquor store. A disappointment this great calls for vodka and cranberry juice."

Sarah smiled. "Oh Marie, you are bad."

"Thank you, my dear. Let's hit it."

Chapter 24

Marie's hands rested on the steering wheel. She fidgeted with the numerous rings gracing her fingers. She spun a large ruby one around her index finger until she abruptly reached down and turned a silver key behind the wheel. The car rumbled to life. The car started to roll backwards. Easy started crying, waking Horc up from a snooze.

"What's happening?" Horc stretched and yawned, his teeth glinting in the dim light.

"We're leaving. We have to get Tess and Judd home before their mother has a fit," said Sarah.

"Mom will understand," said Tess.

"I'm sure she'll be very understanding about a quest to find missing fairy parents," said Marie with her eyes fixed on the mirror atop the window. She executed a quick turn and the car began creeping over the gravel back the way we'd come.

Horc crawled over to Easy, looked at his heaving back, and patted it. He glanced up at me for approval. I nodded and forced a smile. I wasn't thinking about Easy or Iris or even my parents in those long moments crunching over gravel. Whipplethorn Manor had disappeared. Nothing I did would make it come back again. I couldn't fly hard enough or do good enough to change it.

"Thank goodness," said Marie. "The end of that gosh darn gravel."

The gravel ended in another twenty feet and merged with dull blacktop. Marie's rings clinked together as she tightened her grip on the steering wheel and my shoulders tensed, ready for speed. Soon we'd be heading away from Whipplethorn at a breakneck pace. My heart sank a little farther to think of it.

I checked to see if the babies were ready for a burst of speed and saw Easy's head pop up out of the batting. Horc stopped patting him and jerked his head up to look at the window. He seemed to see something in the distance. I followed his gaze. I saw nothing but lengthening shadows and an endless stretch of road.

"Stop," shouted Iris.

The car jolted to a halt as it rolled onto the blacktop. I tumbled off Marie's shoulder and landed in her soft lap. Iris grabbed my hand and yanked me into the air. We flew straight up and landed on the top of the steering wheel.

"Look!" shouted Iris.

In the distance, a tiny sparkling jewel headed straight at us, moving with incredible speed. A second later, Easy's mother was pressed against the glass, her arms spread wide. Her face held such a beatific expression of joy, I sucked in my breath at the sight of it.

"Open the window, Gram," Tess cried.

Sarah pushed a button, the window slid down, and Easy's mother flew in. She lit on the batting next to Easy and Horc, dropping to her knees. She sobbed and clutched both Easy and Horc to her breast. Iris and I flew down and hovered near them, waiting for the right moment to speak. Finally, Easy's mother raised her large brown eyes. She held out her arms and we flew into her embrace. She smelled of home, the forest, and the exotic spices only she cooked with. I cuddled deeper into her embrace. Mrs. Zamora's long brown hair cascaded over me. Even under the darkness of that lovely hair, the world became brighter. My burdens lighter.

"You, too, Gerald," said Easy's mother gently. "Yes, I mean you."

I peeked out from Mrs. Zamora's hair to see Gerald, looking as unsure as I'd ever seen him.

Easy's mother held out her pale brown hand. "Come. Be with us."

Gerald rushed to her and melted into the embrace. I felt him shake once and then be still. Perhaps his burden had lightened, too.

Mrs. Zamora hugged us tight and then released us, leaning back and wiping the tears from her cheeks. Easy clung to her waist and Gerald burrowed his face into the crook of her knee. Mrs. Zamora's gaze fell on me. She touched my cheek, caressing and soothing.

"You have done well." She tucked her lovely thick hair behind her ears, revealing a jagged cut extending from her temple to her jaw. Fine white threads laced the edges together and the swelling was minimal for such a painful wound.

"You know about spider webs," I said.

"I do. Not as much as your grandmother, but perhaps you will teach me the rest."

"You probably know everything in my head already."

"Once we are adults and able to control our mindreading, we do not take what is not offered. For instance, I'm not sure how you have come by a spriggan baby. Nor do I know by what means these human ladies help you. I know the information is there for the taking, but I will not do it if I can possibly help it."

"Former," said Horc from under her left arm.

"What do you mean by former?" asked Mrs. Zamora.

"I am a former spriggan. Now I'm a wood fairy."

Mrs. Zamora nodded. "That makes sense."

Gerald raised his head. "It does?"

"Yes," she said. "Spriggans that leave the nest rarely return to their old ways."

"That's good to know," said Iris, pressing Mrs. Zamora's hand to her cheek. "Do you know where our parents are?"

Sarah and Marie bent over close, their breath ruffling Mrs. Zamora's hair. Tess and Judd leaned over the front seats, bobbing and weaving, trying to get a good look.

"They are out looking for you, as are the rest of the Whipplethorn fairies," said Mrs. Zamora.

"All of them?" asked Iris, her eyes filling with tears.

"Yes, all. You are surprised?"

"I thought everybody but our parents would be out looking for new homes."

"You were the only thought that graced their minds once they knew you were taken away with the mantel."

I clasped Iris's hand and squeezed. We smiled at each other through our tears.

Sarah lifted our box and held it so that Tess and Judd could see.

"Why are you still here, Mrs. Zamora?" I asked as I wiped my eyes.

"I elected to stay in case you returned. I was to search the forest for signs of you while I waited. That was what I was doing when you came." Mrs. Zamora looked up at Sarah and Marie. "Thank you for bringing them."

"Thank you," said Marie. "This is a sight better than Sunday bingo."

"Do you know where everyone is now?" I asked.

"They spread out. Each family took a different route in hopes of finding you."

My shoulders drooped. They could be anywhere. The world outside Whipplethorn loomed huge and unfriendly.

Mrs. Zamora touched my cheek again. "We found out from the humans that a man named Jarvis Hornbuckle bought Whipplethorn and ordered it torn down. Each family is to find him when their route is exhausted. From there we will decide what to do."

"How will they find him?" asked Iris. "One human in a world full of them."

Horc slithered from under Mrs. Zamora's arm. He toddled over the cotton batting and tumbled into my arms. "Your worries are over."

"Oh, really, former spriggan," I said, nestling him into my lap. "How do you know that?"

"Because Jarvis Hornbuckle owns the antique mall."

Marie shifted in her seat and grinned at us. A manic gleam came into her eyes behind her glasses. Her right leg went down and a rumbling shudder went through the car.

"Hold on, everybody!" I yelled.

"To the antique mall," said Marie, as the car shot down the road. Iris and I fell back on the soft batting, feeling the miles flow beneath us.

"How fast are we going, Miss Marie?" asked Judd.

"One hundred and gaining."

"Can you do one hundred ten?"

"She cannot," said Sarah. "Slow down, Marie!"

"Live fast, die young!"

"You're ninety-four."

"And never had an accident."

"Yes, you have," said Sarah.

"I was twelve and in a buggy. Buggies don't count."

Mrs. Zamora handed Easy to me and stood up. "We're almost there I believe. I can hear my husband's thoughts."

"This far away?" asked Sarah.

"Tough luck," said Marie. "I had five husbands and what they said out loud was bad enough."

"You get used to it." Mrs. Zamora smiled. "I'll tell him we're arriving at the antique mall, so that he may gather the others that are there."

"No, don't," I said, jumping to my feet. "They'll know what you are."

She laid a soft hand on my shoulder. "I won't keep them in agony for a moment longer than necessary just to protect myself."

"You don't know what they'll do once they know you're a mindbender," said Iris. "They think mindbenders are dangerous."

"We won't let them do anything," said Gerald.

"That's right and maybe they'll surprise us," I said. "Maybe they won't care."

"In any case, it's the right thing and it's done," said Mrs. Zamora.

"You don't want to hide anymore," I said.

"Perhaps you've got a little mindbender in you."

"Just kindler."

Mrs. Zamora raised an eyebrow at me.

"I don't want to hide anymore either."

The car took a sharp right, a left, and screeched to a halt in front of the antique mall.

"Look at that," said Marie. "I slowed down."

"You need your head examined," said Sarah.

"You're in the car with me."

I looked past Sarah's frowning face at the mall doors. To the left, a luminescent dot of light appeared out of a drainage pipe. Then another and another.

"It's them," said Tess. "I see them."

They were there. My mother. My father. And the rest of Whipplethorn, gathering for our arrival. I couldn't move. I wanted them for so long, so badly it seemed a mirage that I might blink away.

Then climbing out of the pipe came a figure, taller than the rest and painted like the most exquisite maple. Soren joined my family and stood with his strong hands on my parents shoulders. It was right that he was there. He said that I would make it happen, using all my gifts we would be together. My world changed forever, but in exchange I'd received a bigger world filled with more of everything. It was, in the end, quite a gift. I squeezed Iris's hand and decided, no matter what happened or where the mantel went, I would never change my name or pretend to be something other than exactly who I am. I would remain forever a Whipplethorn.

The End

ABOUT THE AUTHOR

A.W. Hartoin is the author of Middle Grade and Young Adult fiction. She can't remember a time when she didn't love reading. The first book she read over and over again was Harry and the Lady Next Door. He was such a bad dog. Anne of Green Gables was the first time she wanted to enter a world and stay there. She began writing her first novel weeks after her second baby was born and never looked back. A.W. lives in Colorado with her husband, children, two cats, one dog, and six bad chickens.

Also By A.W. Hartoin

Away From Whipplethorn Book Two
Coming December 2012

⁊◌⁊

MERCY WATTS MYSTERIES
Coke with a Twist
Touch and Go
Nowhere Fast

18665766R00163

Made in the USA
Lexington, KY
17 November 2012